This Ain't No Gay Romance

Sasha Avice

Cover by: cateashwooddesigns.com

Edited by: copybykath.com

ISBN EBOOK: 978-0-6452714-5-4

ISBN PRINT: 978-0-6452714-9-2

Newsletter

Subscribe to my newsletter via sashaavice.com for regular updates on WIPs, new releases, and thoughts on writing.

You'll receive two free novellas upon sign up.

Just want the books? No dramas: hit unsubscribe after you've downloaded them.

This one's for my Mippy

1

♥

ROLLINS WATCHED AS HORACE clapped Jay on the back. The back slap was hard, too hard. He'd seen Jay around the clubhouse a few times, thought he was a bit of a pussy. Jay didn't flinch when that slap landed though, and Rollins clocked the non-reaction, took a sip of his water.

Jay was pushing his black-rimmed glasses up his nose, grinning at nothing, grinning in a way that was maddening—just smiling, bopping his head every now and then like he was hearing a beat no one else was.

"We've had to push it back, haven't we, babe?" Sarah, Rollins' missus, was saying.

"Yeah," he replied.

"Can't get married if we ain't got no venue!" she honked a laugh and went on about the winery going out of business, about how they'd be doing it at a different winery now, about how this one was better, fancier, and her giggling took on a false note of modesty when Tanya said: "Guess you'll have to wait a while longer to get started then."

Rollins half-listened, most of his attention on Jay near the bar. Horace was holding court and telling everyone about the reappearance of his "long lost son!"

"Did you get a paternity?" Slater—second in charge of this joke they called a gang asked—and even Rollins, who thought this Jay was a pussy wanker from Sydney, frowned at that.

Horace laughed, turned a mean look on Jay next to him. "Course! Turns out one got past the goalie on the old whore," he slapped Jay again, harder this time, and Jay still didn't flinch.

Rollins told himself to stay out of it. Oh, he wasn't planning on getting involved to defend Jay—Christ, no—he was telling his mind to stay out of it. So the newly-minted gang leader had a son reappear after ten plus years. So Horace was trying to pass off the fact he lived with the prostitute in question for almost a decade and that boy there until he was at least seven. So what? The guys gossiped worse than the women and everyone knew Jay was Horace's. Everyone knew he used to beat the shit out of the kid's mum as well. Rollins wasn't much on talking, and he'd only been around for a year, but he was real big on listening. But even if he hadn't been, it would've been hard to miss the chatter when Jay turned up a few weeks ago.

What he couldn't fathom was why Jay had come back at all.

He watched as Jay told Horace, again, "It's JC. Everyone calls me JC," and Horace hit him again and said with inexplicable fondness, "Not around here they don't. It's Jayden."

He'd introduced himself to Rollins as "Jay."

Rollins had caught Jay watching him back in the city; his gaze resting on Rollins a moment too long, a quick smile when he saw Rollins watching him back. He'd even seen Jay give his body an obvious once over, held the eye contact afterwards. That was a clear invitation to hook-up—no homo—if there ever was one. If this was still the army, which it sure as shit wasn't.

Jay bopped his head again now, easy, before excusing himself politely.

Rollins watched him weave through the guys. He stuck out in his baggy jeans, boxers riding over the top of the waistband, his stark white shirt and bright red cap on backwards; the contrast to the head-to-toe black was striking as those bodies refused to part to allow him through. He was forced to bump men awkwardly as he made his way through the bar area, into the house, probably heading for the row of beds where the non-attached guys would be staying as they celebrated opening this new clubhouse in Port Hedland. Yet another small-town paradise to add to the list, Rollins thought dryly.

He was still watching when Jay looked over his shoulder and caught Rollins' eye from inside the glass sliding doors, his smile quick and warm before he turned back and kept moving inside.

Rollins' heart rate spiked. Surely Jay wasn't suggesting they do it here? Jay wasn't his usual type, but since he'd started dropping what was now clearly an invite to fuck, Rollins had taken notice. The idea of manhandling that little body where he wanted it, really digging his fingers into that soft flesh, had taken root in his mind and grown rapidly like a weed.

"Excuse me," Rollins cut Tanya off.

"Course," Tanya smiled.

"Get me a diet coke on the way back, babe?" Sarah asked.

"No bourbon?" Tanya tittered.

"Oh, stop," Sarah replied. "We're not even trying yet..."

Rollins made his way inside through the backroom and into the kitchen. It was old with linoleum floors in mustard and brown, the tiles to match, everything clean on the surface as if that could mask how old the place was. He went through the adjoining laundry and toilet, down the hallway creaking with his tread and emerged in the large room, the addition, nothing but rows of beds with those shitty, grey blankets. It reminded him of the army and yet it didn't; where the army had been sterile in its boring décor, this was inescapably old, tired.

Jay was hunched over his bag on the bed nearest the wall. He went still when Rollins entered, but otherwise ignored him.

Rollins walked over until he was behind him.

He could hear Jay breathing; his breaths coming faster and louder the longer Rollins stood behind him.

Rollins thought about the way Jay had held his gaze when they met back in the city, saying, "Hey, dude," as he'd extended his hand.

Rollins had grunted, shaken Jay's hand tightly, and left faster than usual.

He'd held Rollins' gaze with that easy smile every time they'd met in the weeks since.

Now, when Rollins brought his hands up and rested them on Jay's waist and felt the soft flesh give under the press of his fingers, he knew this was what Jay had been asking for. He squeezed.

Jay stayed still.

Rollins brought his hands around and undid Jay's button, pulled down his zipper. He could hear the sounds outside, the exaggerated laughter of one of the guys, the droning of Sarah's voice over Tanya's and the rest of her minions. He got his thumbs in Jay's waistband over his boxers and shoved the whole lot down roughly.

"What—

Jay cut off when Rollins kneaded his ass with one hand, slipped his fingers around and stroked the padding on his stomach with the other. He slid that hand down and wrapped his palm around a nice sized dick. Jay wasn't hard, but he was hardening up as Rollins stroked him and breathed hotly on the back of his neck.

With his other hand he popped the buttons of his jeans, got his hand around himself and got his dick free.

He used his body to shove Jay forward until he fell on top of the bed and landed on his hands and knees, his bare ass at waist height. Rollins wet his fingers with saliva, then rubbed them around Jay's hole. He gripped Jay's hip with one hand, lined up his dick with the other.

"Fuck," Jay gasped and pressed his forehead into the mattress.

Rollins pressed until the tip popped inside, then brought both hands to Jay's hips to hold him still. He hadn't fucked a dude since he left the army, but as he worked his way inside Jay's ass, he remembered how good it used to feel, why he quietly did it every time he got himself a willing partner out there where everything was sand, and every fuck was a furtive thing in the barracks tent or around the back of a parked Humvee or the occasional cave.

He got a nice rhythm going, dragging Jay back onto his dick as he shoved forward.

Jay started jerking off.

Rollins snickered.

"Shut up," Jay panted.

"I didn't say anything," Rollins replied and fucked him harder.

"Fuck, there," Jay arched his back, really shoved back into Rollins' next thrust and started to come.

Rollins huffed a laugh and brought himself onto the bed, caging Jay's spent body in with his thighs and arms, slid their fingers together.

Jay stayed upright, panting, making squeaks of discomfort as Rollins pounded into him, nice and deep with no space between them. There was a muted slapping of skin, a rustle where their clothes rubbed together; it felt loud above the noise from outside. He mouthed at Jay's shoulder over his ridiculous shirt, licked the skin on his neck beside the cap he was still wearing. He pushed in and went still as he started to come, his soft groan muffled into Jay's pale skin.

The sounds from outside wafted over them as Rollins caught his breath. He sat up, gripped his dick by the base and pulled out slowly. A ripple went through Jay's body and Rollins stroked his ass. Then he gave it a little smack to watch the fat move, to see what Jay would do.

Jay huffed.

Rollins stood, tucked himself away and looked at Jay on the bed, still on his hands and knees, catching his breath, his face pressed into the scratchy grey blanket.

"Shit, dude, where'd that come from?" Jay panted out. He turned his head and squinted up at Rollins from under his skewed glasses.

Rollins' lips parted; a stunned feeling went through him.

He turned and left the room, left Jay lying there with his lazy smile, his eyes squinting with a genuine question.

Rollins' breathing was rough as he got himself a glass of water in the kitchen, looked through the lacy white curtains at the party spilling out to the front of the house.

Where'd that come from?

Had Rollins read that all wrong?

He drained the glass and left it on the sink. He went back out, got a diet coke and another water from the bar, re-joined Sarah. Slater was there now, talking about his new property in Perth.

Jay came back out and went for the bar. Rollins watched him. He ordered a whisky, straight up, took the backslap from Horace as he sipped, made sure not to show a hint of the burn from either.

Rollins thought about his dick in Jay's ass not five minutes ago, thought about how Jay would still be dripping with his come. He couldn't understand how he'd managed to read that all wrong. He was sure he hadn't—Jay had given him the look.

Still, Rollins hadn't done that since he got discharged for good reason. He was off-kilter thinking about it. A carefully packed box had been opened in his mind, next to all the other carefully packed boxes he'd kept up there since he left the army, and contents were being ripped out and scattered around by a force that wasn't him.

He watched Jay nod along as Horace spoke, not once looking in Rollins' direction for the remainder of the night. And that was more infuriating than the confusion. Rollins tethered himself to that anger and held on.

2

ROLLINS

One year later... Somewhere in the middle of the Indian Ocean.

I KNOW WHAT YOU'RE thinking. Whole thing was kinda rapey, even if Jay was into it. But we talked about it, me and Jay, made sense of it.

"Who're you talking to?"

"No one, just talking," I held up the hot pink cassette recorder—an oddity amidst the equipment—and let Jay see.

Jay frowned at it, the red of his sunburn painful to look at. The canopy in our little life raft had ripped and Jay seemed to insist on falling into that streak of sun. I'd gone through the equipment onboard several times and it was apparent Horace had not been adhering to the twelve-month servicing rule. There were no can openers. There should've been three. Enough tinned food to last a month if we could open them—clearly Horace was taking the piss from the grave.

Jay sat up.

"Give it to me."

I huffed and obliged.

Jay turned it over in his hands. "This was mine… Christmas present when I was six."

"Well, it still works, unlike everything else."

Jay shook himself like he was shaking off the memory. "I'll tell it, you're shit at talking."

"Reckon I was doin' alright."

"Tethered yourself to your anger?" Jay gave me his sleazy smile.

I shoved him. His body bounced against the inflatable and he winced.

"Here," I said and started to unbutton my shirt. It's white and long-sleeved, perfectly fitted for my wedding. Jay was left in nothing but a shredded singlet.

"No," Jay shook his head and stilled my hand. "I'm alright."

"No, you're fairer, I shoulda. Fuck, why didn't you make me give it to you earlier?"

"I'm alright," Jay clicked the record button. "C'mon, we'll both tell it, give us something to do while we wait."

I swallowed down that damn lump that kept threatening since we'd started drifting. While we waited. Waited to be found and bluff our way out of this. Or for the alternative. The EPIRB was fucked, and the SART was making an odd sound that probably meant some Egyptian cargo ship would get a blip and nothing more. Still, we had enough water for a while, fishing tackle, a first aid kit and all the safety gear except the life jackets. Another baffling absence. My Nokia had dried out and when it did, I was amazed it worked. No reception out here in godforsaken nowhere though. But even if there had been, who would we have called? A phone call for help was a one-way ticket to prison now.

Still, could've been worse, at least out here I had Jay pressing against my side, the never-ending glitter of sunlight dancing on the surface of the water and a sense I finally didn't need to keep all those boxes shut up tight and in order.

"See, this is why I got to tell it," Jay said.

"Why?"

"No one understands what these damn boxes are, you gotta tell the story. Too many metaphors, that's your problem..."

I pressed Jay closer to my side and hid my smile as I listened to him tell it.

3

♥

JAY

T HERE WERE A FEW things about Rollins I ascertained promptly upon meeting him. One, he was hot. I know, I know; you're thinking, well, duh, this is a gay romance, course he's hot, but you're not listening, not hearing me—he was *hot*, hotter than those GQ models, hotter than any dude I'd ever seen. Tattooed, ripped, perfect face; like, perfect symmetry of the nose and eyes, piercing grey eyes; just the whole makes-you-hard-just-looking-at-him package.

Two, he was an asshole. Course he was, right? Hotness and asshole go hand in hand. Barely said two words to me those first few weeks. The most he said was, "I didn't say anything" when he fucked my ass out of nowhere at that club opening in Port Hedland. I figured it was some kinda hazing ritual. Figured he'd been sent to put the pussy wanker from Sydney in his place. Well, joke was on him 'cos I damn well loved every second of it.

And three, he had a small dick—

One year and two minutes later... Somewhere in the middle of the Indian Ocean.

"**G**IVE ME THAT," I snatched the phone out of Jay's hand. "It ain't small."

Jay nodded along, smile cheesy. "It is but, relative to the rest of you. I mean, I'm half your size and I'm bigger."

"Fuck's sake, would you stop saying that. It's a good size!"

"A good size isn't big though, is it? But I reckon that's why you're so good with it, gotta make up for—

I found the energy to slap my hand over Jay's mouth.

"Stop talking. I'll be telling it like I was before. We've heard just about enough out of you."

Jay licked my palm because of course he did.

5

♥

Now, where were we...

ROLLINS HAD BEEN BACK in Perth a week and he couldn't get the damn incident with Jay out of his head. He would've liked to say it was because he felt guilty, not on account of cheating on his missus—it wasn't cheating if you weren't married yet—but on account of just fucking Jay like that, out of nowhere. Hook-ups in the army had been without the side chatter too, but they'd at least included a, "Hey, you wanna?" beforehand to make sure everyone was willing.

So, when Horace called him in and stated Jay would be tagging along with him for the foreseeable future—"Gotta toughen the little pussy up, his mother's made him into this, this..."—he waved his hand around and his fat face was so red he didn't really need the words to communicate what 'this' was—just hearing Jay's name sent an incomprehensible thrill through Rollins' body.

He clenched his jaw anyway.

"None of that," Horace said and sat forward, the leather of his chair groaning under the strain. "You got them pick-ups, then you got the books. Show him what's what, get him up to speed."

Rollins raised an eyebrow. Letting Jay see that, participate in it, was a one way ticket to prison if they got caught, which never bothered Rollins too much—he'd done some time in military prison after that time he went AWOL, which he never talked about, and again on the outside when he snapped in a bar and did a bunch of shit he couldn't remember and pled guilty on the charges, took the nine months inside because he was terrified of the alternative: getting up on that stand and saying he couldn't say what happened because he didn't remember.

But Jay was barely out of high school and greener than a cadet his first night at camp.

Horace took his meaning well enough anyway.

"Exactly," he smirked. So, the old man couldn't give a shit if his boy went inside, probably wanted it. As much as it seemed like he hated Jay, there was a gruff affection there too—as if he liked the idea of having a son, but warred with the idea the son in question was someone like Jay.

Rollins walked out without another word. He felt his phone buzz in his pocket and looked at the address on his screen. Jay's place wasn't far; a shitty suburb tucked behind the shopping centre.

He felt odd as he got into his lovingly maintained Jeep Cherokee—he'd bought it on his first stint home, before he got the call up to try for the SAS and everything went sideways. As he turned the ignition, he realised he was nervous.

And fuck that noise, he thought as he put it into first. If Jay wanted to confront him about the incident, so be it. Rollins would point out Jay seemed to enjoy himself just fine and that'd be the end of it. Never to be repeated, never to be discussed.

He pulled up outside the address and frowned in disgust. Overgrown weeds, the gutter hanging off the roof, tattered curtains in the windows; the whole vibe of the place said: *don't bother robbing us, we ain't got shit.*

Rollins got out and picked his way up the path through the cracks. A few ravens were hopping around, pecking through leftover food that looked like it'd been tossed off the veranda, their long drawn-out caws imitated back by one of their babies, his reply high-pitched before he swallowed greedily.

There was a doorbell beside the excessively large wooden door, a flyscreen door in front of that. The feel under the veranda was cool in a way that wasn't a comforting reprieve from the heat, but oppressive, dank. Rollins pressed the doorbell. He waited. Nothing.

He belted his fist on the heavy flyscreen a few times. He heard clattering from inside and the door groaned open.

Jay squinted out into the sunshine, his beady eyes slits beneath those black-rimmed glasses.

"Rollins?"

"Can I come in?"

"Why?" Jay blinked up at him. He pushed his glasses up his nose and made no move to open the flyscreen, which, now Rollins looked, was brand new and locked.

"Your dad sent me."

"Horace."

"Yeah? That's your dad, isn't it?"

Jay shook his head, that stupid smile spreading over his face at odds with what he was saying. "Yeah, but I call him Horace. Ain't much of a dad, is he?"

And Rollins didn't want to get into that.

"Are you gonna let me in?"

"You can probably say what you got sent to say from there, eh?"

Rollins stared at him. Jay watched him back.

"I'm not gonna do anything," Rollins found himself saying after they'd watched each other for longer than Rollins expected Jay to hold out.

But Jay just smiled, easy, nodded his head. "Wouldn't mind if you did, but I'm kinda busy."

"Kind of busy with what?" He wasn't touching the *wouldn't mind if you did*. He wasn't making that mistake twice.

"You know," Jay waved his hand behind him, leaned on the door, still smiling.

Rollins was at a loss; he most certainly did not know.

The ravens started cawing more insistently, more of them coming in behind him.

"I'd rather say this without the side of murder," Rollins said.

Jay raised both eyebrows, then cracked up laughing. Rollins held in his smile.

"Okay," Jay said and unlocked the screen door. "But only 'cos you made a joke and I didn't think you were capable of it, I really didn't," he opened the door, stepped back, waved his arm. "Come in, come in, just me and the crew here, workin' some shit, but we can talk in the kitchen. And it's a treachery, but I get it, I get it."

"What?"

"Murder of crows, treachery of ravens," Jay said and smiled over his shoulder.

Rollins shook his head; he was hung up on *the crew*, not debating the merits of naming groups of fucking birds. In his experience, where there were a lot of crows, there were dead bodies and that's all that mattered. But more importantly, *what crew*?

Rollins followed Jay down the hallway, clocked the bedroom on the right—occupied, bed unmade with a red doona, sparsely furnished. He felt the carpet under his feet sinking, giving in a way that meant the floor needed replacing, noticed the soft pink paint peeling on the veneer walls. He clocked the bedroom on the left—also occupied, bed made with a black doona, books on the bedside table, mugs; this one was tidy yet busy. So, Jay and at least one other person lived in this crack house.

Jay led him into the kitchen. A soft sound like beetles scurrying over a bench came from the room beyond. Like a lot of beetles scurrying. Computer keys. He craned his head back. There was at least one guy in his line of sight—black jeans, black shirt, but not in the bikie style; this was a metal head—he was typing on a computer and talking to someone else.

"So, wassup?" Jay asked.

"What's going on in there?"

Jay smiled. He had this easy way of smiling and moving. He was so white he practically glowed with it and yet he had the ceaseless, flowing, rhythmic way about him that reminded Rollins of the African-Americans he'd been stationed with for a while in Iraq. They had a coolness, an internal beat that no white person had. Jay had that. Jay had that encased inside a white man's chubby little body.

"Just messin' around, you know," Jay replied.

"You said working. You and the crew are working some shit."

"Yeah, you know, we're doin' our thing. What can I do for you now?" he asked as he shuffled to the fridge. "You wanna drink? I noticed you only drink water. You want some cold water?"

"What's your thing?"

Rollins peered through to the guy again. Now he listened, he reckoned there were at least two other guys in there.

Jay brought him a water. "Why're you so interested?"

Rollins looked back at Jay in front of him.

"I'm not."

"You're askin' a lotta questions for someone not interested," Jay went back to the fridge and got himself a coke.

"Look, your dad sent me."

"To find out what I'm doin'?" Jay raised both eyebrows, it made the glasses slip down and Jay pushed them up. It was a tick, but Rollins realised it was also because they weren't just too big for Jay's face in terms of style—which was garishly awful—but also literally, they were literally too big for him.

"Why don't you get glasses that actually fit?" Rollins asked.

"Huh?"

"Those glasses," Rollins picked up his water. "They're too big. Hell, get contacts. It's gotta be an improvement on those." He sipped and told himself to stop talking.

Jay was blushing; his skin was so fair it went pink instantly. He pulled the glasses off and examined them in his hand like he'd never thought about it.

"I really like these ones—

"It's not my business," Rollins put his glass of water down. "Your dad wants you workin' with me from now on."

Jay looked away from his glasses back to Rollins, his head tilting and eyes really squinting now.

"Doin' what?"

"You'll see."

"Okay," Jay slid the glasses back on, smiled easy again. "You got my number? You can just text me next time, no point comin' on over unless you need to, eh?"

"I really can't fathom what you're trying to hide here, unless it's the fact you live, well, here."

Jay shrugged. "Why would I be hidin' this place? It's nice."

Rollins stared at him. Jay smiled back; he was being sincere.

Rollins cleared his throat. He needed to address the other thing.

"And I shouldn't have done what I did in Port Hedland, it won't happen again."

Jay shrugged, leaned on the bench. "It's all good, dude."

"No, it isn't. I should've asked first. I thought..."

"I wasn't sayin' 'No' was I?"

Jay was blushing again, but Rollins had to admire the calm way he just took all this in.

"I guess not, but..."

Jay waited. He was good at that, Rollins realised. It was a surprise. To look at, he seemed like the kind of guy who'd need to fill awkward silences. But he didn't. He radiated the calm energy of a sniper. Rollins almost scoffed at the thought—with that eyesight? But his indignation was disingenuous because, yes, a part of him said, with that eyesight and that outfit—another pair of baggy jeans with boxers poking out the top, loose shirt, backwards cap—he had a stillness under the beat.

He didn't prompt on the but and his gaze never wavered, his smile never slipped.

"But," Rollins inhaled deeply. "If I hurt you, I'm sorry."

"Hurt me how? You mean 'cos you went in dry? Nah," Jay grinned, "you're not as big as I was expecting. It was all good, felt nice."

"Whaddya mean I'm not as big?"

"Just, you know," Jay gave him a once over. "You're a big dude, twice my size, eh? But your dick's like, relatively small."

"Small? What the fuck."

"Not small, like you don't have a small dick, but like, mine's bigger and I'm half your size, so like, relatively. You know relativity?"

Rollins couldn't believe what he was hearing.

"I do not have a small dick."

"Never said you did and hey, I reckon you're good with what you got, work well with it, but like, I was just surprised, thought it'd be a monster down there," he waved his coke up and down Rollins' body, took a drink. "'Cos like, you're so big otherwise."

Rollins stared at him. Jay wasn't being insulting, Rollins was pretty sure. He honestly thought Rollins didn't have a big dick.

"You do not have a bigger dick than me," he said.

"I do, but whatever man, I didn't mean to make a big deal out of it, I'm just saying. Didn't hurt."

"You don't," Rollins grabbed him by the arm and dragged him down the hall.

"Where are we going?"

Rollins tugged him into the nearest bedroom, the neat yet busy one.

"I'm the next one," Jay said easily for a man being dragged around.

Rollins turned him, shoved him back into the hall and into the sparsely furnished room, pushed him until he sprawled onto the bed. Jay rolled over, his glasses skewed on his face.

"Get your dick out," Rollins said gruffly.

"Are we actually gonna measure? Are you legit gonna do that right now?"

"Just do it," Rollins snapped and undid his fly, pushed his pants down so he could get his dick out. He was hardening up already.

Jay did the same, his breathing a little fast, his eyes a little wide, but otherwise compliant and easy.

Rollins wrapped his hand around himself and stroked.

"Go on," he said to Jay.

Jay got with the program, but not without an eyeroll. He wrapped his hand around his dick. It was as white as the rest of him. And, as Rollins had noticed last time, a decent size. But it was not bigger. It wasn't.

Rollins watched as Jay shuffled up the bed, propped himself up on the pillow, shimmied his pants down further and got to it. He was thick, definitely long, uncut. He rucked his shirt up to give himself more room to work, the soft padding of his stomach and abdomen a contrast to the steel thickness of his dick as he worked it.

Rollins increased his speed, felt his breath catch.

"Stop," he said and Jay did.

Rollins let go of himself and walked over to the bed.

"Oh my god—you're actually gonna measure, you're actually gonna measure."

"Shut up," Rollins said and straddled him.

He lined them up so he could angle his cock down and press it up against Jay's. The touch of their cocks together sent a tingle of pleasure all over his body. He slid forward and used his hand to press their dicks together in a line. Jay was panting, squirming, but otherwise letting him do it.

Jay was bigger. Quite a bit bigger. And thicker.

"Jesus," Jay breathed out and rubbed his dick alongside Rollins'.

Rollins forgot about the dick measuring and wrapped his hand around both of them.

It was dry, but it felt too good to stop. Jay thrust into his hand, then brought his own hand down to wrap over Rollins' and pushed up into the grip with his pelvis.

Rollins crouched over him, pressing him into the mattress as he got an awkward rhythm going, grinding their dicks together, squeezing and rubbing.

He was panting and looking at Jay's face. Jay watched him back. Those beady green eyes were taking a good look, wide open, hiding nothing of what he was feeling. His lips were parted and little puffs of air huffed against Rollins' lips.

Jay sped up with his hand, urging Rollins to go faster.

"Fuck," Rollins said and started to come, out of nowhere.

He thrust his hips forward, slid through his come and used his dick to spread it around Jay's dick, over his belly, used it to ease the way for Jay to fuck up into his hand, against the flat planes of his abdomen.

"You gonna come?" Rollins whispered. He wanted to sound nasty; he sounded breathless.

Jay squeezed his eyes shut. Gasped.

"Yeah, you're gonna come."

Jay did, his little body going tense, his eyes flying open and meeting Rollins'; he made it look like a surprise, his pleasure.

Rollins let him go and rolled off him. He landed on his back, closed his eyes and felt Jay jerking himself through the last of it, his elbow hitting Rollins in the side, his little whines and cut off breaths loud in the room.

They stayed like that for a moment, catching their breaths.

Rollins expected Jay to say something about having a bigger dick. He didn't. He rolled to his feet, reached for a towel hanging over the edge of the bed, wiped himself down before carefully folding the towel and handing it to Rollins.

Rollins wiped himself off perfunctorily and watched Jay tuck himself away.

"I gotta get back to it, yeah? Can walk you out first if you're ready? No rush, but," Jay smiled.

Jesus, Rollins didn't know what to do with that, with any of this.

He rolled to his feet, put himself away and did up his pants. He was still breathing heavily. He wanted to ask again what it was Jay needed to get back to. As far as he knew, Jay moved here from Sydney a month ago. How did he have a *crew*?

But it was none of his business, and besides, he was pretty out of it from what'd just happened.

"You want another glass of water before you head out?" Jay asked.

Rollins wanted to snap at him, but as his eyes landed on Jay in the doorway he saw the genuine question in his eyes, and all he could do was huff and shake his head.

"I'll text you," he said gruffly as he passed him in the doorway.

"Cool, cool."

"I like to get shit done early and again late."

"'S cool with me dude, I can work around what you got goin' on."

"I ain't got anything going on."

"Okay," Jay said, his tread close behind Rollins' as he walked him to the door.

"I just got a routine, that's all," Rollins said. He didn't know why he was explaining himself.

"Routine is good," Jay leaned around him, his body pressing into Rollins' back. He felt warm and he smelled good. Not like heavy deodorant—which Rollins hated, that and perfume—Jay smelled like the lightest spray of something and then himself, which was earthy with a hint of good-smelling sweat.

Rollins shook his head and stepped outside. The sunshine was blinding, the bitumen road and shithole houses an affront to his senses as he moved away from Jay. He heard the flyscreen shut quietly and lock behind him. He turned back.

"Tomorrow, gotta pick up at night, but I'll do the books in the morning. Your dad," he took a deep breath, blew it out, "Horace—

Jay smiled at him, easy as usual; he was leaning in the doorway, hidden by the shadows.

"Wants you in on that too."

"Cool, cool, but maths ain't really my thing, you know?"

"Yeah, well," Rollins turned and went down the stairs, something twisting in his gut. "See you tomorrow."

"See ya."

Rollins looked back, but the door was closing with a thud.

6

ROLLINS HAD TEXTED JAY the night before telling him he'd pick him up at seven. Jay had replied asking where they'd be working, which had turned into an hour-long exchange, dialling Rollins' fury right up at the audacity of all the bloody questions, and ended with Jay insisting he'd get the bus. This was absurd because Rollins lived in a ground floor unit in Scarborough with a little yard for his dog Nola. Scarborough meant Jay needed to take a bus and a train and another bus and get there by seven.

There was no way he was going to get there by seven and it'd throw Rollins' whole fucking routine out.

He barely slept, frustrated thinking about it, which meant he was gritty eyed and pissed off when he and Nola ran the beach at four, he was stewing and throwing his weights around when he did his workout at five, he didn't enjoy his protein shake at six, and he swore it was all Jay's fault his oatmeal tasted like shit.

A soft knock on his door at 6:56am snapped him out of it.

He opened the door to Jay. He had to look down because he had a good foot on him, and all he could focus on were those stupid glasses atop a beaming smile looking back up at him.

"I bought us some breakfast," Jay said and held up a bag covered in grease.

"From where?"

"Bus station in the city," Jay dropped the bag to his side, hoisted his backpack up his shoulder. "You gonna let me in?"

Rollins stepped back and held his breath.

Jay stepped inside, peering up at him.

"I don't stink," he said around a small smile.

Rollins was about to tell him he fucking well did, but he caught the little flash of hurt behind the glasses and bit back the retort.

"It's not that," he said and slammed the door. He didn't want to say Jay smelled good—he did—and it was making Rollins act insane.

"Okay," Jay said and looked around.

"I don't eat junk food."

"Oh," Jay clutched the bag. "Sorry, shit, I can eat it outside."

"Nola's out there."

"Who?"

"My dog."

"You got a dog?" Jay moved into the unit, beelining for the little courtyard where Nola was dancing on her paws, tongue hanging out, slapping the door with her nails.

"Fuckin' nice one, man, a Lab," Jay opened the door.

Nola jumped up before Rollins could stop her, seized the bag and took off.

"Fuck's sake," Rollins said but missed her as she darted past him, jumped onto the couch and tore into the bag. She swallowed both pastry-encrusted, greasy nightmares in two moves.

"Sorry, man," Jay said.

"Why're you sorry? She's the one who ate your breakfast."

Jay shrugged and came over to her, patted her as she snapped her jaws on the last of it. "You sounded mad, thought maybe she's on a special diet or something."

Rollins snorted. "As if I could control what she eats."

Jay nodded along. "Yeah man, Labs," he was patting her, grinning. "Trainer-wheel dog."

"A what now?"

Jay tilted his head at him. "Trainer-wheel dog. It's like, the dog you get before you get a real dog 'cos they're so easy to handle and shit."

"She's not a fucking trainer-wheel dog."

"She is, but. Nothing wrong with it."

"She's not."

"She is," Jay smiled down at her. "You learn how to handle 'em with a dog like this, then you can get a proper dog."

"Really," Rollins said flatly. "Is that why I had to rescue her from a pack of junkies throwing her against the adjoining wall when she was a pup 'cos she's so fucking easy."

"Noooo..." Jay drew the word out, his face transforming to horror.

Fuck's sake. Why'd Rollins tell him that? He'd never told anyone that.

It was true enough. Fucking assholes. He'd listened to her next door, just being a pup, and those cunts—off their heads, beating on her for pissing and shitting inside, for wanting some attention. He'd let it go for a week. One week he'd sat on that couch, feeling the tight lid on his anger threatening to burst before he'd gotten up, grabbed a hammer, marched over and belted on the door.

"Give her to me," he'd said when one of them opened the door.

"Who?" the fucking tweaker had asked, his jaw grinding away.

"The fucking dog."

The tweaker laughed. "You ain't takin'—

"Give her to me now or I'll cave your skull in," Rollins had said and lifted the hammer, slapped it in his palm a few times. He didn't reckon the dick in front of him had got scared at that; Rollins reckoned he actually wanted to get rid of her.

Next thing he knew, he had a black ball of fur in his arms, her big eyes looking up at him, tongue hanging out as she panted, not a scrap of what they'd done to her marking her personality in any way.

And since then, he'd had a dog. Nola.

His missus wasn't a fan.

"No," Jay said again now and leaned down to cuddle her, his arms wrapping around her big body and squeezing while she vibrated with happiness at the attention, the food.

Rollins cleared his throat, marched into the kitchen. He loved Nola. Seeing her get showered with love made him happy, which pissed him off because he didn't want to feel good around Jay. He was scared he'd let his guard down. And he knew nothing good ever came when he let his guard down.

"You want something to drink? I've got water or green tea."

Jay patted Nola's head. Shook his own. "I definitely don't want either of those. It's all good, I've got a coke in my bag."

"You can't drink coke at seven in the morning."

"I can and I do," Jay grinned over at him.

"It's your funeral," Rollins said and made himself a tea. He brought it to the table where the books were, a couple of duffel bags on the floor—one empty, one half full of money.

He wanted to tell Jay to get over there so they could get on with it, but he loved seeing Nola so happy and couldn't say it. He opened the account book, picked up his pencil and ran it down the column. He had thirty-six thousand to launder and he got to thinking on where to put it.

But the sound of Jay telling Nola she was a "good girl, a very good girl, yes you are," and Nola panting in reply, then Jay unzipping his bag, a can opening, rummaging in said bag was too distracting. He wanted to snap at him, but Nola didn't like that so he focused on the columns.

Jay sat down next to him. Rollins just stopped himself from inching further away. He breathed in and counted to five, breathed out and held the count.

"So, what're we doing?"

Rollins sighed, looked down his nose at Jay. Jay was already smiling back. Rollins shook his head, tapped his pencil on the page.

"I gotta clean this money. Best way to do it is through my electrical business—

"You're a sparky?"

"Yeah."

"I thought you were ex-military."

And how did he know that? Didn't matter.

"I am. Did the trade in the army."

"That's so cool dude. I could never be in the army—

Rollins snorted a laugh. He couldn't help himself.

"What?"

"Nothin'."

"No, what?" Jay was still smiling up at him.

"Nothin', just. No, you probably couldn't."

"Not 'cos of the discipline or whatever, fuck you," but Jay said it like a joke, no heat. "'Cos I hate getting yelled at by men."

Rollins shook his head and hid his smile. "Well, there's some women in there doin' a lotta yelling too. Sure you'd find a unit if you really wanted it."

Jay frowned, bopped his head like he was thinking about it.

"I think I like, hate yelling in general."

"Does anyone like yelling?" Rollins had no idea how Jay managed to drag him into these conversations.

"I reckon some people must 'cos they be doin' it all the time," Jay took a long drink.

"I don't think they like it, I think they ain't got control of themselves," Rollins replied.

Jay tilted his head to the side.

"Anyway," Rollins tapped the page. "I dunno why Horace wants me to show you this, if he's thinking you could be running your own show one day..."

Jay rolled his eyes and Rollins agreed. Even if Horace thought that, he wouldn't be helping Jay do it.

"But you can learn the principles and apply it in another context."

Jay was quiet beside him. Rollins peered at him. He looked puzzled.

"What?"

"Nothin', just didn't think you'd be smart."

"What the fuck. Okay, first of all, ain't need to be a genius to do this and second, why'd you think I'd be dumb?"

"'Cos you're hot."

Rollins clenched his jaw. He felt a thrill run through him at Jay saying that, which was stupid. Rollins knew what he looked like, but no one ever came out and said it.

"Just because..." he shuffled around in his seat, sipped his tea. It burnt his tongue and he put it down roughly.

"So we're gonna, what? Pretend you did a job or something?"

Rollins cleared his throat and took the out Jay had given him.

"That's one way to do it, but depends on the amount. Here, see," he tapped his pencil on the earnings column, "only got thirty-six thousand this time so, yeah, could run it as a job for, say, a sporting club, doing some lights, but that's easily disputed isn't it? Say I get audited; well, he's just gotta head on down to old South Perth Bowls Club and see they ain't got new lights. So, we spread it," he tapped the items in the far column. "Run twelve thousand as scrapped copper. Eighteen thousand five hundred on top of this airport job, 'cos it's big enough we can run it as a variation; say we got in there and they decided they wanted the more expensive light fixtures from Italy. Then we spread the rest across materials."

Jay listened and watched, his body inching closer so he could look at each column.

"Easy," he said.

Rollins sat back, tossed his pencil.

"It's not easy, it's risky and you gotta think real careful about it."

"You really did a job at the airport?"

Rollins felt whiplash from the sudden subject change. "I really did all these jobs."

"Shit, dude, you must be hella busy."

"Full, I got a full schedule, don't know about busy."

"What's the difference?"

"The difference is busy implies I'm doing too much, but I do just enough to fill each day."

Jay snorted. "So no spontaneity for you then, eh?" He finished his coke and got up to put it in the bin, strolled around the kitchen like he was right comfortable in Rollins' space.

The thought of spontaneity made Rollins feel like he was going to hyperventilate; he set that aside and carried on, tried to keep this thing focused on the job.

"Once we got the accounting side of it sorted, we bank it," Rollins said. Jay was opening his fridge.

"What're you doing?" Rollins got up.

"I'm hungry but I can't eat any of this."

Rollins came up behind him and looked at his neatly stacked shelves of weighed portions of meat for the day, eggs, the crisper full of vegetables.

"Whaddya mean you can't any of this? It's food." Not like Rollins would give him any, it was all accounted for.

Jay slammed the fridge shut. "Wanna head out and eat?"

"No, I do not want to head out and eat. We need to get this done."

Jay nodded along.

"Fuck's sake, sit down, I'll make you something."

Jay shook his head. "I can't eat that."

"You can't eat real food?"

For the first time, Jay looked cagey.

"I can make you eggs."

Jay shuffled back to his bag and got out another coke. Rollins wondered if there was a never-ending supply in there. If that was all that was in there.

"You got any music?" Jay asked as he cracked the can open.

"There's a stereo isn't there?" Rollins snapped and opened the fridge, got out the eggs.

"Nah, dude, don't make me anything, I'll wait," he went over to the stereo and turned it on, hit play.

Pink Floyd's *Dark Side of the Moon* drifted into the space.

"I can make you poached eggs."

"I won't eat 'em."

Rollins slammed the fridge shut.

"Why?"

"Don't eat eggs."

"Why?"

Jay slipped back into his chair and looked at the book.

"Just don't, c'mon, let's get this bit done 'cos then I can eat on the way to the bank."

Rollins felt his temples throbbing. He wanted to say they most certainly could not eat on the way to the bank—he went to the bank, then directly to the gym—though he had no idea what he was going to do with Jay while he was at the gym.

"What bank do we gotta go to?"

"Northbridge," Rollins said and scraped his chair on the tiles as he pulled it out.

Jay scrunched his face up.

"What?"

"Nothin', just not much open there during the day."

"There's a deli," Rollins said gruffly. "I'm sure they'll sell whatever cancer-inducing shit you like to eat in there."

Jay giggled. "Cool."

Rollins shook his head and got to assigning the amounts, explaining each to Jay as he went. Jay moved his head next to him, nodding along. He was smiling and cutting Rollins off with inane questions, but Rollins got the feeling he was taking it all in just fine; in fact, a lot better than he let on. Rollins got to wondering if part of the chill-dude-vibe was an act.

7

♥

A FTER HE DID THE bank and dropped Jay at the deli, Rollins went to the gym. He used the old kickboxing place because it had an old-school set-up, same as the army, and it was always quiet. He was a big fan of quiet.

He'd done the treadmill for forty minutes, finished the hand weights and was dropping the dumbbell on the ground after a ripper set when he was assaulted by the sound of gun fire. His heart seized in his chest. It felt like it stopped before it galloped ahead of him too fast, too much. There was dust and he couldn't see, he couldn't see what happened—an explosion? Derek was in front of him holding his arm, but his arm wasn't attached to his body anymore, he was holding it near his thigh and looking around. Gunfire rained down on them from the hill—

Rollins stumbled through the gym, crashing into machines, scrambling for the showers, for his bag, for his pills, he needed, if he could just make it all slow down, he could get home...

Rollins rolled over on his couch. Nola was nudging his hand.

Everyone called Labs stupid, said they didn't know when to turn it off. But Nola always knew. When Rollins got like this, she sat real quiet near him, nudged him awake when it all came crashing back in, whined at him until he got up and took his pills.

"Good, girl," he said to her, patted her head and rolled to sit up.

It was late. Night beyond the open door, the sound of the waves crashing on the shore reaching him out of the blackness.

He got up and Nola padded along behind him.

"Good, girl," he said again as he got out her food.

She whined up at him and he smiled down at her. He set her things aside and grabbed a pill, washed it down.

"Happy?"

Her tail thumped on the floor.

He got her food, watched her whoop it down before looking for his phone.

Ten unread texts.

Fuck. Jay. He must've left him in Northbridge. He couldn't remember. He never remembered.

Yo dude im all done just waitin in the park.

An hour later, which, Rollins was impressed he held out like that; if he made his missus wait an hour longer than intended, she'd have his balls.

Just checkin u got me b4. Im in the park. Headin back to the deli.

Rollins' heart clenched when he saw Jay waited another hour before texting again.

Wow u really like to work out eh?
Im at the deli.
Im gonna eat more, just be inside.

Forty minutes later:

U alright dude?

Rollins couldn't quite believe he waited another hour before calling it.

Im guessin u ditched me.

It's cool.

Im out.

Hope ur alright.

And just fuck Jay for that last one. He should be angry—for all he knew, Rollins just left him there.

Sorry, he wrote. *Sick. Had to bail.*

It was lame as fuck—who got so sick they had to leave someone behind? But fucked if he was going to tell Jay he left him because he'd had... whatever, an episode or something.

Dude!

Rollins snorted, he didn't know what to do with that. He really didn't want to explain he was a walking time bomb that exploded every time he heard a car backfire. He'd left his missus at a restaurant once. She went nuts when she found him at home, then got all pissy when he refused to elaborate on the sick line. It was nobody's business. A man can't walk around in the world telling people his weaknesses. Hell, no. If he wanted to advertise his liabilities like that, he might as well just take out an ad in the fucking paper: *Rollins here—if you wanna take me out, just set off some firecrackers.*

So, he really wasn't looking forward to the interrogation from Jay.

We still doin this pick-up?

Rollins raised his eyebrows. He looked at the clock. They had a few hours. He felt washed out, exhausted, but he refused to let this shit get to him.

Yep. Be at yours in an hour.

If Jay was planning to give him the run around and insist on getting a bus like last night, Rollins was going to punch him in the face when he saw him—

Kay. U sure u up to it?

And that pissed Rollins off as well.

He ignored it.

See you in an hour.

He went and got in the shower.

8

♥

HE EXPECTED QUESTIONS, BUT Jay got in the car as soon as Rollins pulled up, looked him over, said, "Yeah, lookin' like hell, eh?" and put his seatbelt on.

"Where we headed?" he asked before Rollins could defend his appearance.

Like Jay was one to talk. Rollins could make cancer look better than the awful hoodie Jay was wearing. It was actually psychedelic.

"Think the eighties called." He couldn't help himself.

But Jay laughed and plucked at the material on his chest.

"'S alright, eh? Used to be my mum's."

"I wouldn't advertise that," Rollins said and headed for the freeway.

"So, where we goin'?" Jay looked out the window. He was really good at dismissing what he chose not to hear.

"You'll see."

"Ominous."

Rollins snorted.

"Why didn't you bring Nola?"

"Huh?" Rollins glanced at him. The streetlights were whipping by and lighting him up before he dropped into darkness, flashes of light reflecting off his glasses, his easy smile on Rollins from where he was huddled into the seat.

"Nola. Dogs love going for drives."

Rollins gave him a look like he was insane, because he was. He wasn't wrong—Nola did love the car.

"It's not safe."

And maybe he shouldn't have said that, he didn't want Jay to feel unsafe.

But Jay just nodded along. "Yeah, makes sense."

"I mean," Rollins said and took the exit, headed south. "It's not like anything's ever happened. Especially not since Tara took over. What's that whore gonna do?"

"Is she a prostitute?"

Rollins glanced at him; he sounded uncharacteristically serious.

"Yes?"

"Is that a yes or you're just calling her that?"

"What're you, the union for whores?"

Jay huffed at him. "Dude, you know my mum is, was, c'mon."

And, well, Rollins did and yet he didn't. He couldn't fathom it. His own mum was a bookkeeper and a housewife, went to church on Sundays, he was pretty sure she was in a quilting group for fuck's sake. A mother as a prostitute? Unfathomable.

"Yeah," he breathed out. "Yeah, I heard something like that."

"And it's just a job, ain't no reason all you guys think you can use them then have all this fucking attitude about it. I mean, she wouldn't have a job if you didn't need her."

"I've never been to a prostitute," Rollins shot him an affronted look.

"Yeah, 'cos you don't mind tappin' ass and guys always be up for it. Still, don't think you can just go round callin' them whores."

"Look," Rollins ground his teeth together. He had a headache. He also didn't know what to say. He'd never developed an opinion on prostitution beyond the usual shit that floated around about it.

Clearly he'd hit a nerve with Jay though. Maybe his only nerve.

"Look? Look what?" Jay went on while Rollins floundered. "Just don't say that shit, alright? It's not cool. Now," Jay sat up. Rollins could feel his eyes on the side of his head. "I'm asking again, is this Tara a prostitute?"

"No... I dunno. She used to be a skimpy, a stripper. Now she cooks."

"A skimpy and a stripper is not a prostitute," Jay said.

"Alright, what're you? HR for the sex workers now?"

Jay huffed. "No, although I could be if that were a job. I'm just saying, don't use their job as an insult. It's hard work."

Rollins bit his cheek to stop himself from a very inappropriate snort of laughter.

"Don't laugh," Jay said. "It is, you haven't seen the shit I have."

Rollins glanced at him. Jay was being serious.

"No, I know, I wasn't gonna laugh at that, just," he looked over his shoulder, checked the blind spot and sped around a long line of cars, "hard."

Jay snorted. "For real, dude?"

But he was laughing and Rollins felt oddly relieved.

"Anyway, all I was saying before," Rollins gave him a pointed look, "before I got the lecture from the prostitution PC union," he shot Jay a smile. Jay scoffed. "...was Tara never makes any trouble with pick-ups. Sometimes Carl's with her, since he chopped his balls off and went back to her, and he's a dick, but there's never any trouble." He drummed his fingers on the steering wheel. "Still."

"Still?"

"Still, never trust them. Any of them. Anyone. And that's why I don't bring Nola."

"You don't trust anyone? What about your girlfriend?"

Rollins snorted at that.

"Especially not her."

"But she's your partner, gotta trust your partner, dude. You believe in soulmates?"

Rollins features contorted as he glanced back at Jay. There was barely any traffic this far down the freeway and the old Jeep glided along smoothly.

"I can't quite believe you just asked me that. And I'm guessing you haven't had any relationships if you reckon you can trust your... your..."

Jay cracked up. "Can't even say it. And yeah, man, course I had partners. I've had a few boyfriends. Two of 'em real serious."

Rollins gave him another bewildered look. "You're that gay?"

"Wasn't aware there were degrees of gayness," Jay chuckled. "We ain't all fucking ass and pretending it's all no homo."

"I'm bisexual," Rollins defended himself. Contrary to what Jay was implying, he was self-aware enough to know that: fuck you very much, Jay.

"Nice, nice," Jay nodded along and looked out the window. "We almost there? Or does this chick live in the country?"

Rollins was again vexed by the subject change. He wanted to keep talking about relationships. He never had before.

"Technically, no, still Perth, but urban sprawl so it feels like it."

He didn't know how to bring the conversation back without letting Jay know he wanted to discuss it. He couldn't stop himself from being curious about Jay having boyfriends either. There was no way.

"Yeah, yeah, I been noticing that. In Sydney, me and mum had a flat—

"You've really had two boyfriends?"

Rollins felt awkward at blurting that out and he could feel Jay's eyes on him. He gave him the side-eye. Yep, he was watching him, smiling small and easy-going, the orange of the streetlights between the moments of darkness casting him in a glow, then shadow.

"Yeah, man. Aiden when I was in high school, then I dated this dude who shall remain nameless before I came out here."

"Remain nameless," Rollins scoffed. "Was he famous?"

"Nah, nothin' like that, just turned out to be a bit of an asshole and so I don't wanna speak his name, you know?"

Once again, Rollins did not know.

"But for real, before that, those dudes were my dudes. Not my soulmates, but you know, my partners. I'd tell 'em everything, trusted 'em to try all the shit, you know?"

Rollins jerked his head to stop the conversation. He did not know and he regretted asking.

"That's why I can't get you not trusting your woman. That's the whole point, eh?"

Rollins pulled off the freeway. "It is most definitely not the whole point. You get a missus 'cos you need to have one, gotta get married and shit."

"Who says you need to have one?"

"Life."

"I never heard anything about that, but I don't reckon that's a good reason to be with someone, 'cos you need to have one? You don't need anything except the basics, man. Beyond that, you can do what you want."

"You can't just do what you want."

"Yeah, you can."

They were stopped at a red light, nothing and no one around.

Rollins looked at Jay. Jay wasn't watching him back, he was peering around the nondescript edge of the suburb.

"You can't," Rollins insisted. "If you just go on doin' what you want everything will be out of control."

And okay, Rollins, he said to himself, it was really time to stop talking.

Jay frowned over at him.

The light turned green and Rollins accelerated so hard they skidded out. Jay didn't say anything about it or even flinch.

They were quiet as Rollins drove through the suburb, beyond it, made the turn off for the beach.

"I don't reckon you should get a partner so you feel like you got life under control."

"Yeah, well, I don't reckon you know shit all about it," Rollins snapped.

"Nah, man, I get I'm like ten years younger than you or whatever—

Rollins peered at him then refocused on the dirt track, the dunes high on each side of them illuminated by the high-beams. So Jay was around twenty. And here he was, lecturing Rollins on relationships. And prostitution.

"But I reckon you're wrong on this one, man. Don't wanna go getting something outside yourself to control the inside, you know? That's askin' for trouble."

The little caravan came into view and Rollins threw the car into neutral.

"No," he said slowly. "Placing yourself in someone else's hands is askin' for trouble. We're here," he finished even though it was obvious.

"This is nice, eh?"

"It's a fucking caravan."

"Man, I'd love to live in a caravan."

"No one would love to live in a caravan," Rollins said and opened the door.

"Well, that's just not true, is it?" Jay was still talking as he got out on the other side and they both made their way around the hood. "Cos I'd just love it. Pick up, be movin' on whenever you felt like it, all self-contained—

"Shut up."

Jay did, then had the audacity to look affronted.

"Dude, not cool. We were chatting—"

"And now we need to stop," Rollins said, voice low. "We're on the job now."

"Well you coulda just said that," Jay whispered back.

"Stop whispering."

"You were."

"I wasn't."

The door to the caravan opened and Tara appeared in the doorway, cigarette in her mouth, those dead eyes of hers surveying them like she thought they were nothing but trash.

Rollins squared his shoulders, did his best to pretend Jay didn't exist beside him.

Tara took a drag and looked between them. If she was surprised by Jay, she didn't show it.

"Carl's just packing it," she said.

Rollins groaned internally; he hated seeing Carl.

"You got the money?"

"Jay, in the back," Rollins said.

"I'm on it, dude," he said. Rollins cringed on the inside but kept his face blank. Tara watched Jay, smoked. "Nice to meet you, Tara. I'm JC," he said to her.

She quirked her lips. "JC."

Rollins clenched his jaw.

"Didn't know you'd be needing muscle to come on and visit me now," she smirked at Rollins.

Rollins felt his eye twitch. Jay laughed. Rollins listened to his feet crunching in the sand as he went to the rear of the jeep. He stared at Tara. She stared back, smoked. She twitched as Carl came up behind her, his hand resting on her waist, other hand holding a black duffel.

"Rollins," he said as he handed her the bag.

Rollins grunted.

"Is it the black one?" Jay shouted from the rear of the vehicle.

Carl quirked an eyebrow, Tara smiled, and Rollins felt his temple throb. Instead of answering he turned and went to the back of the jeep.

Jay was standing there, surveying the duffel with the cash, Rollins' gym bag, and another duffel Rollins liked to think of as his post-apocalypse escape bag. They were all black.

"They all look the same," Jay said.

"They do not all look the same," Rollins hissed. "This one is clearly packed with cash. Look at the shape of it."

It was rectangle at the edges, the cash pressed in nice bundles against it; whereas the other two had the look of being packed with luggage, gear.

"Dunno, man, I wouldn't wanna grab the wrong one, accidentally give her your weekend getaway gear," Jay stepped back as Rollins tugged the cash bag forward.

"I don't have weekend getaway gear," Rollins snapped.

"Alright, alright," Jay grabbed the bag and walked off.

"What the fuck is weekend getaway gear," Rollins muttered and followed on the other side of the vehicle.

Carl was sitting on the caravan step, Tara in front of him with the bag. They were both smirking.

"Who's your friend?" Carl asked.

"No one," Rollins snapped.

"Dude," Jay said to him then turned and made his way over to Tara with the bag. "I'm JC. Nice to meet you, eh? We got this one for you," he dropped the bag next to the other one, "and this'll be for us, eh? Nice, nice. You wanna count the cash?"

"Nah," Tara winked. "I know where this one lives," she inclined her head behind Jay, indicating Rollins.

Rollins held in the eye-roll. As if that tiny skank could ever get the jump on him.

"Fair enough," Jay clapped his hands. "We'll be going then. Nice to meet you, Tara, Carl."

Rollins couldn't watch anymore. He got back in the driver's seat. He started the engine while Jay fucked around at the back, rearranging the bags and nattering on about what was in said bags.

Tara and Carl didn't move, just watched them, their mouths moving like they were having a conversation. Probably discussing the ludicrousness that was Jay.

Jay finally got in, did up his seatbelt and said "They seem nice."

"They're not," Rollins replied and reversed out of there.

"You know, I get the feeling you don't give people much of a chance. If you spent time with them—

Rollins scoffed. "I am not spending fucking time with them. Jesus Christ." He spun out and straightened, headed back for the main road. "I'd rather stick bamboo shoots under my fingernails than spend time with those two."

"Visceral, dude."

Rollins grunted.

"I'm just sayin'..."

And Jay promptly continued to just say all the way back to the clubhouse. At least it took Rollins' mind off the drive, the stash in the back, and the usual terror that lingered whenever he drove this part.

"Jayden, get in the back and help cut this shit," Horace said once they made the drop. He jerked his head at Rollins, dismissing him.

Rollins felt an odd protectiveness flare to life. He also felt incensed on Jay's behalf. Cutting was fraught with potential catastrophes: the gear itself was nasty to handle; the ever-present anxiety that Horace, in a state of paranoid madness, might accuse the cutter of fudging it and pocketing pure gear; and then there was getting busted actually doing it—can't get caught more red-handed than literally cutting pure gear.

"Cool, cool," Jay said, easy going as usual. It pissed Horace off; he hid it, but Rollins didn't miss the narrowing of his eyes nor the clench of his jaw as Jay strolled past him. "Later, Rollins."

"Hang on," Rollins said.

"Yeah, man?" Jay smiled over at him.

"Don't you need a lift home?" Rollins wasn't sure where that was coming from but it sounded plausible enough.

Horace scoffed. "He can fucking walk from here. Do him some bloody good too, work off the fat."

Like Horace was one to talk, Rollins thought and eyed the old man's gut straining over his belt. Jay though, his smile dimmed a bit, like he'd been called out as unbecoming in front of his crush, which was a ludicrous thought—Jay clearly enjoyed their little fucks, but he wasn't into Rollins, Rollins knew that much.

"Ain't safe to be walkin' around here at two in the morning. I'll wait," Rollins surprised himself and went to the bar.

"It's all good, dude. I can walk," Jay said.

"He can bloody well walk!" Horace reiterated.

"Water," Rollins said to the skimpy. Then turned to Jay. "Go on, get on with it, I don't wanna be here all night."

Jay smiled—a stupid exaggerated thing with all his teeth—and hopped to it, rushing through the door that'd take him to the office where the gear was.

"What's gotten into you?" Horace asked. "He can fucking well walk."

Rollins shrugged and sipped his water.

"You gettin' soft? Maybe I shouldn't have paired you with the little pussy."

Rollins drummed his fingers on the bar.

"You ain't helpin' him toughen up, which is why his whore of a mother sent him here in the first place," Horace held up a finger to the skimpy and she reached for the rum.

His mum sent him? That got Rollins' attention.

"You should know this, weren't you some hot shit in the army?"

Rollins stared at him. "SAS," he sipped his water. "And we worked in pairs, if you catch my meaning."

Horace slurped on his drink. "Perfect, baby," he winked at the skimpy. "Yeah, well, this ain't that," he said to Rollins.

Rollins hoped Horace wasn't planning to join him for the entire dawn patrol. But he couldn't help from answering. "Actually, it's exactly like that. Never leave your partner behind."

"Bunch of fuckin' faggots," Horace replied and chugged the drink.

"They also taught us how to kill a man with whatever we got layin' around."

Horace raised an eyebrow. "You threatenin' me, son?"

"Just making conversation," Rollins said and picked up his glass, looked at his fingers. "Even bare handed, we learnt that too," he sipped.

Horace chuckled and drained his drink. "Alright, you do you. I'm out," and with that—thank Christ—he left.

One thing about Horace, he wouldn't retaliate unless someone actually did something. Man didn't rise to the bait of talk. But if he thought you'd done something? Well, then, different story. Not that Rollins needed to worry about that; he was just doing this on the side to get the cash to build the dream home for the missus in the suburbs, square away his own little stash so he could finally buy a boat.

As for Jay? Well, it's not like he was actually going to do something, was he?

9

IT WAS CLOSER TO three by the time Rollins pulled into Jay's driveway. He was antsy at having broken his routine, but when they saw a pack of drunks loitering around the shopping centre, he was damn glad he'd stayed. Those guys would've beaten Jay and stolen his sneakers, no doubt about it.

"Thanks, dude. For real, my whole body hurts," Jay said. "You wanna come in?"

Rollins raised both eyebrows. Was Jay asking for something or was he just asking to be polite?

"Why?" Rollins replied. He needed to get to the beach and run Nola in an hour.

Jay shrugged. "To fuck around? Why else? Pretty sure you got like, water and shit back at your place," he looked down at his hands.

He seemed nervous. Like it cost him something to ask. And, well, Rollins' dick was interested just from the invite, fuck the rest of it.

He got out of the car and followed as Jay scrambled to get in front of him.

Rollins was balls deep in Jay's ass for the second time that morning. Christ, he was a good fuck. Responsive, needy, Jay totally abandoned himself to his senses the moment Rollins shoved his dick into him.

"Oh, fuck, here we go," Rollins grunted as he slid out and slammed back in.

"Yeah, dude, just there, just there," Jay panted and arched his back, pushed himself back onto Rollins' cock.

"Don't call me," Rollins pulled out and shoved in again, "'dude' when I'm fucking you."

Jay laughed. Rollins thrust in harder. Jay threw his head back, his baseball cap finally gone and his surprisingly clean blonde hair brushing his nape while Rollins fucked into him from behind.

Rollins slid his hand into his hair at the base of his skull and gripped him, tugging his head back so Jay's throat was taut, his eyes on the ceiling. He grabbed him by the hip, his fingers digging into the white flesh, marking him up with bruising indents. His dick moved like a piston in and out of him, and he watched himself disappearing again and again into that heat, that tightness. Jay clenched around him, moaned like an absolute slut and Rollins pumped his hips faster

"Yeah, you fuckin' like that?"

"Fuck yeah, just there," Jay panted out between thrusts.

"God, listen to you, such a slut for it."

Jay moaned and shoved back, tried to rip his head free. Rollins tightened his grip and fucked him harder.

"Oh, fuck," Jay gasped.

"Yeah? Already gonna come for the second time," Rollins increased the pace.

Jay keened, tried to get more of Rollins' dick into him but he was pinned, manipulated, and could only move where Rollins let him go.

"Nuh, uh," Rollins leaned down to whisper near his ear. "You come on my dick or not at all."

"Go faster then."

Rollins huffed. "Such a slut," he said and kissed Jay's ear and did as he was told.

He was sweating, puffing, he felt like he'd done a marathon of a workout by the time Jay came, crying out as he did it; that did it for Rollins—he shoved in deep and held himself there, came with a long, drawn-out groan. He stayed like that for a minute, rocking his hips into Jay with little twinges of pleasure, burying his come in the little slut.

A low groan came out of his throat as he pulled out and flopped onto his back next to Jay on the bed.

Jay laughed, breathless. Then he had to go and talk.

"Such a slut, really?" he nudged Rollins in the side.

Rollins felt himself blush. "What? You seemed to like it."

Jay chuckled and Rollins could feel him rolling over to look at him. "Yeah, dude, it's kinda hot, but like, your kinks are so vanilla. It's a good thing you're good with that dick of yours."

"Vanilla? Since when is being called a slut vanilla? I don't reckon my parents would be doing that skanky shit," Rollins rolled up to sit. "We weren't all raised by whores." He stood, looked for his clothes. He couldn't believe he'd just said that. But he wasn't taking it back. Fuck, Jay. Just fuck him.

Rollins yanked his pants on, grabbed his shirt off the floor, pulled it over his head and looked at Jay without wanting to.

Jay was staring at the ceiling, still catching his breath, naked—his big dick still half hard even though he'd come, the length and thickness of it striking against his soft belly. He was breathing loudly, doing a pretty good job of pretending Rollins wasn't there anymore. But he had a shit poker face. He was hurt.

Rollins was about to apologise when Jay sat up; he did it quietly. He reached for his pants and didn't make eye contact when he said, "Well, fuck you, I guess."

Rollins shook his head and got the fuck out of there. What the fuck was he doing fucking around with Jay of all people anyway? His missus was a ten, a solid fucking ten! And alright, fucking her was not like fucking Jay. At all. Fucking Jay was good in a category it fucking shouldn't be.

He slammed out the front door—fuck Jay's roommate, like he wouldn't have woken up from all their fucking anyway. He got in the jeep, turned the engine over. The sun was already peeking over the horizon, lighting up the front of Jay's crack whore of a house.

Rollins saw the man himself carefully locking the flyscreen door, and carefully not looking up when he shut the main door.

10

ROLLINS PUSHED THE STEAMED fish around his plate. Sarah was still talking about the centrepieces for the wedding.

"So, what do you think?" she asked.

"Think it sounds great."

"Really."

Rollins looked up at her. She was leaning back, folding her arms over her chest—the low-cut top accentuated her breasts perfectly. Rollins knew they stayed like that even when she took the top off. And yet, all he could see in his mind was Jay's stupid fucking face staring at the goddamn ceiling.

"Babe, you know I don't care. C'mon, even if I had an opinion—which I don't—you'd overrule it."

"Yeah, but," she glanced around. The restaurant was nice with low lighting and cosy tables in an old converted house. The food was a bit rich, but fortunately they always made something off the menu for Rollins and so he routinely picked it as their Friday night dinner spot. Fuck what Jay said about partners and soulmates and all that shit. Taking the missus out to dinner once a week and fucking after was a solid relationship. Sometimes Sarah even stayed all weekend, so suck on that, Jay.

"It'd be nice if you were more into it," she flicked her eyes up to meet his, sat forward, picked up her fork and speared a garlic fried prawn. Just the sight of that much oil made Rollins shudder, but it pissed Sarah off no end when he talked about nutrition so he kept it to himself.

"I'm into building the house."

"I know, but..."

"But?"

She chewed, swallowed, met his eyes. "Do you even want to get married?"

Not really. But it's what people did wasn't it?

He didn't say that; he didn't fancy getting stabbed in the eye with a fork.

And besides, he knew everything would be better once they were married. He'd have to stop fucking around, she'd stop turning a blind eye to it—though to be fair, he was pretty sure she assumed he was fucking other women, not small, plump dudes who had too many opinions on everything and prostitutes for mothers.

"I want to get this done with you."

She snorted. "How romantic. You make it sound like a mission."

"You know what I mean."

"Yeah," she smiled. "I think so, sometimes I just wish..."

He wasn't touching that. If she had something to say, she could come on out and say it. Jay always did. And fucked if he was thinking about that shithead again. He hadn't seen him again all week and Jay was meant to be shadowing him. The little asshole ignored his text about a pick-up the first day after that morning, and Rollins didn't try again.

"Anyway," she brightened. "Just don't go complaining on the day when you hate everything."

Almost a year from now with the venue change and he couldn't see his opinion on fuck all changing, but he nodded in agreement and asked how things were going with her hair and beauty salon.

That set her off and he tuned out. He absolutely wasn't apologising to Jay again. He'd tried to after Port Hedland and look how that turned out? And he was most definitely not fucking him again. It was good with Jay—there was a desperate energy to it that made no sense—but that was not a good enough reason to keep fucking the dude.

He paused with the fork halfway to his mouth—maybe Jay had reawakened that part of him? Now he thought about it, he hadn't felt like this with sex since he was fucking an American marine before the incident that turned everything to shit. Mr New Orleans. Slayer? Slash? Some fucking name, point was, guy was an incredible lay. And the complete opposite of Jay—black, fit, fucking cut, and hung. And okay, Jay was hung too, but otherwise, completely different. The marine had also never talked, which Rollins had really appreciated.

"Shall we get dessert?" Sarah asked.

"I think we should get out of here."

"Oh yeah?" she smiled up at him.

"Yeah."

"Get the bill then, I'll just use the bathroom."

It was pitch black in his room, Sarah sleeping softly beside him and Rollins was wide awake, staring at the ceiling. The sex had been no different. No fireworks, but nothing to complain about either.

Rollins lifted the covers, slipped out of bed and got his pants and shirt on like he was on a stealth mission.

He went downstairs and Nola whined at him.

"Yeah, girl, I know," he said and patted her.

When Sarah stayed over, Nola lost her place in the bed. She was a Lab so she didn't do pissed off, but she did the Lab version of it—sad. Sad like the world was ending sad.

Rollins found his phone, sat on the couch and she curled up next to him.

He opened the thread to Jay.

Just his sad line about the pick-up.

If nothing else, Jay needed to sort what he was doing with Rollins so his dad didn't kill him.

He wrote and erased some texts—*Where the fuck have you been.* That one sounded like he cared too much. *If you don't keep working with me Horace will find out.* That sounded like a threat and hell was freezing over before Rollins told Horace what was going on. *Where are you?* He settled on the last one. It got to the point. He hit send.

An uncomfortable feeling spread through him after he sent it. He pushed his hand into Nola's fur, worked his fingers through the strands. She sighed next to him. The clock in the kitchen ticked with the second hand. The waves beyond the closed back door crashed onto the sand, then drew back with a long, drawn-out drag.

Jay wasn't going to reply. And now Rollins was the stupid guy who was messaging like a desperate, needy, whining little bitch.

It was almost midnight. Jay would be up. He drank coke like water and seemed the type to stay up late and sleep in. It was really going to fuck with Rollins' routine again, but he was not spending an entire night feeling like this.

"C'mon, Nols," he said and stood.

She jumped off the couch, tail wagging manically, nails skittering on the floorboard in her rush to get to the door.

Rollins followed, got his boots on, car keys, and headed out.

11

♥

Sure enough, when Rollins pulled up at Jay's place all the lights were on, several cars were parked out the front on the dead lawn, and the low drone of music buzzed from the place.

"So, he's having a little fucking party is he," Rollins said to Nola.

She panted and looked at him; she looked like she was grinning. Rollins cracked a smile back.

"C'mon," he got out. He felt her nose pressing into his back as her big body vibrated with the need to get out and explore.

He left her to it and stepped onto the veranda.

He belted on the screen door with his fist a few times. It wasn't that loud inside, but fucked if he was waiting out here.

The door groaned open and the metal head peered around it.

"Yeah?"

"Is Jay here?"

"Yeah."

Rollins waited. The metal guy looked at Rollins, then at Nola charging up the steps, and turned around and disappeared.

Rollins tried the screen door and found it locked. Jay appeared and he dropped his hand.

"Rollins?"

He was wearing the backwards cap again, a shirt so white it was blinding, and some kind of parachute tracksuit pants that seemed way too big for him; his feet weren't even visible.

"We need to talk," Rollins said and thought that was news to him and he hoped he thought of something to say.

"Okay," Jay said and leaned on the doorframe.

Then he noticed Nola.

"Nola," he said and unlocked the screen door, opened it.

She bounded inside, her whole body shaking as Jay made a big fuss over her. She pushed past him and bounded down the hall.

"She'll be alright, my dudes will take care of her," Jay smiled, his eyes on the doorframe.

"Are you gonna let me in?"

"Nah," Jay was still smiling, but it wasn't his usual easy one, it was dimmed like when one light globe blows in a room leaving half the light as before.

Rollins wasn't apologising. Jay was the one who should be apologising. Rollins finally got into some dirty talk and this little shit goes and mocks him for it?

"You need to turn up for work," Rollins said. "If Horace finds out…"

"I been going in," Jay said. He was picking the paint on the doorframe.

"And doing what?"

"Cleaning, cutting gear, you know."

"With who?"

"Horace, Chad sometimes."

Chad was a first-class moron and the best person to hang out with if your plan was to get arrested or murdered.

But what could Rollins say? If Jay preferred to work with them, so be it.

"Alright, well, you coulda let me know. Saved me driving out here and fucking my routine. Again."

Jay snorted. "I never made you come out here, dude."

"You don't answer your texts, what am I supposed to think?"

"You sent one message and I was busy."

"Two."

Jay fished his phone out of his pocket and huffed.

"Obviously I'm here."

Rollins took a deep breath. "Yeah, you are."

He watched Jay picking at the paint. He hadn't met Rollins' eyes since he arrived.

"Well, I guess that's that then," Rollins said.

"Guess so."

Rollins blew out a breath. "Can you get Nola for me?"

"Sure, dude," and then he was gone too.

Rollins shoved his hands in his pockets, clenched his jaw.

It was a while before Jay reappeared with Nola and Rollins was dialled right back up by the time he did.

"She was getting spoiled, eh, girl?" Jay opened the door and she bounded out, raced into the front yard and started sniffing everything. "See ya," Jay said and went to shut the door.

Rollins' hand shot out and stopped him.

"You mocked me," he said.

"Huh?" Jay glanced up at him.

Rollins couldn't believe he just said that.

"Nothing."

He let his hand drop and turned away.

"C'mon Nols," he called and power walked to his car.

Jay didn't say anything else, and Rollins didn't hear the door close.

12

"I NEED SOMEONE TO take over in Port Hedland," Horace said and leaned back in his chair. "Cal's too fuckin' old to run it and I was gonna send Chad but he's too fuckin' dumb. You're up."

Rollins stared at him. He was standing in front of Horace's desk, and he couldn't quite believe what he was hearing.

"I have a life here."

Horace snorted. "You ain't interested in working the mines for a bit?"

Rollins frowned. He could easily get sparky work on the mines, and Horace knew that was a lot of cash to turn down. Still.

"And you can run the books from up there, got a computer installed and everything."

A computer?

"Gonna send Jayden with you."

Oh, hell no.

He and Jay had not spoken since that night and Rollins finally felt his inner peace being restored. Not that Jay had disturbed it that much—it had been a blip, an awkward detour in his otherwise well-structured life.

Rollins ground his teeth together.

Horace laughed. "What? Thought you liked him after the whole chivalrous, but he needs a lift home, Horace!" he mimicked.

Rollins shook his head and headed out.

"Gonna get you settled up there by the end of the month."

Rollins paused in the doorway. Something unnameable fluttered in his stomach and it was a half-hearted protest when he replied. "Chad's not that bad. Send him."

Horace scoffed. "If I was looking to put out the welcome mat for a full takeover of the north, I'd send Chad."

Rollins held his retort in and walked out.

Sarah was not going to like it.

Nola was going to love it.

And fucked if he cared what Jay thought about it.

Turned out he didn't have to wait too long to find out. Jay texted him that night after Sarah had stormed out saying, "You're not taking us seriously!"

Let me know when we leaving.

Right fucking now would be good, Rollins thought but didn't say.

End of the month.

His phone buzzed.

Duh. But like when? What's our flight.

Flight?

We're driving.

Driving! Dude! That's like 24 hours! Noooooo!!!

Rollins snorted. What a fucking drama queen.

Try 18. And I'll pick you up at 4am on the 31st. Don't make me wait.

I aint made u wait yet have i?

And Rollins wasn't answering that.

He felt giddy, tingly—his heart was fluttering for fuck's sake. All from a short text exchange. He hadn't interacted with Jay for almost a month and it felt like... like he'd missed him.

"Nols, run," he said and tossed his phone on the couch. He went and got changed, Nola skittering around and whining behind him.

Nola was always up for breaking routine.

13

J AY WAS SITTING ON his veranda with a duffel and a box stuffed
with electrical shit beside him when Rollins pulled up just
before four on the thirty-first.

Nola was pressing up against Rollins' back as he opened the door.

"Alright, alright," he said to her and let her through.

She bounded over to Jay and he made a big fuss, scratching
her behind the ears, holding her face and kissing her nose as she
wriggled.

Rollins walked over.

Jay looked the same as he always did. His outfit was ridiculous,
his eyes were squinting under the glasses, and his smile was goofy.
But his smile was still smaller than it had been. Rollins did his best
to ignore it.

"What's all this?"

"Just gear from the crew."

"Gear for what?"

"Working."

"What kinda work?"

Jay shrugged. "Just our shit, you know." He shouldered the
duffel and picked up the box.

"So this is really only eighteen hours?" he asked before Rollins could press him.

"Yeah, we'll drive straight through."

"You can drive for that long?" Jay called from the back where he was stuffing all his gear.

"We'll split it," Rollins said and watched Nola urinating on a very sad looking patch of flowers. "I'll take here to Geraldton. You do to Carnarvon. C'mon Nols."

She bounded over and Rollins let her go past and into the backseat.

He got in. Jay was putting his seatbelt on. He was blushing. It was dark, but Rollins could see it clear enough.

"You can drive, can't you?"

"Yeah, but..."

Rollins didn't start the car.

"Yeah, but what?"

"I got an automatic license."

"You can't drive a manual?"

Jay shrugged.

"Fuck's sake," Rollins started the car. "Why?"

"Dunno." Jay was looking out the window. He sounded small. He sounded like he did after Rollins said that nasty shit about his mum.

"Fuck it, I'll teach you."

Jay looked at him. "Isn't it, like, hard?"

Rollins scoffed. "Maybe for you."

"Hey, fuck you, I'm like hella smart, dude."

Rollins cracked a smile.

"There's a salt flat 'bout sixty clicks outside of Carnarvon."

"Won't it take us longer than eighteen hours to get there then?"

Rollins cruised out of Jay's suburb, shrugged. "Yeah, well... Who gives a fuck."

Jay laughed. Rollins shot him a smile.

They stopped in Geraldton for something to eat after Rollins had managed to prod Jay into talking more like he had before. Rollins was feeling good and figured he'd push on through to Carnarvon no problem. They could bed down in the back for the night after he showed Jay how to drive, then see where it was at before making the final push to Port Hedland.

"Grilled steak, two boiled eggs," he said to the waitress in the pub and handed her the menu.

"And for you?" she asked Jay.

"Umm, can I get chips, bread with margarine, you got margarine, yeah? Not butter?"

"Reckon it's Flora," she said.

"Margarine," Jay nodded, "cool, cool, and some lettuce. And a coke."

Jay handed her the menu.

"Drink for you?" she asked Rollins.

"Water," he replied, eyes fixed on Jay.

"Be about twenty," she took the menus and wandered off.

"What the fuck was that?" Rollins asked.

Jay straightened his knife and fork.

"Food."

"No, what kinda order was that?"

"I dunno, guess you're not the only one who likes to order off menu."

"Yeah, but, I got my reasons."

"Which are?"

"Health."

Jay shook his head.

"So you reckon—

"You don't eat eggs either."

Jay sighed. "Dude, what can I say, I like what I like."

"Hmm. And no butter. You don't like it?"

"Never thought about it, just don't wanna eat it."

Rollins stared at him. Jay rearranged the salt and pepper shakers.

"You're so fuckin' weird," Rollins said.

Jay looked up, raised his eyebrows. "I'm weird? Mr everything must be steamed and all hours accounted for. And, oh yeah, I like sticking my dick up guy's asses but I'm getting married soon."

"Jesus, keep your voice down" Rollins hissed.

Jay looked around the empty dining room, then back at Rollins.

Rollins shook his head.

"So, I reckon what?" he asked as the waitress came back over with their drinks.

"You reckon," Jay looked up at the waitress, "thank you," sipped his coke through the straw, "I'll be able to drive the last leg?"

"No."

"Then why teach me?"

"So this doesn't happen again."

"When will we get there then?"

"Tomorrow."

"We're gonna stay the night somewhere?"

"We'll sleep in the car, find somewhere to park."

"Haven't you got like a tonne of cash?"

"Haven't you?"

Jay snorted. "Nah, dude."

"Horace isn't paying you?"

"Nah, he is, but I got like, expenses."

"What kinda expenses?"

"You know, just life shit."

Rollins sat back and crossed his arms over his chest, sized Jay up. Sure, his clothing left a lot to be desired in the fashion department—though Rollins was hardly a fashion star himself, favouring khaki pants and a black t-shirt or black jeans and a black t-shirt—but Jay didn't look expensive. Clean, yes, but his shit was department store bought. Then there was all this computer shit he was lugging around.

"Is it your computer shit?"

"Dude, why so interested?"

"I'm not."

The lapsed into silence. Rollins watched Jay fiddling with his utensils, straightening the table cloth, tapping the table.

"What are you doing with those computers at your house?" Rollins broke first.

Jay smirked at him like he knew it too. "Nothin' much, we just like building them."

"Building computers?"

"Yeah, get all the parts, build a PC. It's fun. Then we go online, meet people, do shit, you know."

Rollins tilted his head to the side, studied Jay watching him back, gaze steady. There was more to it, Rollins was sure of it.

"So, you spend all your money on that."

"Nah."

The waitress came with their food. Rollins watched Jay make a sandwich with chips, squeezing the bread into the chips so the margarine melted before he piled it with lettuce and took a bite.

"Why're you being so cagey about this?"

Jay smiled around his mouthful. Swallowed.

"I'm not, just you know, not much to tell."

"Hmmm."

Rollins started eating.

As they walked back to the car, Nola stuck her head out, her big nose getting a whiff of the bag Rollins had the kitchen make up for her, her body vibrating to get out, and he couldn't let it go.

"Are you doing something illegal?"

Jay snorted. "Like more illegal than what we're already doin'?"

"I just can't figure out why you wouldn't come out and say it."

Jay was shaking his head, taking the bag from Rollins and letting Nola out. He was focused on her eating when he answered.

"It's for my mum. I send it to my mum."

Rollins didn't know what to say or why he hadn't expected it.

"C'mon," he said. Nola was finished anyway, such a guts. "Nola, in."

Nola jumped in. Jay tossed the bag in the yellow bin next to the car and went around and got in.

Of course he was sending it to his mum. And of course he wouldn't want Rollins to know that.

All conversation over.

Or so he thought. He wasn't convinced Jay had forgiven him for that remark about his mum, but Rollins thought fuck him anyway: he hadn't forgiven Jay for the whole thing either.

But Jay was not a fan of long stretches of silence.

They were in the middle of nowhere, nothing but land stretching in both directions, the jeep dipping and rising at one hundred and twenty down the smooth bitumen when Jay started talking.

"Why'd you call her Nola?"

"Dunno."

"Yes you do, c'mon, when you went, oh hey, this one is called Nola. Why? I had a cat and she was called Pikachu because I liked the show—

"Christ, shut up. I've always wanted to go to New Orleans."

"Why don't you?"

"Why don't I what?"

"Go to New Orleans? You're a grown ass man with a lot of cash, why don't you go?"

"Why do you keep implying I've got a lot of cash?"

"'Cos we're doin' the same work? And I've seen your books?"

"Fuck, whatever. The missus isn't into it."

"So? Go without her."

"That's not how it works."

"How what works?"

"Relationships. Happy wife, happy life."

Jay squinted at him. "That doesn't make any sense."

"Yeah? Had a lot of relationships, have you?"

Jay rolled his eyes. "You know I've had boyfriends, dude. C'mon."

Rollins wasn't touching that. He didn't like the idea of boyfriends in general, never mind associating it with Jay, which made him feel sick and uncomfortable. Lucky for him, Jay could be counted on to bumble along with wherever his brain went.

"Why New Orleans?"

"Dunno."

"Yes you do."

"Fine, fuck, I'll tell you so you'll shut up, okay? Promise you'll shut up until we hit the next town and I'll tell you."

"That's like, six hours."

"Exactly."

"I'll shut up for one hour."

Rollins worked his jaw. "Fine. There was a guy in an American unit we got stationed with in Iraq from New Orleans. Thought it sounded like a good place." That was the guy who was also a great lay, but Jay didn't need to know that part.

"Oh, that's right. What was that like? Did you wanna be there? 'Cos I don't reckon we shoulda been there—

"One hour."

Jay smiled at him. Rollins could feel it on the side of his head. He heard Jay rummaging around in his bag for his CD Walkman and headphones.

Jay started bopping along, looking out the window.

And Rollins was beginning to think it was safe to say he'd liked Jay from the start. But he wasn't going to admit that then, least of all to himself.

14

"**A**ww, you liked me from the start?" Jay pinched my side, but it was weak.

He was tucked under my arm to stay out of the sun, the sound of the ripped canopy flapping in the wind becoming the new beat of our lives.

"Like you didn't know that."

"Seriously, dude? You were such an asshole to me, always."

"I was nicer to you than I am to anyone else!"

Something you have to understand, dear listeners: Jay is insufferably stupid.

Jay scoffed. It was raspy. He kept refusing to drink enough water. Even out here, he was insufferable about water. And I was gonna need to fish soon and deal with that argument.

"I'm smarter than you and I ain't eating fish."

"You know, this might not be the time to get all moralistic," I sat up and looked around. Water, shimmering with sunlight, calmness, unbroken blue.

"Dude, I reckon you're delirious. You get all poetic when you're tired."

"And I reckon you're gonna need to start pulling your weight on this expedition."

"I reckon we'll be alright. Tell me more about how you liked me from the start."

"Shut up," I slumped back down, my smile completely out of my control.

Because, unfortunately, it was true.

15

THERE WAS NO RATIONAL reason for Rollins to like Jay. Once they got to a suitable salt flat—miles and miles of open space to drive on—Rollins explained the clutch, the gears, adjusted the seat, hopped into the passenger seat and told Jay to get to it.

Jay stalled. Tried again. He complained about the coordination required to shift from the brake to the accelerator and use the clutch with his other foot, and stalled again. He kept revving it in second and trying to go faster.

"Right, stop," Rollins said.

"Give me a second."

The gears crunched and Rollins had a horrible thought Jay was going to flood the engine. They'd be stuck out there. In the middle of godforsaken nowhere, just each other for company.

"Stop."

Jay hit the brake and the engine stalled.

"Get out."

"I been tryin' for like two seconds."

"That's two seconds too long."

"You're the fuckin' worst, you know that, man? Don't ever have kids, that's all I'm sayin'."

"Wasn't planning on it," Rollins snapped and got out.

"Maybe tell your missus that then," Jay slammed the door.

Rollins felt his eye twitch. Yes, he knew what she wanted. Yes, he'd end up giving it to her. Because that's just what you did in relationships: rolled over to keep the peace. He did not need that thrown back in his face from Jay of all people.

As he and Jay crossed each other in front of the hood, Jay pushed his glasses up his nose and gave Rollins the stink eye for a change. Rollins couldn't help it, he laughed.

"What?"

"Nothin'," Rollins got in the driver's side.

"No, what?" Jay asked as he jumped in.

"Nothin', really."

"So, what? You just got it first time?"

"Course not," Rollins started the car.

"So what's so funny then?"

Rollins focused on heading back to the road. "Nothin', just, never seen you pissed like that. It's funny."

Jay scoffed. "Sorry we can't all be default assholes."

Rollins shook his head. "I'm not an asshole."

"Yes. You are."

"Maybe you're just a pussy."

"And maybe you're just a dick."

Rollins laughed again.

And so did Jay even though it was clear he was trying not to. He had his arms crossed tightly over his stomach, his eyes out the window, but he was smiling, Rollins could feel it.

After they got food from the nearest town, Rollins pulled off and parked in a shaded spot near a dry riverbed.

"We'll sleep here," he said.

"Ugh, why can't we just go to a motel."

"If you wanna pay for a motel, I'll sleep in a motel."

"We could split it?"

"I'm not wasting my money on shit I don't need."

"How is it a waste if you're enjoying life?"

"I'm enjoying life out here," Rollins gave him a look. "Or at least I would be if I had better company."

Jay snorted, shook his head and looked at the cracked ground of the river through the windshield. "Your missus is one lucky lady, I'm sure you take her to all these nice places too."

Rollins opened the door and let Nola scramble over his lap. She launched herself into the bush, her paws crunching in the brush. He kicked his leg out.

"You seem pretty interested in my missus for a faggot," Rollins said.

"Dude!"

Rollins looked at him, startled. "What?"

"You can't go around calling gay people faggots! You do realise you're kinda gay, yeah? You do get you're like, insulting yourself."

"I told you, I'm bisexual, fucked a lot of guys in the army, ain't nothin' wrong with that. But I'm not gay and I'm certainly no faggot."

Jay pushed his glasses up his nose, squinted up at Rollins.

"I reckon you believe that."

"I reckon I don't say something I don't believe," Rollins replied.

Jay shook his head and looked around.

It was getting dark so Rollins jumped out and got to folding down the backseat, rolling out the bedding.

Soon he had a nice fire going, his lean chicken fillets cooking in a pan and carefully not touching whatever the hell the crumbed fillet looking thing Jay had bought was.

They managed to eat, wash, clean up and get to bed without further argument, and Rollins was settling in for a good night's sleep when Jay refused to lay still beside him.

"Quit it," Rollins said after Jay rolled over and bumped him. Again.

"I'm so uncomfortable."

Rollins snorted. "This is fuckin' luxury. Try sleepin' in a burnt-out building on a concrete floor with no blankets, no warmth, nothin' but the knowledge you better not be makin' a fuckin' sound."

"Why would I want to imagine something like that? Have you done that?"

"Of course I've done that. Whaddyathink I just make shit like that up for fun?"

"I dunno what you do, man," Jay sighed. "Was it in the army?"

"Sort of," Rollins closed his eyes.

"What does sort of mean?"

"It means go to sleep."

He could feel Jay shuffling around, bumping into his arm, his face so close Rollins could feel it pressing up against his shoulder.

"There's the army and then there's what?" Jay asked like he was talking to himself.

"SAS," Rollins mumbled.

"SAS?"

"Yeah. Go to sleep," Rollins said.

"No shit, dude? You must be hella skilled."

Rollins snorted. Well, that was one way of putting it. Shame he was fucking useless now. No way he could get dropped in enemy-held territory now. Imagine if he had an episode in a fucking sand hellhole? No, thanks.

"You were in Iraq, eh?"

"And Afghanistan. Timor, Kuwait," he mumbled. Why was he still talking?

"Dude, that's fucking amazing. I'd love to get out of Australia."

Rollins started laughing. He couldn't help himself. It started as a low rumble and then he was heaving with it.

"What?"

"It wasn't a fucking holiday. Who goes to Afghanistan for a holiday?" he was absolutely losing it laughing.

"Nah, but, like, you been out and about, eh? Seen some shit."

Rollins got himself under control.

"Yeah, I guess."

"Can you kill someone with your bare hands?"

"Yes."

"What about with a rock?"

"You reckon if I can do it with my bare hands I need a rock? But yeah, course."

"Have you killed people?"

"Course."

Jay scoffed. "Don't reckon you should answer 'of course' to something like that."

"What? You reckon we went into enemy territory for a fucking tea party?"

"No, but like, don't you avoid killing if you can help it?"

"Trust me, if someone tries to kill you, you kill first. And over there, everyone is trying to kill you."

"You kill any innocent people?"

"Probably."

"Have you got PTSD?"

Rollins groaned. "Who just asks that?"

"What? Lots of soldiers have it."

"Maybe so, but it ain't something you fucking talk about."

"Why?"

"Because it's a fucking liability."

Jay was quiet for a minute. Rollins' breaths sounded loud in the confined space. Nola was snoring. At least someone was sleeping.

"I don't think so, eh? I think it's like any injury."

"All injuries are liabilities."

"Well, yeah, if you're in Afghanistan or wherever, but not here."

"Yes, here."

Jay rolled onto his stomach. Rollins looked up at him. He was peering at Rollins, his expression obscured by the darkness.

"Is that why you're such a control freak?"

"I'm not a control freak."

"Yeah, dude, you are. Gotta have everything in order, but it makes sense, eh," he was nodding his head, "if you can't trust yourself."

"I trust myself, what the fuck."

"Nah, like, if you lose control 'cos of something? 'Cos that's what happens doesn't it? Something sets you off."

"What the fuck do you know about it?"

Jay rolled onto his back. "Nothin'."

And that was cagey as fuck.

Rollins rolled onto his side, he poked Jay.

"What do you know about it?" he was curious now.

"Nothing, whatever, I was just thinking it through to the end, you know? Imagining it."

"No," Rollins said slowly. "Something sets you off, you said. How do you know that?"

"I don't."

"You do."

Jay fiddled with the blankets. "Reckon my mum's got it, that's all."

"How would a prostitute get it?"

"Could you stop just calling her that like that's all she is? And how could they not?"

Rollins frowned.

"Dude," Jay huffed. "They get beaten up, like, on the regular. Some of them get killed. You know that, right?"

And well, Rollins had never thought about it. But now Jay mentioned it.

"Yeah," he breathed out and lay back down.

They lapsed into an uncomfortable silence.

"What sets her off?" Rollins asked.

Jay sighed. "I dunno."

"Yes, you do."

Jay was fiddling again.

"I'm not gonna make fun of it."

"What sets you off?" Jay shot back.

"No way I'm telling anybody that."

"Well then I ain't tellin' you either."

"You don't get it," Rollins rolled over again. "It's like telling someone your kryptonite. You don't tell anyone that shit."

"Well then, why'd you reckon I'd tell you that about my mum?"

Rollins scoffed. "I ain't gonna hunt your mum down to set her off, c'mon."

"Well, I ain't telling you if you don't tell me."

"Fine, shut up and go to sleep then."

Rollins shoved himself onto his back and tugged the blankets up.

Jay yanked them back.

They got into a tussle, which Rollins obviously won.

Jay groaned. He shoved himself right up against Rollins' side.

"Get off."

"No, give me some blankets."

"Get your own."

Jay snuffled into his arm; he was giggling.

Rollins wanted to kiss him. His mind screeched to a halt with that thought. What the fuck? No, he absolutely did not want to kiss Jay. He didn't want to kiss a man, period.

He freed some of the blanket and chucked it over Jay hoping it'd make him go away. He did and then Rollins wished he'd come back.

Christ, this was insufferable.

They were silent for a long time, but Rollins could tell they weren't sleeping.

"Wind chimes," Jay said quietly after a while. "And like, those bells on doors, like in shops."

Rollins knew what he was talking about. He exhaled roughly and didn't reply. He couldn't sleep. Jay didn't say anything else.

Rollins wasn't sure if Jay was asleep or not when he said, "Cars backfiring. Fireworks," he exhaled slowly through his nose. "Thunder if I don't know it's comin'... sometimes even if I do."

He didn't think Jay heard him—he didn't stir—but it felt good, just a little bit, to say it out loud.

16

IT WAS ALMOST NOON when they slowed to enter Port Hedland. Red dirt—buildings, roads, houses, cars, even the pigeons—everything was tinted red-orange with the dirt. The place felt old, worn down; tired under the steady hum of work and the incessant humidity.

Rollins navigated the few suburban streets and pulled up in the driveway of the clubhouse. It looked worse than he remembered, the house bordering on dilapidated save for the slapped-up paint job and minor renovations pasted on top to keep the place together. There was an old tree out the front—one of those ugly trees that wouldn't have looked out of place in a Gothic horror movie.

"It's nice, eh?"

Rollins cut the engine and looked at Jay to see if he was joking. He was not.

"No," Rollins said. "It's an absolute shithole."

"Dude, you and me got very different taste."

"This isn't about taste," Rollins opened the door and Nola scrambled over him to get out. "This is about reality, and the reality is," he got out of the car and listened to Jay doing the same on the other side, "this place is a rundown hole that should be condemned."

"Well," Jay leaned back, cracked his back, "compared to some of the places I've lived, this is a sweet set-up."

"Then you've obviously lived in places boarded up by the Department of Health."

"Dude, you have no idea."

Rollins gave him the side eye. Jay was stretching from side to side. He managed to make it look all wrong, like if someone was teaching a yoga class, he'd be the example of what not to do.

The key was in the metre box, so Rollins ignored Jay's exercise attempts and went inside. It was dim, the floorboards creaking, everything dank and musty smelling. He heard Jay coming in behind him, Nola close on his heels.

Rollins made his way through the living room where the last occupant had left empty beer bottles, overflowing ashtrays, and used plates. He shook his head. The bedrooms in the main house were off this room and Rollins poked his head into the front one. Sparsely furnished with a bed, chest of drawers, and a cupboard. There was another overflowing ashtray on the bedside table, but otherwise it was clean enough.

"I'll take this one," he said.

Jay didn't respond.

Rollins turned around. He followed the noise of Nola on the other side of the house. He passed through the kitchen—similarly used with dirty dishes, the refrigerator purring away like an outboard motor—and went into the games room.

There was a futon on the floor and the space was huge.

"You want this one?" Jay asked. He was on the other side of the room, looking out the sliding doors at the backyard.

"No," Rollins did not. It was too big, too many windows, and with two entry points from common areas—he'd never sleep.

"Cool, cool," Jay said and stepped outside.

Rollins followed and stepped into the backyard. It was also huge, the bonfire burnt to coal, the outdoor bar area an absolute mess, and the grass brown from a lack of water.

"What're we doing here anyway?" Jay asked from where he was picking his way through the debris on the bar.

"You're only asking now?"

"Yeah, well, I go with the flow," Jay gave him a cheesy grin.

Rollins shook his head.

"Occupying the territory, doin' whatever comes up."

"What'll come up?"

"Dealing. Maybe a fight if someone is stupid enough. And I'll be workin'."

"Cool, cool."

"What will you be doing while I'm at work?"

Rollins realised he just sounded like his mother. He wasn't taking it back though.

"I got my own work, remember?" Jay smiled over at him.

"Building computers," Rollins replied flatly.

Which reminded him.

"Horace said there was already a computer here, said you'd be doin' the books with it."

"News to me," Jay walked over and went back inside.

They searched every room in the house. There was no computer.

"You know," Jay flopped down on the futon, "Horace is a dick, but he ain't a liar. Where d'ya reckon it is?"

"Stolen."

"For real?"

"For real."

"Who by?"

"Well," Rollins looked around the room Jay was claiming as his. He imagined the computer would've been sitting on the table near the wall on account of the power point under it. "Could've been someone around here."

"Good thing we got Nola then, eh."

"But, I doubt it."

The lady herself charged into the room and jumped onto Jay on the bed.

"It was the guys here before us," he went on as he watched the two of them rolling around—Jay was using the doona to play tug-of-war.

"For real?"

"For real." Rollins nodded. Idiots.

"What're you gonna do?"

"What do you mean?"

"Are you gonna tell Horace?"

"Can't you build another one?" Rollins arched both eyebrows at Jay as if to say—you're up, hot shot.

"Course, but kinda not the point."

"What's the point?"

"They stole shit."

"Well, I can't prove that," Rollins headed for the kitchen. "And I ain't gonna get them killed on a hunch. A pretty good fucking hunch, but still a hunch."

Jay snorted. "Don't reckon they'd get killed for stealing a computer, c'mon, man."

"And I don't reckon you know Horace then."

Rollins went and got their shit, unpacked the car by himself, which was okay since Jay was playing with Nola.

17

HE'D MADE A FEW calls before he left Perth and secured some work on the nearest underground mine. He was starting on a night swing and wasn't looking forward to it. He was fixing the last of the black tarpaulin to his windows when Jay wandered in and flopped down on his bed.

"What're you doin'?" Jay asked.

Rollins wanted to ask the same thing—Jay was making himself quite at home on the bed, shuffling up so he was against the wall, crossing his ankles over each other. At least his feet were clean.

"Blocking out the sun," Rollins said and got back to it, fixing the final corner.

"Bleak, man."

Rollins shook his head, shot Jay a look. "I'm on night shifts."

"Whaddya mean? Like, you're gonna work all night and sleep all day?"

"Yes? What do you think night shift means?"

He stepped back and surveyed the room. It was pitch black. Perfect.

"Nooo," Jay groaned. "I hate when the person I live with works nights, it's so boring." Jay really dragged the last part out, like he was singing.

Rollins hid his smile.

"Who else you know works the night shift?"

"My mum, duh."

Rollins kept forgetting about the practicalities of his mother's work. Of course she worked nights.

"She never blacked out her room though."

Rollins flicked on the light. Jay squinted up at him.

"She should've."

"Yeah, well she should've done a lotta things," Jay replied wistfully.

Rollins wasn't touching that.

"Have you built the computer yet?"

"Dude, it's an art, don't rush me."

Rollins turned back to the window to hide another smile.

"Well, have you at least cooked us some dinner? I got a bunch of food this morning when you were still dead to the world."

"Yeah, course."

Jay bounced over and went out.

Jay placed a plate in front of Rollins at the old kitchen table—it was one of those tables with the steel legs, the corkscrew top, and it felt like it'd been sitting against this wall since 1950. Rollins looked at the food. It was some sort of mush on a bed of rice. Leaving aside that it was not what Rollins had bought, he almost gagged at the amount of carbs on the plate.

"What the fuck is this?" he asked.

Jay was at the stove, plating his own dinner.

"Dahl," Jay said and grinned over at him. "My mum taught me how to cook. It's good, trust me."

"Dahl as in lentils?" More fucking carbs. Also...

"Where's the meat?"

"Don't gotta eat meat at every meal," Jay said and sat opposite him.

The table was so small, Jay was right there, in his face. Rollins could see he was trying not to laugh.

"You little shit," Rollins said. "Where's my dinner?"

Jay cracked up. He stood, took Rollins' plate and added it to his own smaller portion and went back to the stove.

He brought Rollins a surprisingly well-cooked and nicely presented plate of grilled chicken and steamed vegetables on a clean plate.

"Good," he said.

"Thanks, boss."

"Shut up," Rollins said and ate. He could probably add some carbs now he'd be adding twelve hour shifts underground to his days, but the thought of it made him queasy.

Jay was digging in, moaning. "So good, man. You're missin' out."

"Why don't you eat meat?" he asked.

Jay shrugged. "Don't like it."

"Hmmm," Rollins ate, watched him.

"You can afford it now," he said after a while.

Jay shook his head. "It's not about affording it. I don't like it."

"You're not just saying that because you couldn't afford it before?"

"No? Why would I lie like that?"

"Dunno," Rollins got up and cleared their empty plates. "People be lying like that all the time. Better to lie than admit something they're ashamed of."

Jay scoffed. "Well, this ain't that. There's icy poles in the freezer."

"That's pure sugar."

Jay laughed. "I dunno what you do to unwind, man. What's your treat?"

"Treat?" Rollins leaned against the sink and crossed his arms over his chest.

"Yeah, you know," Jay got out an icy pole and tore into it. "How do you reward yourself?"

"Why do I need a reward? I'm not a dog."

Jay sucked on the icy pole. It was not sexy and it did not make Rollins think of other things because this was not a fucking porno and Jay was not a porn star. The thought almost made him laugh out loud.

"Dunno, just nice to treat yourself sometimes, you know?" Jay sat down, leaned back against the wall and sucked on the icy pole.

It was hot as balls with no air conditioning; Jay was doing a full man-spread and rearranging his package under his baggy jeans. His white shirt was clinging to him with sweat.

"Don't you have any shorts?" Rollins asked.

"Huh?" Jay rubbed his package a bit more. "Oh, nah."

Rollins tapped his fingers on his biceps. Jay sucked on the icy pole.

"Are you gonna buy some?"

Jay let the icy pole pop out of his mouth. His lips and mouth were bright red-pink.

"Where from?"

"South Hedland?"

"How am I gonna get there?"

"I'll drive you?"

"Is that a question?"

Rollins huffed.

"It's all good, dude. When you get a day off, we can go to this fancy South Hedland of which you speak. I'm sure it's as nice as this," he waved his hand around as if to indicate Port Hedland in general.

Rollins pushed off the bench. "Think it's cooler outside," he didn't know that but he needed to get away from Jay.

"Cool," Jay's chair scraped and Rollins felt him at his back.

Nola was on the lawn in a full sprawl, the sprinkler turning over her, soaking into her black fur.

"Put it on for her earlier. She loves it," Jay said from so close behind him, Rollins could feel the cold air from his mouth on his back through his singlet.

"You didn't put it on to water the lawn?"

"What?" Jay laughed. "I didn't even think of that. Never had lawn."

"Didn't you ever live in a house?"

"Nah," Jay sprawled in a plastic lawn chair next to Nola, the sprinkler hitting him. Rollins imagined that's how he'd spent the morning while Rollins was shopping and sorting his job for tomorrow. "We always had like flats? Units? That kinda thing. Shared places with other girls. No house. Oh, well, 'cept when I was younger here, but I don't really remember it."

He said he didn't remember it like he did remember it but didn't want to discuss it. Rollins didn't want to discuss it either. If Horace was an asshole now, he didn't want to imagine what he was like when he was a much younger man with more testosterone and more stupidity. The stories were enough.

"How 'bout you?"

"How about me what?"

"Where'd you grow up?"

"In a house."

"No shit?" Jay sucked on the icy pole. Rollins looked away at the fence, the expanse of blue sky beyond it, listened to the steady sound of metal clanking and trains moving from the port nearby. "Thought you were raised in a tent, eh?"

"Idiot," he couldn't help turning a quick smile on Jay. "I grew up in Girrawheen, suburb north of Perth. Same house all my life. Nothin' special. It was a bit rough back then, getting gentrified now."

Jay sucked down on the icy pole so his cheeks were hollowed out; he held it like that and seemed to be sucking the sugar out of the ice. His face was blotchy red over his pale complexion from the heat, his eyes drowsy under his glasses. He moaned faintly as he drew out the juice.

"You are not sexy," Rollins said to him.

Jay raised both eyebrows and pulled off. "Huh?"

"Nothing," he kicked out another lawn chair with his boot and sat down.

Jay looked at his icy pole in his hand. "Oh...oh!" he cracked up laughing. "Dude, I never meant to make it look like that."

Rollins was blushing, he could feel it. He sat forward, focused on his hands.

"But I mean, if you wanna..."

He flicked his eyes up—Jay was bouncing his eyebrows up and down, giving Rollins a sleazy grin.

"We're not doing that!"

Jay chuckled. "Alright dude, settle down. I'm not gonna jump you. You're the one who brought it up. Feelin' a bit wound up are we?"

"I'm not gonna fuck you again," Rollins sat back, kicked his legs out.

"Or suck my dick," Jay nodded around his smile and went back to finishing his icy pole.

"I don't suck dick."

Jay pulled off again with a loud, wet, popping sound. "You don't reciprocate?"

Rollins worked his jaw, but found himself answering. "Usually just fuck."

"What if someone sucks you off?"

"I'll give 'em a handy. Finger them."

"You don't go down on your missus even? Dude!"

"What? I don't like it."

Jay shook his head, finished his icy pole. "Then you're not doin' it right."

Rollins did not want to get drawn into this conversation. He blew out a breath. Fucking Jay, though, what'd he know about it?

"And I guess you're the expert then," Rollins couldn't help himself.

"Yeah, dude. I always hit my partner back. Reckon I'm pretty good at it," he was folding the plastic and tucking it into his pocket, "paid a lot of attention to what makes the other person feel good, you know?"

Rollins grunted. He did not know. The sprinkler clicked between them, intermittently making the quick clicking sound as it wound back around before beating out a slower rhythm as it wet the lawn, Nola, and Jay.

Jay's shirt was wet now, clinging to him, his soft flesh visible in small lumps against the material, his pink nipples evident against the sheer fabric. He was smiling a soft smile as he looked out at the horizon, head bobbing faintly like he was lost in thought.

"Well," Rollins finally said, "good for you, but I'd rather jerk it alone than fuck anyone who expected me to get on my knees."

Jay laughed. "Once again I gotta say, your missus is a lucky woman."

"It ain't all about the sex."

"Nah, but, the sex is like the physical expression of the other stuff isn't it? Like, both my dudes, even the dick without a name, with both of 'em the sex was where we said what we couldn't say, you know? Where we showed each other what we felt."

"I can't believe you talk like this about fucking dudes."

"Dude!"

"What? You fuck around with a dude to get off."

"I'm gay, but."

"Yeah, well. It's not the same."

"What's not the same?"

Rollins shook his head. He had no idea what he was on about. "Nothin'. I'm just sayin'. We won't be doin' anything like that. Best to clear that up from the start."

Jay laughed, humourless. "Dude, with the way you're talking, I wouldn't even if you were payin' me."

"Oh, so your mum never fucked dudes she didn't see eye to eye with?"

"Okay, once again, stop bringing her into shit. You're a bit obsessed, you know that? And second of all, I ain't a prostitute, am I?"

Rollins snorted. "No one would pay you for sex."

"Well, no one would pay you, Mr I ain't goin' down on you."

Rollins shook his head. People would totally pay him for sex. Had Jay seen him?

"I'm just saying," Rollins went on, "better get used to your own hand for a while."

Jay snorted. "Dude, trust me, lotta fellas around here, if I feel like it, I'm sure I can find someone who's willing."

Rollins clenched his jaw. "Not in this house you won't."

Jay raised both eyebrows. "It's like that, eh? Well, I can always go to their place."

"You do that."

"I will."

"Good."

"Good."

At least Rollins wasn't sporting a semi anymore. No, he felt all twisted, out of sorts.

Jay got up. "I need a shower, I'm all sticky."

Rollins grunted. Jay disappeared inside the house.

No, he was most definitely not thinking about Jay fucking random dudes. In fact, he was going to shower after Jay and go to bed.

18

♥

THE PROBLEM WITH WORKING nights was the first night. Trying to get to sleep during that first day before a twelve-hour shift. Rollins was so irritated by the time he tossed around after an hour of lying there, he almost wanted Jay to do something to piss him off so he could yell at him. But Jay was so quiet, Rollins wasn't even sure he was in the house.

And that thought had him sitting up in the pitch blackness of his room. Had Jay actually gone out to fuck some random dude? Already?

What a little slut, Rollins thought as he tossed the blankets off and banged out the door. Jay could fuck whoever he wanted, of course he could, but he was still affiliated with this house and so if he was going to do it, he needed to be discreet, and Rollins was going to have a few choice words with him about—

Jay was sitting on the floor in his room, computer parts scattered around him.

"Shit, dude," he said when Rollins walked in, "was I too loud?"

"No," Rollins exhaled roughly. Why was he so fucking relieved to see Jay sitting there? "Couldn't sleep," he mumbled, "building it?" he waved his hand at the mess.

"Yeah, my crew sent me the best shit though, so won't take much. You ever take a sleeping pill?"

Rollins shuddered. He had, once. He had dreams. Nightmares. And he couldn't wake up. He could always wake himself up from within a dream, say, 'Wake up, it's just a dream,' but with the pills he was stuck, he couldn't get out.

He jerked his head. "Don't like 'em."

"Yeah, my mum's the same. Just gotta get through the first night, eh? Then you'll be on moon time," Jay went back to screwing a panel on the back of a white box.

Rollins grunted. "Moon time," he rolled his eyes.

"Yeah, that's what I call it. Hand me that panel," he said and gestured to a stack of white panels.

Rollins did.

"Did you try jerking off?" Jay asked after Rollins had been standing there watching him for a while.

"Jesus Christ, I'm not telling you that."

Jay shrugged. "So, that's a no."

"How do you know it's a no?"

"Well, for a start," Jay leaned back and looked at the box he'd made. He pushed his glasses up his nose and ran the cord from the back of it to the power point, "I've seen you after you orgasm, and you're slightly less wound up than usual."

"I'm not wound up any of the time."

Jay laughed. "Yeah, dude, you're Mr Relaxed." He flicked the switch and the box started to hum. Jay turned it off, nodded, and went for the screen. "And for another thing, you'd probably just say if you'd done it."

"No I wouldn't. We're not talking about that shit anymore."

"I thought we weren't doing it."

"Same thing."

Jay looked up at him, he was smirking. "No, it's not."

"I'm not fucking you," Rollins said.

Jay cracked up. "Dude, I know, and I told you, I don't want you to."

Rollins could not get past that. "I reckon you do."

Jay smiled up at him. "I reckon you reckon that, yeah. But for real, dude, I'm good. I don't wanna fuck you, eh."

"Why?"

"Whaddyamean why?"

Rollins glared at him sitting on the floor, looking between his work and this conversation like it was an afterthought. *He* didn't want to have this conversation.

But, fuck it, he was in it now.

"Why don't you want to fuck me?" And that sounded more desperate than he would've liked. He crossed his arms over his chest to toughen it. Now he looked defensive.

Jay paused in screwing the panel off the back of the screen and looked up. "Do you want me to want that?"

"No."

Jay shrugged and went back to working. "I'm just not feelin' it with you anymore, nothin' personal."

"If you're not feelin' it with someone anymore, it's personal."

Jay sighed. "You're right, dude. You're right," he shrugged and kept his eyes on his work. "I dunno, I guess you kinda put me off with the shit about not reciprocating. And then that shit about my mum," he trailed off at the end.

Rollins clenched his jaw.

"I'm going back to bed," he said and walked out.

"'Kay, night."

"It's fucking day time," Rollins muttered and stormed back to his room.

An hour later and Rollins gave up. He couldn't stop thinking about Jay's mouth, about his lips around that icy pole. How would it feel to have that cold mouth sucking his dick? He tried to think of his missus. Hell, to think of some of the guys he'd fucked overseas. His mind kept drifting back to Jay.

He slipped his hand under his trackies and wrapped his palm around his hard dick. He stroked. It was dry, but it didn't matter because the thought of Jay coming in, crawling between his legs, wrapping his lips around his throbbing dick and sucking him down to the root had him pushing up, keening, desperate.

Rollins groaned and shoved up into his hand. He stilled. Could Jay hear him? The little pervert would probably like that. He was such a fucking liar. He totally wanted to fuck him, of course he did. He was gay and Rollins was hot as fuck. He rubbed himself, tried to slow it down but it was useless—he was fucking into his hand, panting, the image of Jay choking around his cock too much, he was coming suddenly with a long, drawn-out sigh.

He was sated, he was sleepy, then he thought about getting off thinking of Jay like that and he was awake again. Fuck his head, seriously. He rolled out of bed and went for the shower. He needed to clean up anyway, he might as well just give up and get ready to go in.

19

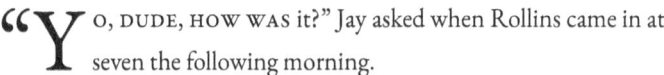

"**Y**O, DUDE, HOW WAS it?" Jay asked when Rollins came in at seven the following morning.

Jay was sitting at the computer, the screen on, all in order like the thing was store-bought and not pulled together with random parts and Jay's hands.

"It was a fucking mine shaft in the middle of the night," Rollins said without heat.

Jay chuckled, kept typing something. "I cooked you some dinner. It's on the stove."

Rollins grunted. Jay stayed focused on his screen. It was irritating. Nola bounded over and he gave her a pat. He didn't want to hang out with Jay, of course he didn't.

He headed outside with Nola, went to find her ball. He was dead on his feet; his shoulders, arms, and neck sore from hauling cable and screwing it above his head for twelve hours. And he had another twelve hours of it to look forward to in another twelve hours. The least he could hope for was a fucking blowjob.

He threw the ball and Nola bounded after it. Because that was the other thing—he was growing obsessed with it, Jay was right. Now it was out there, it was all he could think about. Jay on his knees sucking him off. Jay crawling between his thighs while Rollins dozed, waking him up with an ice-cold mouth while Rollins fucked in, gripped him by the hair and fucked his mouth as he woke up. He didn't know what he'd do if Jay got another icy pole.

He looked inside. Jay was focused on the computer. He was still in sleeping gear—trackies and an oversized Metallica shirt, his hair in disarray, a steaming mug of coffee next to his hand.

It was because Jay rejected him, it had to be. There was nothing appealing about Jay, which is probably why him refusing to sleep with Rollins again was pissing him off so much, consuming him. He knew how that sounded—like he was a stalking asshole, a crazy person. He wasn't, normally. He was controlled. Well, aside from his episodes.

"C'mon, Nols," he said and padded back inside. "Did you cook last night? It'll be no good," he said to Jay.

Jay didn't even look at him when he replied. "Nah, dude, course not. I cooked this morning."

"When did you get up?"

"Like, five."

"What're you doing?"

Rollins peered at the screen. It looked like a series of rectangular boxes with words in it.

Jay did something and the screen disappeared. A black screen with gibberish came up.

"Coding."

Rollins didn't know what that was, but he knew Jay wasn't telling him the whole truth.

"I don't care about your secret society or whatever the fuck you nerds are up to," Rollins leaned away.

Jay snorted. "Secret society. I like it, but nah, me and the crew just chatting online about what we're doing."

Rollins looked back at the screen. He had no idea what Jay was talking about. He'd used computers briefly when he was in the army, but never without help from one of the resident nerds. Regular people were starting to get them and he'd been able to email his family in those last few years away, but he was, like most people, fairly computer illiterate.

"Hmmm," he focused on the screen. "If this is what that looks like I don't reckon it's gonna take off."

Jay crossed his arms over his stomach, tilted his head, rocked from side to side. "It is. Before you know it, everyone will have one."

"Why?"

"For life."

"What life? You can't live life looking at a screen."

"True that, true. It'll be a different kinda life. Like me and my crew, eh? We only met in person when I got to Perth, but I already knew those dudes for like a year before I came out."

"How?"

Rollins was glad to be getting some answers on that front.

Jay inclined his head at the screen. "Online. Chat rooms."

Rollins shook his head. He didn't want to know.

"What did you cook?"

"Two boiled eggs, grilled steak, steamed spinach."

Rollins grunted. "Good." It was actually perfect.

Jay smiled. "Glad to be of service. Now," he spun back to his screen. "I gotta get back to it, my boys got questions and I'm a man with the answers."

Rollins shook his head and went back inside.

"Let me know when you turnin' in, dude, I'll make sure to be quieter," Jay called after him.

Rollins thought he was surprisingly quiet and considerate on that front already. But Jay didn't need to know that. What he really wanted was to drag Jay into bed with him and fuck him. Jay also didn't need to know that, and Rollins wanted to scrub his brain of the goddamn thought.

20

"D UDE," JAY SAID AGAINST my shirt, "you were so salivating over my dick, I had no idea!"

"Shut up, I wasn't. I was just... hot." I said and rearranged my arm so Jay could rest more comfortably against my body. It rocked our little life raft and Jay slumped into my side.

"You were," Jay chuckled.

"Like you weren't into it."

"I wasn't dude, I seriously wasn't. I mean, yeah," Jay glanced up, eyes like slits. He'd lost those damn glasses in the melee back on the boat, "you're hot as fuck, that's like, just a fact, but you were such an asshole and you said you wouldn't go down on your partner. Total turn off."

"I wouldn't." It was absolutely true. The thought of being down there, bloody servicing someone, the thought alone made me gag. Until Jay.

Jay shook his head and nudged under my arm more. He was like a little dog, which made me think of Nola and my heart clenched.

"We'll bump into Africa soon. I can feel it, dude," Jay said softly into my shirt, his breath warm on my skin.

I doubted it. Chances were we'd drift aimlessly until the winds pushed us towards Antarctica and we'd freeze to death. But I didn't say that. Jay was an optimist, and I decided to borrow a bit of that for a change.

21

S MOTHERED. AFTER A WEEK on nights, Rollins was feeling
smothered. Working underground didn't help, but the main
problem was Jay. Rollins wanted to call him out on being constantly
in his face, keeping him awake, only it wasn't true.

Jay never made a sound during the day when Rollins tried, and
wholeheartedly failed, to sleep. He cooked but was unobtrusive about
it, pointing it out and then going back to his work.

Rollins wanted to snap at him about something else, accuse him of
going out and fucking half of Port Hedland while he was at work. But
Jay looked like he barely left the house—he walked Nola twice a day,
he worked on his computer, he showered and changed into the same
jeans and a different, hideous shirt and his cap—so if he was getting
some, he wasn't making any effort with his presentation to do it. He
looked the same when Rollins left each night and again when he came
in.

But his presence was suffocating. His easy smiles. The sound of his
soft breathing when they were in the same room. The way he sat and
sprawled out, talked to Nola, played with her whenever she wanted.
Rollins wanted to grab him and shove him against a wall and—

And there the thoughts dropped off. He didn't want that.

He didn't know what he wanted.

"Dude, I reckon you gotta feel this," Jay was saying now while Rollins sat outside and drank a water, unwound from his shift.

"What."

"C'mon, Nols," Jay said softly and brought her over. "This." His hand was under her belly, rubbing. He reached up, grabbed Rollins by the hand and pressed it to her abdomen.

A lump. Rollins felt around it. He shot out of his chair.

"A vet, we need to find a vet—

"Yeah, already did it, but they're not open yet."

"What time do they open?"

"Like, nine."

"Alright, alright," Rollins crouched down and looked at Nola. She panted into his face, wagged her tail.

"It's probably nothing, she looks alright otherwise, eh?"

"It better be fucking nothing," Rollins sounded vicious. He didn't know who it was directed at, all he knew was he couldn't lose his fucking dog. He swallowed, regained his composure. "Let's head over there, we can wait out the front."

"Okay," Jay said, pretty easy about it considering Rollins was suggesting they sit and wait in the car for two hours.

Rollins grunted.

"C'mon, Nols, drive," he said, his voice cracking on her name. Nola went ballistic—spinning in circles and then charging for the front of the house.

Jay, probably aware of protecting his life, didn't comment on how choked up Rollins already felt.

He pulled up at a non-descript building in an empty carpark, VET emblazoned in blue across the top.

Nola was already pushing at the side of Rollins' face to get out. He opened the door and she charged over him, scampered around the carpark sniffing everything. Rollins got out, heard Jay on the other side doing the same.

Rollins swore to God, if Jay so much as hinted at a platitude, he was going to punch him in the face.

Jay didn't. He cracked his back in that awkward move he had, glanced around at the empty street and the sky, the way the blue looked heavy with the humidity around them, spun his cap the right way round and tugged it over his face. He brushed his hair back on either side of his ears, smiled over at Nola investigating the bitumen and scaring the crows.

"You got a lot of work on?" Rollins found himself asking for something to talk about.

Jay turned his smile over to him. He had a nice smile, kind. "Nah, dude, found myself kinda mirroring you a bit, workin' real late then napping in the day, got ahead of myself."

"What're you actually doing?" Rollins leaned against the roo bar, crossed his arms over his chest.

Jay crouched on the ground in front of him, watched Nola. "Coding mostly, which is like, building shit online."

"Is that for Horace?"

"Some of it, he's got me building a shell company with a dodgy connection in Hong Kong, tryin' to see if he can start running his cleaning that way, funnelling small amounts to test it out. But some of it's like, freelance work, contracted hacking, that kind of thing."

"Where'd you learn to do it?"

Jay shrugged. "Taught myself, mainly, but one of the girls my mum lived with for a while, her dad was an electrical engineer. Anyway, used to stay at his place when I was little and mum was working and didn't want to leave me alone. He was right into computers, showed me what's what."

Rollins frowned down at him. He was beginning to think what Jay was doing might actually be hard.

"Did you go to uni?"

"Not yet," Jay replied and smiled up at him.

Right, he was like, twenty at most.

"Got a good score on the HSC, but. Can go if I want... don't reckon I will."

"That's stupid. What're you gonna do instead?"

"What're they gonna teach me at uni that I'm not already doin'? I could teach them," he gave Rollins a sly grin.

Rollins snorted. He looked at Nola—trying and failing to catch a crow—and felt a sharp pain shoot through him at the thought of her being sick.

"I joined the army straight outta school," he said quickly. Anything to avoid talking about Nola being sick, even talking about this. "I dunno why. My parents are fine. I got a brother, one year younger, he's fine. But I had to get outta there. Went straight to the ACT for basics, then up to Queensland for army, did the electrical license. Joined the air force. Came home when I joined the SAS. Then I reckon I wasn't here for... musta been ten years. More. When I got back, my parents looked so old, but like, the same. The exact same... and I still felt like I didn't know these people at all. And I realised I never had, which is fucking stupid. Anyway, I'm just talking shit."

"Geez, how old are you, dude?" Jay asked.

Rollins laughed. "Thirty-six."

"Fuck, for real?"

"No, I'm lying."

Jay chuckled. "Wow, man, you're not much younger than Horace and you look so much better."

Rollins snorted. "Yeah, well, I ain't bought a one-way ticket to the grave with booze, drugs and cigarettes, have I?"

"No," Jay huffed, "nor beating up on women and kids. I mean, you've killed people, but like, I guess that's different."

"You reckon Horace hasn't?"

"Has he?"

Rollins squinted down at Jay. Maybe he shouldn't tell him. Then again, he reckoned there was absolutely no love lost there.

"Not directly, he gets other people to do it."

"You?"

"Course not! I ain't going to prison for murdering some fuckwit he doesn't have the balls to take care of himself."

"Yeah, I guess killing in combat ain't murder, is it?"

"It ain't murder if they're trying to kill you, no."

"Were the people Horace had killed trying to kill him?"

"You on his side now?"

"Huh?" Jay looked up at him. "Duh, no. I'm just pondering."

"Those people got in his way, that's all. It ain't the same."

"Nope," Jay agreed.

They lapsed into silence. Nola got sick of her lack of hunting skills after a while and came and sat next to Jay. He patted her and Rollins took deep calming breaths.

The vet was a solid looking lady, had a no-nonsense manner about her, which Rollins appreciated.

She felt the lump. "Gonna need to biopsy it."

"Okay."

"Put her under, remove it, send it off. It's gonna cost at least a grand."

"Okay."

"If it's cancer, then we're looking at thousands for treatment," she felt around the rest of Nola's body. "But I'm not feeling anything else. I can do some X-rays, ultrasound to check. Another five hundred."

"Okay."

"If you want me to put her down, it'll be cheaper."

"Treat her. I don't care what it costs."

"Alright," she smiled at Rollins. She must've been at least fifty and working up here, well... no, she probably didn't put that many animals down—most guys used a bullet.

"Book her in for some time this week."

"Is she in pain?" Rollins asked.

"Is she exhibiting signs of pain? Open mouth breathing? Tender to touch?"

Rollins looked at Jay.

"Nah, she seems the same."

"Then we'll hold off on meds. I can give you some tramadol just in case if you want."

"Yes."

"Okay, c'mon Nola, you can come down now," she said and Rollins lifted her down.

The vet gave her some treaties and Nola wriggled her whole body in ecstasy.

Rollins huffed. It sounded throaty and his eyes felt wet. He couldn't remember the last time he cried. Well, he could, but that was because a bomb exploded in front of him and his partner lost his arm and he had shrapnel fucking everywhere. This wasn't that.

"Take Nola out to the car, eh?" Jay said to him. "I'll deal with your appointments and bill, Missy," he patted Nola's head and she did the dog smile up at him, her tongue hanging out. "Yes I will," he crooned.

He opened the door and Nola raced out. Jay avoided Rollins' eyes when he let him go past, let him get the fuck out of there.

Rollins would pay him back. He'd get under control first.

"Nols, c'mon, girl," he said when he got outside, his voice a husk. He cleared his throat a few times. He was overreacting. He was being ridiculous. She was just a dog for fuck's sake.

"Nols," he tried again, but his voice broke.

She whipped her head back to him; her ears went up and her tail stopped wagging.

"No, I'm okay, girl," he crouched down and let all his tension drop.

She bounded over, whined up in his face.

"No, this ain't that. I'm good girl, I'm good."

His fingers sank into her fur. He pressed his face into her neck and just breathed. She smelled good, like tea tree oil.

The door banged open behind him and Jay's sneakers scuffed the ground.

"All good, dude? Want me to drive?"

"Did you bath her?"

"Yeah, yeah. Couldn't believe they had such good stuff at the little shop. She smells good, eh?"

"Yeah," Rollins stood. "She does." He cracked his back. "And you're not fucking driving."

Jay chuckled, smiled over at him.

"What?" Rollins snapped as he let Nola jump in and followed her as Jay got in the other side.

"Nothin', just," Jay smiled at him, pulled his hat down, "you're welcome, dude."

Rollins started the car. Fucking Jay. Only person fluent in Rollins.

"Good... glad. I'm glad."

Jay started laughing. "C'mon, we need to get this girl home and stuff her 'cos she's fasting tomorrow to get ready for her surgery. Yes you are," he put on that sing-song voice and she shoved her head at him while he patted her.

Rollins sucked in a breath. "Okay."

22

J AY WAS SO CHILL about everything, Rollins had no idea what
he'd do without him. After they dropped Nola in for her
surgery, Rollins thought he'd have another breakdown but Jay
just rolled along, told him, "Nah, dude, head outta town, I heard
about this waterhole."

"You want to go swimming? Get eaten by a crocodile?" Rollins
snapped.

Jay guffawed. "I ain't falling for that."

"Falling for what? It's true."

"Here, here, turn here," Jay indicated for the turnoff that'd take
them out of town, heading inland.

"And what do you mean you heard about it? From who?"

"Got my lady at the shops, don't I?"

"I thought you were gay."

Jay laughed. "I am, but even if I wasn't, I reckon sixty-year-old
ladies are a bit too old, even for me."

Rollins grunted and followed Jay's directions.

They drove for about an hour in companionable silence and
Rollins felt the worry easing. Oh, he was still tense as fuck every second

he thought about his girl on the table back there—what if she was scared? What if something went wrong? What if...?

"Shit, the vet's gonna call—

"At two. We'll be back by then."

"Okay."

"Here, follow this road, just at the end here."

Rollins did as he was told and was soon pulling up at an out-cropping of rocks, the large boulders and sleepy-looking gum trees flanking a waterhole beyond them.

"Shit, it's nice, eh?" Jay said and hopped out.

It was. Rollins followed.

Jay came to a stop at the edge of the water, started stretch-ing—twisting his body from side to side and swinging his arms.

"Jesus, who taught you to stretch like that? You're doing it all wrong."

"Huh? Oh, no one, it's just instinct, man."

"Well, you've got the instincts of a dildo."

Jay cracked up laughing. "Dude, that doesn't even make sense. Anyway, you wanna go swimming? Don't reckon there's any crocodiles here, how would they get here? How would they leave?"

Jay was right. In fact, there probably weren't crocodiles this far down, he just liked fucking with city people. He was a city person himself, but any city gullibility he'd had was lost long ago in a haze of sand. As far as he could make out, everyone was a filthy fucking liar and it was best to try and figure out their angle as soon as possible.

Jay was pulling his shoes off, then his shirt, undoing his pants.

"You going in naked?"

Jay shook his head. "Got my boxers on."

Rollins didn't know why he felt oddly disappointed. It's not like he wanted to gawk at Jay's big dick. Men's dicks were a means to an end, not something to fucking well look at.

"You comin'?" Jay asked as he walked over to the edge. He was so pale—his white skin bright against the red dirt, the red rockface, the black surface of the still water. He glanced over his shoulder at Rollins, still in his cap, and smiled. It was a disarming smile, nothing new in it, the same friendly, kind one he always had, except for a little while there after he was hurting over Rollins' crass remark about his mum, and Rollins didn't know why it caught him off guard in that moment. If it was because he was terrified about Nola and felt all cracked open; if Jay wanted to slip in, now would be the time to do it.

"Yeah," he heard himself reply and pulled his shirt over his head. But that wasn't it. He liked Jay. And he already knew that, had liked him from the start, but as he shucked his jeans and boots, made his way to the edge and glanced at Jay swimming with his head poking out, red cap on over his blonde hair skimming the surface, he realised he actually liked him as a person, felt good around him. He hadn't felt like that around another person since Derek. His SAS partner. And if there was one topic Rollins refused to think about, it was Derek.

He jumped in, the cold water plunging around him as he disappeared under the surface before launching back up with a gasp.

"It's cold as fucking balls in here!"

Jay was cracking up. "I know, fuck. I know."

"Jesus, it's like ice."

Jay was still laughing. "It's like, so cold it's not a reprieve from the heat." He looked around. "It's like, you got two options up here, sticky and hot or freeze your fucking balls off. Where's the middle ground, dude?"

"I dunno, but it ain't here," Rollins said and swam quickly to the edge, turned, and swam to the other edge.

Jay swam breaststroke slowly in the middle.

"Dude, what are you doing?"

Rollins stopped and trod water. "Warming up."

Jay shook his head, smiled. "Relax. We're supposed to be relaxing."

"Are we?"

"Yeah, man, why else would we come to a waterhole?"

Rollins had no idea. He reclined onto his back and floated on the surface. The sky was so blue, so expansive, the white puffing stream from a plane in the centre of it looked tiny. The sun was hot on his face, the water cold on his body. He closed his eyes and tried to let it all go.

They got back with plenty of time to take the vet's call. It rang once and Rollins scooped it up.

"Yep?"

"It's me, surgery went well, she's just waking up now."

"Oh, thank God," Rollins sat down at the kitchen table. Jay was hovering. Rollins glanced up and jerked his head.

Jay punched the air and grinned.

"Is it cancer?"

"Won't know that 'til I get the biopsy back, but I can't see anything else on the X-ray or ultrasound. So, probably looking at benign even if it is."

"Which means?"

"Which means we just cut it out."

"So she's gonna be okay?"

"Probably, I took some bloods as well, we'll see what they show up, but yeah, it's looking best case scenario at the moment."

"Thank, God. Thank God," Rollins breathed out.

The vet huffed a laugh. "What're you thanking him for? Haven't seen him holding a scalpel lately," she chirped. Before Rollins could reply, she went on, "Ah, here she is, waking up now. Come down in a few hours, I wanna make sure she comes out of the anaesthetic alright."

"Okay."

The line went dead.

Rollins hung up.

"All good?" Jay sounded so hopeful, gleeful.

"All good," Rollins beamed at him. "Might still be cancer, but benign."

Jay punched the air again and whooped. "Best kind!"

"Don't think anyone should be cheering cancer, but yeah, that's what she said."

"Can we go get her now?"

"Few hours, gotta wake up from the anaesthetic."

"Oh," Jay deflated. Then reanimated. "Fuck, I need a beer. That was stressful, you want?"

And Rollins rarely did, but yeah, for once, he bloody well needed it.

"Yeah."

Jay grinned at him, got them both one of his beers.

They sat outside in the shade, drank their beers and stared at the grey asbestos fence, the blue sky beyond it.

"I think we should have sex," Rollins said.

Jay spat a mouthful of beer all over the patio. He was choking on it.

Rollins leaned over and slapped him on the back. Jay heaved, shook his head and seemed caught between choking and laughing, his eyes streaming, mouth spluttering.

"Fucking hell," Rollins muttered as he looked at him. He didn't know why he was so hellbent on getting another shot at this, but for reasons that went beyond his understanding, he was.

"What the fuck, dude? What?" Jay said once he got himself under control. He was smiling up at Rollins, eyes and lips wet from his outburst, but he looked genuinely unsure.

"I can't sleep," Rollins said.

Jay watched him like he was waiting for him to go on. Rollins didn't have anything else. That was it.

"Are you asking me to fuck you so you can get some sleep?"

"Yes."

Jay cracked up. "Dude, you are somethin' else," he kicked his foot out, refocused on the fence and drank his beer.

Rollins didn't know if that was a yes or a no. He drained his beer, rolled the bottle between his palms.

"I got tonight off, but tomorrow before my next swing," Rollins said.

"Dude," Jay turned to him, smile easy, but his eyes were guarded. "We ain't fucking again."

"Why not?" And Rollins really could not get past this.

"Because of all the reasons I said and also... Also! It's not cool to ask someone to fuck you just 'cos you can't sleep. What am I? A walking fucking dildo?"

"I would fuck you."

"No you fucking well wouldn't," Jay snorted. "I got zero interest in fucking around with someone who just wants to use my ass and mouth. And also, it's like I told you before, you put me off."

Rollins huffed. Jay, unfortunately, had a point. He mulled it over. He was actually surprised how much it stung, to get rejected like this. Though he'd never chatted to anyone he was fucking as much as he chatted with Jay. Maybe that was the problem—Jay knew him too well now. He didn't even chat to his missus this much and they fucked every Friday.

Jay started laughing.

"What?" Rollins asked.

Jay shook his head. "Nothin' dude, it's just, you're kinda weird."

"I'm weird?" Rollins looked over his shoulder at Jay's computer stuff pointedly, back to the man himself in his weird rapper outfit, his ugly glasses. "You're the definition of weird."

"No, I mean," Jay smiled over at him, a bit more open, "you just come on out and ask that like you expect I would obviously say yes. It's like, you really don't get it do you? Like, you honestly don't?"

Clearly not because he had no idea what Jay was on about.

"Get what?"

Jay nodded, smiled. "Yeah, that's what I thought. Tell you what. You figure out what you don't get and I'll think about sucking you off so you can sleep. If," he ginned wide, "you agree to hit me back."

Rollins frowned. "I ain't sucking you off."

Jay stood, shrugged. "Then I guess you better go find yourself someone else to fuck or make friends with insomnia."

Rollins narrowed his eyes at him but Jay just laughed, asked if he wanted another beer and went inside the house to get them.

23

NOLA WAS SO EXCITED when they brought her home, Rollins thought it was hard to believe she'd just had surgery. She had antibiotics in case of infection and a bunch of other shit to do while she recovered. Jay had plucked the instructions out of Rollins' hands, "I'll take care of it."

Rollins raised both eyebrows.

"I work from home."

Rollins grunted.

He hated to think it again, but he didn't know what he'd do without Jay in this with him.

The vet said she'd have the results in a few weeks and that was that.

One thousand and five hundred dollars later and Rollins had his dog back. Fucking beauty, he thought as he smiled at her laying across Jay's bed.

"Fuck, I'm tired," Jay said.

"She can sleep in my room," Rollins replied. Nola had been hanging out with Jay every day and hadn't been sleeping with him.

"Cool, but she's fine with me. Anyway, I'm not going to bed yet, gotta eat, might watch a movie."

"What movie?"

"Dunno, there's a bunch of films under the TV."

"What're you having for dinner?"

"Well," Jay said and went into the kitchen. Nola charged behind him. "She can eat now, but only half her normal amount," he said to Rollins. "And I was gonna have some of these schnitzels my lady, Nelly at the shops, ordered in for me."

Rollins looked at him looking at a green box in front of the freezer. He had his cap backwards again, his nose scrunched up while he read the instructions and scratched the back of his leg with the big toe of his other foot.

"Fried," Jay said and tossed the box on the counter. "And I got you some fish. You want fish?"

"Yeah," Rollins breathed out. "With spinach—

"And two boiled eggs, I know, dude," Jay winked at him.

He wasn't sexy. He looked stupid with his hat and glasses, the fluid way he moved around the kitchen, patting Nola as he passed her and commended her on her appetite.

"You need help?" Rollins wasn't sure what he'd do with himself otherwise.

"Yeah, actually, I'm gonna have some potato gems with my schnitzels. Turn the oven on—

"I know how to cook fucking potato gems," Rollins said and got to it.

"Do you? Really? How?"

"Whaddya think I grew up eating?"

"They had potato gems back then?"

Jay laughed when Rollins flicked him with a tea towel for that.

"Not gems, no. Chips, frozen. Same deal."

"Gross, dude."

Rollins shook his head. "Yeah, well, it's not like I liked them then either."

"Man, I love potato gems, and hash browns."

"It's basically pure trans fats. And carbs," Rollins spread the gems on a tray.

"Give me more than that, dude," Jay bumped him, "I like to snack on 'em through the night."

"You shouldn't snack," Rollins replied but did as he was told and poured half the packet onto the tray. When he put the bag back, he noticed another three packets. "Jesus."

"No, just Jay," he grinned over his shoulder.

Rollins shook his head and put the gems in the oven, set the timer. "Now what?"

"Now go pick the movie, I'll bring this all in when it's ready."

There were a bunch of movies stacked in the cabinet under the TV. It was a small space, but so many were wedged in there, Rollins reckoned there'd be at least a hundred videos and DVDs. The videos were bought, the DVDs were those pirate jobs from Bali and Bangkok.

He pulled the lot out and started flicking through them. The sound of Jay cooking, his voice crooning at Nola, and the smell of fish and fried food wafted into the living room, drifting over him as he went through the pile.

Action films mainly, which he preferred not to watch on account of his problem. He set them aside. And, hello. Porn. A lot of it. Straight stuff, obviously, and most of it cheesy shit. He started reading the back of some them, tried to find at least one with a storyline. There was one about an investigation into illegal activity at a club. The images made it seem like there'd be quite the cast of characters—girls at the club, the boss, cops. He put that in just as Jay came in with his food.

"Find something?" Jay asked.

"Yeah," Rollins grabbed the remote, sat on the couch and started eating.

Jay returned with two schnitzels and a can of coke.

"That's your dinner," Rollins stated flatly.

"Yep, gonna eat the gems too when they're ready."

Rollins shook his head, pressed play.

The synthesiser beats started up, the image of the nightclub against a backdrop meant to be the night sky.

It started out with a guy in his office asking a scantily clad girl if she knew anything about some missing cash. The acting was terrible.

"What's this?" Jay asked. He was next to Rollins on the old, stuffy couch, close enough to touch if either of them leaned to the side.

"Some arthouse crap," Rollin replied.

"You went with an arthouse film? Isn't there like, a comedy or something?"

"This was on top."

"So you just grabbed the first film? Dude, don't you ever just relax? It's like you don't know what that means."

The boss on screen was telling the girl he could find other ways to get the information out of her.

"Hang on," Jay said around a mouthful.

The girl got on her knees as the guy undid his belt, his other hand wrapping around her hair.

"Dude!"

Rollins was chewing and trying not to laugh.

The guy's thick cock flopped out—fat and long like a sausage, half hard—and he yanked the girl's face in until she was licking him and moaning.

"This is porn!"

Rollins let out his laughter.

"You went with porn?"

Rollins shrugged, finished his dinner. He set the plate on the coffee table and leaned back. The guy onscreen was thrusting into the girl's mouth and saying all kinds of filthy shit—*yeah, take it, slut, that's it*—and Rollins realised he'd seen this. It was a long time ago; he and his brother had found it in his dad's closet.

He also realised, cheesy dialogue or not, he was getting hard. Which, let's be honest, was kind of the point.

Jay was squinting beside him, eating his schnitzel and leaning forward as he watched.

"You reckon they reshoot these scenes a lot?"

"Huh?"

Rollins stretched his legs out and rearranged his dick against his pants, gave himself a surreptitious rub.

"You know, to get the different angles. This is using like," Jay paused, took a bite, spoke around his mouthful, "at least three camera angles. They'd have to stop and reshoot, especially for these close-ups. See? Like that."

It was a close-up now of the girl's head, her mouth stretched around the guy's dick, her lipstick smearing along his length as he dragged her up and down his shaft by the hair. This was rougher and more explicit than Rollins remembered.

"Yeah, probably," Rollins mumbled.

"I wonder how many times he has to come. If it ruins sex for him."

"How would getting to fuck ruin fucking?"

"You know," Jay set his plate down and sat back, "making it work."

Rollins bit his tongue on his reply—*why don't you ask your mum?*

But his silence didn't go unnoticed. Jay peered at him, then looked at his dick and laughed.

"Dude, are you hard?"

"And you're not?"

Jay chuckled. "Little bit. I might be gay, but," he swigged on his coke, "sex is sex, think it's the sounds." He readjusted himself and refocused on the screen.

"You wanna?" Rollins asked as he rubbed his dick over his pants. It felt nice, really nice.

Jay shook his head. "I told you. If you can figure out why I don't want to, and let's face it dude, I actually told you, come on. And—

"Because of your mum," Rollins rushed out.

"And hit me back."

Rollins scrunched his face up.

"But yeah, you ragging on my mum all the time is part of it."

Jay crushed his can and leaned back. He was rubbing himself through his pants as well. The guy on screen was thrusting faster and harder, really spewing filth at the girl now before he yanked out and jerked himself off until he was coming over her panting, waiting mouth.

"Jesus," Rollins said.

"Yeah, wow. Is this eighties shit?"

"Think so. Early. Maybe late seventies."

Jay cracked up, but it was breathless with the way he was rubbing himself off.

"Are you a porn connoisseur?"

"No," Rollins snapped, "I'm just a man who lives in the fucking world."

Jay snickered.

The scene shifted to the police station. Two cops. One woman had been arrested.

"C'mon, please?" Rollins said.

Jay shot him a look. "Wow."

"What?"

"You must be really fucking desperate if you're using your manners."

"Shut up," Rollins shoved him.

Jay laughed, but he did not fall into his lap.

This fucking guy, Rollins thought. He didn't reckon he'd ever worked this hard to get laid. Not even with a woman.

"Fine," Rollins said, still pressed against Jay's side so he could feel his arm moving as he rubbed himself slowly through his jeans, "I'm an asshole 'cos I said shit about your mum."

"And?"

"And, I dunno, I have a bad attitude about sex or whatever."

Jay cracked up but it was breathless. "Gonna need you to be more specific, dude."

"Fine, I put you off because I'm selfish in bed."

"Yeah, that's—

"I'm not though."

"Huh?" Jay was looking at him now. The sounds of two cops fucking the woman from both ends was loud from the screen and driving Rollins crazy, but this suddenly felt more important.

"I made you come. Every time."

"Yeah, it's not all about coming though, is it? If you go and make your partner feel like shit about themselves after, it's not a good experience. I mean like, overall."

"Yeah, but you did that too and you don't see me being all withholding. Also, we ain't partners."

"No shit," Jay said and returned his attention to the screen. "And whaddya mean I did that too? No I didn't."

"Yes, you did. You made fun of me for, you know."

Jay glanced back at him, pushed his glasses up his nose. "You mean 'cos of your shit dirty talk?"

Rollins stood, huffed. He didn't know why that stung so much, why it made him so irrationally angry and hurt. At least Jay wasn't bringing up his dick size again. But now he was thinking about that as well, fuck it all.

"I'm goin' to bed," he said and stormed into his room.

"Dude, c'mon," Jay was saying, but Rollins slammed the door and flopped down on his bed face first like a fucking teenager.

There was a soft knock on his door. "Dude, I was just joking," Jay said softly.

Rollins rolled over. "No, you weren't," he breathed the words out but he was sure Jay could hear him.

Jay didn't say anything, but Rollins could see his feet under the door, two small dark shadows.

"Well," Jay said eventually, "I didn't mean to bother you by it so much then. It's good that you're making some effort in that department, I mean most guys—

"Oh, God. Shut up!"

Jay was laughing on the other side of the door, but Rollins could hear him as if he were doing it against his ear.

"Okay, well, I'm gonna watch a comedy if you feel like hanging out again," Jay said and went away.

Rollins lay there, looking at his ceiling and listened to the sound of the studio theme song. Jay hadn't apologised; Rollins made a mental note of that.

After a while, he had to concede that if he stayed in there, he'd seem like a tantrum-throwing child and he wasn't letting Jay have that over him. Bloody Jay with his smooth criminal attitude about everything. He got up and came out like nothing had happened. Jay smiled over at him, murmured the name of the film and shuffled over so Rollins could sit. Nola was there, tail wagging, head up and mouth smiling. Rollins patted her and took a seat.

"What's this shit?" Rollins asked but he knew.

"There's not much selection, eh. It was this or some slapstick shit, which just ain't funny, is it?"

Rollins grunted. He agreed. He settled into the couch, kicking his legs up on the coffee table and watched. The guy on screen was threatening an old lady in a nursing home after her son left, but in a funny way. Rollins snorted a soft laugh.

He could feel Jay smiling at him and not the film. He did his best to ignore it.

24

ROLLINS DECIDED TO LEAVE it alone after that. If Jay was going to keep bringing up his humiliation all the time, Rollins didn't want to go there.

He had other shit to deal with anyway. Horace wanted him to start running the pseudo from a new contact in China out of the port and send it with a truckie down to Perth. He'd made arrangements for that same truckie to do a money drop and Rollins was now expected to clean hundreds of thousands of dollars, while Jay needed to do something on his computer with "the numbers," as Jay put it. Rollins didn't pay too much attention to that part—Jay seemed to know what he was doing—because he was too preoccupied with one, how fucking dodgy it was to shift that much pseudo, and two, how he was going to run that amount through this job. Sure, he was sub-contracting for the mines to refit all the cables, but scrapped copper and materials on a job like that only went so far.

He was mulling it over at the little kitchen table when Jay walked in and grabbed himself a coke from the fridge.

"You havin' any issues with the numbers?" he asked. The question felt funny in his mouth because he didn't really understand what it meant.

"Nah, dude. Me and the crew got a funnel sorted with Mr Hong Kong and besides, we ain't dealing with much, just testing it, running some numbers. All good, eh. You?"

"Me what?"

"Havin' any problems?"

Rollins shook his head slowly. Then said, "It's too much. I can't run this much in that timeframe without raising red flags."

Jay came over and leaned over his shoulder, looked at the book, the columns.

He was so close, Rollins could smell him. Even covered in sweat, he smelled good. Rollins couldn't fathom it—Jay was hygienic, sure, but so were a lot of guys; none of them smelled this good.

"Run it as labour," Jay pointed at the column.

"I ain't running tradies on this one."

Jay shook his head and leaned back. "Me."

Rollins snorted.

"You can't use a TA on this?"

"We don't use Trade Assistants, come on. What'd you know about that anyway?"

"The South African sparkies use them."

Rollins snorted. Of course they did. "How do you know that?"

"My boyfriend," Jay stepped back and leaned against the counter, "the one without a name?"

Rollins rolled his eyes but jerked his head in acknowledgement.

"South African. Dad was a sparky."

Huh.

"Still, we don't use them here."

"Maybe you do on this job."

It wasn't the worst idea. Labourer would be better. Rollins tapped his pencil on the column.

"Yeah, alright. You're gonna have to come and do some work though."

He expected Jay to fight him on it, but he just shrugged. "Yeah, alright. I'm gonna need some clothes though."

Rollins looked him up and down—baggy jeans again, one of those singlets where the arm holes went down to the waist revealing his soft sides, white skin.

"Yes," he said slowly. They'd go to South Hedland later. In the meantime, Rollins was thinking about this boyfriend.

"What'd this guy do that you don't want to mention his name?" he asked because he couldn't help himself.

Jay scrunched his face up. "I'm not talking about that. Let's just say, he wasn't boyfriend material."

Rollins scoffed. "What is boyfriend material?"

"Well, not you."

"What the fuck, I'd make a great boyfriend," Rollins was honestly offended.

Jay finished his coke, crushed the can and pitched it into the bin. It made it with a clatter but the bin was right there, so it's not like it was impressive.

"You'd make as shit a boyfriend as he was."

"I would not."

"You would. But it's not like it's relevant dude, I'd never go out with you."

"What the fuck, I'm the one who wouldn't go out with you."

"What's wrong with me?" Jay asked.

Rollins' eyes widened in surprise. Was Jay joking?

"Are you kidding?"

"No," Jay frowned at him, his eyes serious behind the glasses.

And, well, unfortunately, Jay smelled good, he fucked good, and he was nice to Rollins' dog. But!

"You're a nerd," he said triumphant.

Jay laughed. "And you're an asshole, but that's not why I wouldn't go out with you."

"Why then?"

"Because if you wanted to be with me, you'd have to change everything about yourself and that's not a good way to start a relationship, is it?"

"I'd have to change everything? Are you fucking kidding me? I'm a catch. You're the one who'd have to change."

Jay scoffed. "I'm the shit. And also, you're a catch if someone was into watching paint dry on a wall."

Rollins stood, he didn't know why. He was so affronted he just found himself needing to stand. He towered over Jay in the shitty little kitchen. Jay didn't even flinch. He wasn't smiling, but he wasn't not smiling either.

"Let's go," he said to Jay.

"Where?"

"Shopping," Rollins blurted. He desperately felt the need to cover his sudden movement.

"Okay," Jay said, "let me just turn my shit off, turn the sprinklers on for Nols."

Rollins wanted to snap at him to make it quick—but, Nola—so he just stood there and waited for Jay to come back.

Jay returned with his cap on—backwards—still in the same jeans and singlet, thongs on his feet. Jesus.

"Do you have another shirt?"

Jay looked down at the red monstrosity he was wearing.

"What's wrong with this one?"

"What isn't?"

Jay huffed a laugh. "Sorry we can't all pull off black on black every fucking day," he said and went out the front door.

Fucking hell. Now Rollins was going to have walk around the shopping centre with Jay dressed like that. In South Hedland.

Jay was a surprisingly good shopping partner. Sure, people gave him the side-eye—not many people dressed like white gangster wannabes in this town—but Jay never reacted to it. Rollins saw he noted it, but he ignored it like he was genuinely unaffected by it. He was also acquiescent to Rollins' suggestions. So much so—easily taking everything Rollins handed him with a gruff, "this, you'll need this, and this, now boots"—Rollins eventually had to ask.

"Why're you just doing what I ask?"

Jay was pushing the trolley, browsing the DVDs as he moved past them.

"'Cos you've done this shit and I haven't."

Rollins frowned. It was true, but he thought Jay would have a bunch of opinions about everything.

"Yeah, but, you're just agreeing with me."

"Do you want me not to? Over work pants and high-vis shirts? Isn't it like, a uniform?"

"Yeah, but you haven't even commented on it."

Jay stopped looking at a film with weird cartoon characters on the cover and peered up at him. "I don't really have any thoughts on it."

He chucked the DVD into the trolley and kept pushing it.

"None?"

Jay tilted his head to the side. "No," he peered over his shoulder at Rollins, "I don't like wasting my thoughts on shit that I can't change."

"Saving them for your geek crew?"

Jay snorted. "Yeah, me and the crew get into it, eh? But, nah, I just don't see the point getting all riled up about things that don't matter."

"How do you know what matters?" Rollins couldn't believe he'd had that thought, never mind voiced it in a tone like he was contemplating it. "Here," he stopped too quickly to cover it, "get some of these socks. Good with the boots."

But Jay was looking at him, the little divots in his white forehead creased, his eyes squinty behind his glasses as he really thought about it.

"I guess..."

Rollins busied himself with the socks. They were all black but there was a variation in the texture.

"I guess it's what you're really feelin', you know? If you get, like, a super strong feeling about something. Well, then, it matters, doesn't it?"

"Anger's a pretty strong feeling and I think we've all been told to let it go."

"Not necessarily," Jay said and started pushing the trolley again. "Sometimes anger's pointing you toward what you need to do. Besides, anger isn't really anger, is it?"

"Anger is anger," Rollins replied.

"Nah, anger is hurt."

Rollins scoffed.

Jay shrugged. "That's been my experience," he mumbled.

Rollins wasn't touching that.

So why did he find himself continuing the conversation as they crossed the carpark, both hands full of shopping bags, the humidity like a blanket between them and the impending storm—the large sky dark blue above them, the redness of everything more severe against it—why in the midst of that did Rollins say: "I dunno about hurt, but I reckon anger is valid."

He felt frightened as soon as the words left his mouth. He didn't know where they'd come from. It's not like his anger had been in-validated—he'd had a regular life, 'children are to be seen and not heard' and all that shit from his parents; do what you're told without question in the military and he'd signed up for that, he wasn't angry.

"Course, dude, course it is," Jay replied easily and looked up at the sky. "Cyclone?"

Rollins scoffed. He felt charged with adrenaline after making that comment and relieved Jay had heard and moved on.

"Just a storm," he replied.

"Nice," Jay said still looking around at the rapidly changing sky, the liveliness of the horizon.

Rollins felt like he'd jumped off a cliff, and now he'd made the leap, he could finally breathe. He felt giddy with it.

"What're you smiling about?" Jay asked as they got in the car.

Rollins turned to him. "Nothin', just like storms. Especially when I can see 'em coming."

"Yeah? Me too, man, me too. Especially summer storms."

"Well, this is one endless summer. So, you're gonna like this one."

25

THEY WERE SAFELY ENSCONCED in the house when the storm hit. The humidity was so high, Rollins' face and throat, his whole body, was covered in a film of sweat; it trickled down his neck, beaded on every inch of him like a second skin. The wind smashed into the house, repeatedly announcing its violent arrival below the rumble of thunder. Bursts of crackling lightning painted the sky like flashing spider webs.

"Fuckin' sick as," Jay said from where he was perched at the back door to his room, Nola beside him as they watched the show on the horizon.

"Yeah," Rollins said as he came up beside him and wiped the sweat off his face with the hem of his shirt.

Jay whistled.

Rollins peered at him as he let his shirt drop, then rolled his eyes.

"You know what my abs look like."

Not a lot of dudes Rollins could say that to since he got back to Australia, except for Jay and the odd guy he ran into at the gym in the locker room.

"I do, but it's a show every time, dude. Damn. Is it all work or you got some natural genes goin' on as well?"

Rollins raised both eyebrows at him, couldn't help his smile. "I still can't believe you just come out with this shit."

"What? It's a legit question. I need to know if it's worth making the effort or if there's some unfair natural advantage I'm never going to have."

Jay stretched up out of his crouch and leaned against the doorframe. He was still in that hideous singlet with the long arm holes, the soft indents of his sides visible. He wasn't fat; he had an extra layer of padding everywhere and he was short so it squished up on him like little rolls.

Rollins found himself reaching out and stroking his fingers along Jay's side, trailing over the divots in his skin.

"Diet," he murmured as he watched Jay's breath move through his body where Rollins' hand followed, "if you changed up your diet, you'd shed this then you can worry about abs," he ran his hand down and rested it on Jay's hip, "but I don't reckon you need to."

Jay was silent. Rollins realised what he was doing and pulled his hand back.

He refocused on the horizon.

Jay still didn't say anything.

A clap of thunder so loud and sudden it felt like the house shook with it made Rollins flinch. Nola flicked around and sat to attention at his feet. She whined up at him, tapped his knee with her paw.

"Yeah, girl," he said. She was right. He should take a pill. His heart was starting to pound and he was on the edge of it, he could feel it coming.

"You got something for it?" Jay asked.

"Huh?" Rollins thought he'd replied but it was coming in, the rushing scenes above the reality of here, of now.

"Dude, c'mere," Jay's voice was soft, close, his hand on Rollins' elbow as he tugged him inside.

Rollins didn't like anyone touching him when he was like this, but Jay's hand was gentle. He felt himself being moved, pushed down. Then he was alone. Everything was dark and his heart was pounding and he needed to get under control, he needed to get out.

"Here," Jay was opening his palm. Rollins felt his pills against his skin. He took them around his gasp, felt the rim of a glass pressed against his lips.

Nola jumped up and sat behind him, so still and quiet: on guard. He felt Jay moving away and his hand shot out, met a soft hip. He gripped him. A moment passed before Jay huffed.

"Alright you big baby," he heard Jay as if from somewhere far away, but then he was against Rollins' chest, pressing his body in so Rollins could tuck Jay's head under his chin, hold on, that lovely smell filling his lungs.

He drifted. He was terrified, but he felt anchored, he felt okay. He felt Jay's ribcage expanding and contracting against his own, his soft breath whistling over the sweat in the hollow of his throat.

He didn't remember falling asleep, but when he woke the rain was battering the side of the house, the wind still going strong. The thunder and lightning had passed, and Jay was in his arms.

"You good, dude?" Jay murmured.

Rollins heaved a drawn-out sigh. "Yeah."

He needed to move away, get up, stop clinging to his chubby little workmate. He felt Jay wriggling like he was reading Rollins' thoughts.

Rollins tightened his arms around him.

"Just five more minutes," he whispered.

Jay was quiet.

"Okay," he said.

Rollins squeezed him and felt Jay's answering grip in the flexing of his fingers against his back.

26

"SO, WHAT'RE WE DOING exactly?" Jay asked as he peered around the mine site from his window in the jeep.

"Upgrading all the cable," Rollins said as he came to a stop and threw it into neutral.

"Like rewiring?"

"Exactly," Rollins got out.

It was dusk, the pink of the sky dimming around them but barely visible against the bright lights on-site.

"Rollins," the site manager said as he walked towards his office—a white demountable flanking the carpark.

"Tim."

Jay came around the bonnet. He looked the part in his brand new pants, high-vis shirt and boots. He refused to lose the cap—backwards and holding his hair back under the hard hat—and nothing was to be done for the bloody glasses under the safety glasses.

"This is Jay," Rollins said.

"Jay," Tim said and then disappeared into his office.

"So, you want me to carry something?" Jay asked as he looked around.

"Already down there. C'mon."

Jay followed him to the site elevator that'd take them underground.

"You probably shoulda asked if I was claustrophobic."

"Are you?"

"Nah."

Rollins shook his head, ushered Jay in front of him.

"It's not cramped anyway."

"Yeah, but like, there's gonna be a fuck tonne of soil between us and the surface isn't there?"

The lift started moving down, the carved-out shaft glowing with lights, the fine trickle of water seeping down the dirt around them.

"Don't think about it."

Jay pushed both pairs of glasses up his nose and looked up at him. "You mean, don't think about it like, you're telling me not to think about it or you never think about it?"

"The second one," Rollins replied and crossed his arms over his chest.

"Mental discipline to match the muscle discipline, nice, nice," Jay nodded his head and glanced around.

The cage clanged to a stop and Rollins tugged it open.

"Oh, wow," Jay said from behind him.

Rollins looked around the cavernous space to look for what he was gushing about.

"What?" he shot over his shoulder.

"It's so big."

And Rollins guessed it was. Like a spacious, cavernous carpark.

"We doin' the whole thing?"

"Just this level for now, might upgrade the rest later. We'll see. C'mon."

He got to his gear and explained to Jay what he'd need him to do—pull cable mainly—and finally got to wondering about Jay's fitness.

Jay surprised him though. He was clearly unfit, huffing and red as he pulled the cable through the conduit Rollins had already put up. But he was determined, and he managed to chatter away the entire time.

Rollins thought that'd piss him off—he liked working in silence—but he found himself snorting when Jay said, "Almost makes me think we mighta been better off sticking with fire," after they'd been pulling cable for four hours. And he listened intently while Jay described his plans to become a 'blogger.' Rollins didn't ask, but he learned Jay was going to write a 'daily log' on his 'observations of man.'

"Whaddya mean 'man'?" he couldn't help himself once Jay got done detailing how he'd set up this screen where he'd write all this shit and, apparently, people would come and read it.

"What people?"

"People on the internet."

"Nobody's on the internet."

"Some people are and soon everybody will be."

Rollins doubted that, but whatever. Then he'd asked: "Whaddyamean 'man'?"

"Like," Jay huffed and tugged the last of the cable for that run, "you know, the species, man."

"What kind of observations then? Here's man, taking a shit."

Jay laughed. He headed over to grab the next cable.

"Smoko," Rollins said.

"Okay."

They settled on top of the toolboxes and Jay ate the deep-fried patties he'd brought in alfoil and drank a coke, while Rollins ate a few hard-boiled eggs and drank a smoothie.

"No, like, take Gaz," Jay said.

"Whose Gaz?"

"My housemate. You met him."

Must've been the metal-looking dude. Rollins grunted.

"Gaz is studying, right? Wants to be an engineer. Like, he legit wants to do it, loves all that shit. But when he gets assignments from uni, he like, just doesn't do them. He waits until the night before when he's like, sick over how much work he's gotta do and then turns in a real pile of shit. Why? I mean, what does that say about the species?"

"That we want to avoid pain," Rollins replied.

"Yeah, but like, we want things and to get them we gotta go through the pain. Why can't his brain put two and two together?"

"And this is what you'll be writing about."

"Yeah, with pictures as well."

"Pictures of what?"

"Well, like in this one Gaz."

"So you're gonna write about Gaz not doing his assignments and then stick in a photo of him."

"Sort of a bit more complex than that, but yeah."

"No one wants to know about Gaz, never mind see him."

Jay laughed. "I reckon they do."

"They don't."

"Alright, well maybe I can blog about you."

Rollins narrowed his eyes at him. "Over my dead body."

Jay laughed again. "Definitely make for a better picture."

"You ain't getting a picture of me."

"I dunno, if I got you after, well..." Jay gave him a sleazy once over.

Rollins blushed and finished his smoothie to hide it.

"Except we're not doin' that anymore," he said.

"Yeah," Jay replied wistfully.

"It was your idea not to."

Jay smirked. "I'm just messing around, dude."

Rollins didn't want to be feeling all flushed and tingly with Jay's brand of messing around down here.

"C'mon," he stood. "Let's finish this run."

"'Kay."

By the time they got home, Jay was dramatically extolling the virtues of his bed and a hot shower.

"How do you do that every night?" he asked as he flopped down on the couch after making a big fuss over Nola.

"Used to it," Rollins replied and went into the kitchen to cook dinner. Breakfast. Dinner-breakfast.

Jay was in the exact same position when Rollins brought in their food. He snorted.

"Here," he held the plate out.

Jay brought his hand up and didn't move any further.

Rollins shook his head at him and closed the distance.

"Oh, fucking nice, dude," Jay said as he rested the plate on his stomach and started eating the disgusting patties and potato gems Rollins had cooked for him.

He sat next to him and took a bite of his fish.

"Don't you ever get hungry, dude?" Jay asked around a mouthful.

"No?"

"What about carbs? You need carbs to feel full."

Rollins scoffed. "No, you don't. You see many cavemen eating carbs?"

"You see many cavemen eating like, ever?"

Rollins shook his head. "You know what I'm saying."

Jay chewed. Rollins could hear him thinking. Could feel him looking at the side of his head.

"What?" he broke first.

"Nothin', just thinking it'd be really great if you'd let me blog about you."

"Not even if you paid me a million dollars."

"I ain't got that kinda money and anyway, all this shit is free."

"Then why do it?"

"It's fun."

"It's fun to write about Gaz failing at uni," Rollins said and set his plate down. Nola looked at it, then up at him. "Alright," he said to her and got up to get the oil from Jay's pan to pour in her bowl. He'd seen Jay doing it and she loved it and he figured what's the harm. Well, a lot, but whatever, she probably had cancer, she could live a little.

"You'll see, this shit's gonna take off," Jay said when Rollins came back in, his eyes sleepy.

"I doubt it, but if it makes you happy then whatever," Rollins sprawled out next to him. He thought about clicking on the TV.

"Thanks, dude," Jay nudged him.

"For what?" Rollins expected some appreciation for the dinner.

"For supporting my dreams."

Rollins huffed a laugh. Jay was grinning at him.

"Shut up and go to bed."

"You go to bed."

"We've gotta do it all again in eleven hours."

Jay yawned. "Fuckity, fuck. Fuckin' fuck."

"Exactly," Rollins clicked on the TV.

And between one atrocious news story on this joke they called morning television and the next, he was asleep, and the last thing he remembered was his head falling to rest on Jay's shoulder.

27

J AY HAD BEEN RIGHT about labour covering a lot of the cleaning; Rollins was moving the cash through at a nice click and enjoying the pleasure of not hearing from Horace. He was also having fun on the job, which had never happened. The last time he remembered happiness like this was in the military, particularly with Derek. He'd forgotten how good human company could be, how it could lift him up.

Speak of the devil, he thought as Jay strolled into the kitchen.

"You heard from Horace?" Rollins asked.

"Nah, not lately. Why?"

"It's good," Rollins shrugged and went back to his accounts. "Means we're good."

It also meant they could relax over the one week break they had coming up. Rollins had been thinking of heading up to Broome, seeing if Jay wanted to do a fishing trip. Then he remembered Jay didn't eat fish, and he got a curt text from his missus telling him if he didn't come back for the break, it'd be over. He'd read that with relief and the sudden feeling of freedom before he'd shut that down.

"You heading down to Perth for the break?" he asked Jay.

"Dunno, maybe."

"You wanna make a decision so I know what to do with Nola?"

"What're you gonna do if we both go?"

"Take her with me and drive."

"And if I stay?"

"Leave her here with you and fly."

Jay nodded, drank his coke. "I'll stay then."

"You don't have to."

"It's not like I need to do anything in Perth and besides, I can talk to the crew from here," he waved his hand at his room, his computer.

Rollins heart sank with that pronouncement, but that was a ridiculous thing to feel so he shoved it aside.

"Right," he said and stood. "You ready?"

"Yeah, just gotta pack our lunch."

"Did it," Rollins said and grabbed his keys.

He felt Jay at his back as they went out and tried to shake off his bad mood.

The bad mood persisted to his arrival in Perth. His missus picked him up and he felt annoyed with her from the moment he got into the car.

"Shall we grab a drink?"

He could see she was dressed for it, and normally he made the effort to do things he didn't want to do because she did. Not today.

"Maybe tomorrow, I need to sleep."

It wasn't a lie. He'd finished that morning at seven, told Jay not to bother dropping him at the airport—he'd need to learn to drive better before Rollins left him on his own for the short drive home from the shed they called an airport—and then he'd sat on the front porch with Jay waiting for the taxi, his agitation and melancholy growing.

"Got a lot of plans with your missus?" Jay had asked.

"No," he looked over at Jay. "What're you gonna do?"

"Me and Nols got all the plans, haven't we girl?"

Rollins snorted. He'd wanted to berate Jay for something, but nothing had come to mind.

Then he thought of something. "She's not gonna like strange men in the house."

Jay raised both eyebrows at him. "What strange men are comin' round?"

"I'm just sayin', if you're thinking about doing that, she might not like it."

Jay's eyes widened and he cracked up. "Noted, dude."

Rollin clenched his jaw. His taxi pulled up and he was saved from further embarrassing himself. He wanted to hug Jay goodbye, but he didn't see any reason to do that, so he shouldered his duffel, grunted a goodbye, patted Nola and left.

Now he was here, his missus frowning as she drove, her pissed off silence filling the space between them.

"I just got off a month of nights and I ain't slept yet today," he defended himself.

"Didn't you sleep on the plane?"

"No, I ain't sleeping around a bunch of miners, Christ."

She scoffed. "What're they gonna do?" She shot him a dirty look. "Your paranoia is ridiculous."

Rollins sat back and looked at her. She rarely brought up his condition directly. He didn't know what to say. He said nothing. By the time they pulled up in front of his unit, she was vibrating with anger and for the first time, Rollins seriously thought about ending it.

But then she blew out a breath and said, "Can you at least be available tomorrow so we can go over wedding stuff? We need to meet the priest and I'm sick of going to all these tasters with fucking Tanya."

"Yeah, okay," he said and got out.

"I'll pick you up at eight."

He grunted and slammed the door. Then he went inside and face-planted on his bed and wondered what Jay and Nola were up to.

The whole visit was like living in a waking nightmare. More than once, he thought about ending it with his missus. He didn't know what stopped him. Something about the trajectory he found himself on with her felt safe in a way breaking up with her felt like the opposite—freedom, yes, but that freedom utterly terrified him.

By the time he stepped off the plane back into the humidity of Port Hedland, he felt the sweat prickling his skin like a warm blanket welcoming him home. When the taxi pulled up in front of the house, he was excited, nervous.

As he stepped onto the porch, he felt a stillness to the place. He knew before entering a building if it was occupied or not and this one was not. His feeling was confirmed when he went in and quietly checked each room. No Jay. No Nola. Then he saw the note on the kitchen table.

Gone to Sydney. Emergency. Nola's with me – all good, dude.

Sydney?

He pulled his phone out and hit Jay's contact.

It went straight to voicemail.

Did he have his fucking phone turned off?

He left the house, calling his taxi back on his phone as he walked, and went straight back to the airport.

He messaged Horace for Jay's mum's address. He got—*how the fuck should I know?*—in reply.

By the time he stepped out of another taxi into Jay's front yard in Perth, he was quietly furious. Who did Jay think he was? Taking off with Rollins' dog and then turning his fucking phone off?

The metal head answered the door.

"Yeah?"

"What's Jay's address in Sydney?" he asked. He had a flight to Sydney in two hours and no time for fucking small talk.

"Jay's address in Sydney?" the guy, Gaz, Jay said his name was, gave him a bewildered look.

"That's what I said."

"Ah, yeah, I dunno who you are, man," Gaz looked him up and down through the flyscreen.

"Jay's got my dog."

Gaz frowned at him. "Were you hurting the dog?"

"What? No, of course not, she's my fucking dog. I just need to know where he is so I can get her back."

That's what he'd been telling himself since he left Port Hedland. A transparent lie because if Nola was safe with anyone, it was Jay. But then he'd remembered they stocked dogs like cargo under planes and he'd been enraged. This wasn't the military where the guys with dogs kept them with them in the plane then parachuted out the back with the dog strapped to their chest, this was fucking commercial where everyone was treated like cattle and pets like luggage. Rollins had never hated this apparent civilisation more.

"You got some problem with Jay, then?" Gaz asked.

"No, I just need to get my dog."

"Hmmm," Gaz drummed his fingers on the doorframe.

"We're friends. Me and Jay. He was looking after her then he had to go to Sydney for some emergency—

"Yeah, got sick family over there," Gaz said and disappeared down the hall.

Sick family? His mum?

"You got a pen?" Gaz asked.

"I'll remember it."

Gaz gave him a look like he doubted it, but he rattled off the address in Newtown and then said, "I'm gonna let Jay know you're comin', so if you're thinking anything dodgy, he's gonna be ready for it."

Rollins had a moment to wonder what on earth Jay could do to him for this guy to make a threat like that, but then he realised this guy could contact him on his computer.

"Good," he snapped. "I want him to know I'm coming."

Then he turned and headed back to the taxi.

The hospital carpark was a hospital carpark—plain, bitumen, parking metres no doubt so overpriced that if you were a person living on the edge of your finances, this would be the tipping point. Rollins crossed it quickly, eyes taking in the ugly brick building in front of him. After much haggling with the woman who lived next door to Jay's mum, he found out 'the family' were likely here. What family?

It didn't matter. His tiredness was receding under his desperate rage to see Jay and hit him.

He saw Nola first.

She was sitting at a woman's feet out the front of the hospital. And she was wearing some kind of jacket. The woman was smoking, eyes on the carpark. She shifted her gaze as Rollins approached, narrowed her eyes, but otherwise continued to smoke as he held his line straight for her.

Nola saw him and stood, her whole body wriggling, tail wagging.

The woman took a drag, but didn't move.

"That's my dog," he said as he came up to them.

Nola was leaping up, hew paws landing on his thighs, and he held her head in his palms and scratched behind her ears.

"So it is," the woman said.

Rollins straightened. "Where's Jay?"

"Why're you looking for him?"

"Because he took my dog," he thought that was pretty obvious.

The woman shook her head slightly, tilted her face down to look at Nola. She would've been pretty once—cute—but she looked old, probably older than she was. Her dark roots were visible against the bleached blonde strands, her wrinkles prominent in her tan skin. Even her clothes looked tired—faded jeans and a flannelette shirt.

But her eyes were shrewd and eerily calm. "He's been taking good care of her, no need to rush all the way here from Port Hedland."

"Who are you?"

"Friend," she looked up and met his eyes, "of the family," she finished after a pause.

"Okay, is Jay inside?"

She dragged on the butt of her cigarette, blew the smoke in his face—which he thought was really unnecessary—and dropped it and crushed it under her boot.

"Yeah, but he's with her now and she's dying so I wouldn't bother him if I were you."

"Who?"

"His mum."

Rollins sucked in a breath. She was watching him carefully.

The sliding doors opened behind them and Jay came out. He was holding his glasses and wiping his eyes and Rollins suddenly wished he'd stayed home and trusted Jay with Nola like he knew he should've in the first place.

"Rollins?" Jay asked as he walked over. He was surprised. Obviously he was surprised.

"Came to see his dog," the woman said, looking at Jay. "How's your mum? I told him she's dying."

Jay stared at her. He'd put his glasses back on and his red-rimmed eyes blinked slowly. Rollins had a horrible thought that maybe she'd just died and here he was, right in time for it with his bullshit excuse and no idea what to do if that happened.

"She's sleeping," Jay replied after a moment. "You wanna go up?"

"Yeah," she said and handed Jay Nola's leash. She squeezed his shoulder roughly, pressed a firm kiss to the top of his head. "This one seems alright, but call me if he gets any ideas," she said against his hair so Rollins could hear.

She gave Rollins a once over, didn't smile, then went through the sliding doors.

"What're you doing here?" Jay asked once she was gone.

"Nola," Rollins replied and felt ridiculous.

"She's alright," Jay said and looked down at her, "she was real good on the plane."

"How would you know?" Rollins asked and tried to keep his voice steady. He couldn't lay into Jay like he wanted to if his fucking mum was dying.

"Because she was with me? How else?"

"Oh, so they just let her sit in a seat then?" Rollins sneered.

"Nah, we sat at the front near the emergency exit, both flights. They gave her some blankets and everything, lots of food, she loved it."

Rollins looked at Nola panting up at Jay and looking between them. The jacket she was wearing was high-vis and had 'support' in large black writing across the back.

"They let her on the plane."

"Course."

"Why?"

"She's an emotional support animal. I mean, she's not mine, but she does do that job so I figured I'd just fudge the truth a bit and say she was mine for like, that reason."

What the fuck was an emotional support animal?

"Did you come all the way here to get her?" Jay asked.

"Yes," Rollins bit out.

Jay frowned.

"And you turned your phone off so I couldn't check on her," Rollins said.

"My phone died. Forgot the charger."

Rollins stared at him. Jay watched him back.

"I'm sorry about your mum," Rollins said.

Jay frowned; he looked over Rollins' shoulder, jerked his chin.

"You wanna go get something to eat?" Jay asked.

And well, Rollins couldn't see why not. But.

"Nola?"

"That jacket gets her in everywhere," Jay patted her. "C'mon, there's a good dumpling place a few streets over and I reckon they'll do you some strips of steak or whatever."

And Rollins couldn't think of any objection to that so he fell into step with Jay and wondered what the fuck he was doing in Sydney.

"Who was that woman?" he asked for something to say.

Jay was trudging along beside him, hand in his pocket and the other one loose on Nola's leash as she marched ahead of them, tail wagging. He blew out a long breath before replying. "Janet. Friend of my mum's," his voice cracked as he finished.

Rollins desperately cast about for something to say.

"She seemed nice."

Jay cracked up laughing. He looked up at Rollins, his smile wide around his washed-out complexion and bloodshot eyes. "Yeah, a real people pleaser."

Rollins huffed a laugh.

"I'd never let anything happen to Nola, dude," Jay said as they made their way down a busy street, weaving in and out of the people.

"I know."

"And I'd never let 'em fly her like cargo."

"I... yeah, I know." He didn't know how Jay had managed it, but he did know Jay wouldn't have let that happen. Hell, he'd probably have risked driving if they said they were going to put her down there.

Jay nodded and steered them into a Chinese restaurant. The lady seemed to know him and Rollins listened as he explained how Nola was Rollins' emotional support animal "'cos of shit in the army," and the Chinese lady tutted, smiled, replied, "Sit, sit! I make special for her."

Rollins clenched his jaw and sat. Jay wasn't wrong but Rollins didn't like to think about it, never mind advertise it.

"Dude, relax. It's not like she's Viet Cong," Jay whispered.

"And it ain't 1965," Rollins snapped.

He was about to apologise—it was actually great, having Nola with him—but then he saw Jay burying his face in his menu because he was trying to hide his laughter.

Rollins kicked him gently under the table.

Jay let his laughter out.

"I get it, you know," Jay said. "Not wantin' people to know, but I reckon you gotta take the odd risk to keep her with you 'cos, like, it's safer."

Rollins really didn't want to talk about it even though Jay had a point.

"I don't know how safe she's gonna keep me if shit actually hits the fan," he looked down at her—she was sprawled on the ground, resting her head on her paws and watching the bustle of diners and waiters, her side pressed against Rollins' boot.

"Wouldn't underestimate her, man. Just 'cos she's a lab, doesn't mean she can't get aggressive if someone tried it on."

Rollins grunted. Jay was right; she was friendly but she was still a dog and somewhere in her clever DNA before her kind snuggled up with cavemen for scraps was a vicious killer. He leaned down and rubbed her head. She looked up at him, gave him her dog smile as her tail thumped on the floor. He smiled.

"I'm getting the vego dumplings, shredded potato, broccoli with garlic—

"You're ordering a vegetable? Are you feeling alright?"

Jay laughed. "It's fried."

"Of course it is."

"And I reckon you'll like these steak strips and May can do you some boiled eggs," he handed Rollins the menu.

Rollins scanned it. "Might get some prawn crackers as well."

"Dude," Jay said, eyes wide. "Are *you* alright?"

Rollins kicked him gently again, then left his boot resting against Jay's sneaker.

"Just order it," he retorted and settled back in his chair.

When May asked him what he'd like to drink, he ordered a beer and couldn't help smirking over at Jay's mock cheer.

"Dude, I gotta go back up, but here," Jay said as they arrived back at the hospital.

Rollins was dead on his feet but pleasantly buzzed from the two beers, good food and the rhythm of conversation he only seemed to enjoy with Jay.

Jay pressed a set of keys with a blue ribbon for a keychain into his hand.

"You can use my bed."

"No, I can get a hotel."

"Dude, why? It's fine, I'm gonna be here and Nola likes it there, so," Jay shrugged and headed for the entrance. "You should be able to tell my room from Mum's and Janet's," he winked as the doors slid open, "I hope."

And then he was gone.

"Well, Nols, looks like we're sleeping in Newtown," he said to her.

She looked up at him, tongue hanging out, tail thumping on the pavement.

"Right."

Jay was right about the room. But there were only two bedrooms so he didn't know what Jay meant about different from both women, but clearly the room exploding with posters of gangster rap bands, psychedelic art and a faded ninja turtles bedspread was Jay's room.

He kicked off his boots, shed his pants and got into the bed. Nola curled up on the dog bed Jay had put out for her, eyes on the door, and sighed deeply.

"I know," he said to her and rolled over to look at the ceiling.

The bed smelled like Jay. There was no way Rollins was going to sleep. He still didn't get what he was doing there and for a moment he had the crazed sense he'd lost complete control of himself. He closed his eyes and let the last twenty-four hours catch up with him. He was safe here, in Jay's bed, Nola on guard. He was safe.

Rollins woke to the feel of the bed shifting.

"Go back to sleep, dude," Jay whispered. "I'm just gonna top and tail it and catch a few."

Rollins groaned. He grabbed Jay around the waist and hauled him up beside him.

"Oof," Jay said. "Fuck you're strong."

"Shut up and go to sleep."

Jay chuckled. It whistled across Rollins' throat.

"She alright?" Rollins mumbled.

"She's stable but she's gonna... you know," Jay said.

"Sorry," Rollins said after a while.

Jay's breath gusted out of him, warm on Rollins' skin. "Dude, me too. Me fucking too."

Rollins wrapped his arms around Jay, gave him a squeeze.

"Get some sleep."

"I will. You stayin' for a bit then?"

Rollins hesitated. He had no idea what he was doing. He had a shit tonne of work waiting for him. And Horace would start riding his ass if he dropped the ball.

"Do you want me to?"

Jay didn't say anything, but Rollins felt his hands go around his back and rub him over the material.

"I dunno. Yeah."

"Is that a yes or a no?"

That hand was distracting. It felt nice.

"It's a yeah, but I know you got shit on."

"It'll keep."

"Okay," Jay said and tucked himself under Rollins' chin.

Rollins held Jay close and drifted. He wasn't asleep, he was in between and he could feel Jay was too—his hand caressed Rollins idly, the feel of his breath soft on Rollins' skin.

After a while, he tilted his face down so Jay was forced to move his head out from under his chin. In the same movement, Rollins pressed further into his space and Jay lifted his face to meet him. It was dark, but his eyes were adjusted enough to see where Jay's lips were. He moved forward and Jay met him, their lips brushing in a hesitant caress. It sent a jolt of excitement through Rollins' abdomen. He did it again and Jay kissed him back, firmer this time, their lips brushing, the kiss getting wetter.

"Okay?" Rollins asked against Jay's mouth.

"Yeah. Yeah, fuck dude," Jay whispered against his lips. "I just want to forget."

Rollins frowned. He didn't know why that bothered him, but Jay pressed their lips together and Rollins had to answer him, deepening the kiss, adding tongue. Jay groaned.

Rollins rolled Jay under him. They were both hard and Rollins wanted to get off, but he liked the feeling of kissing Jay too. He didn't want to stop. Neither did Jay apparently, because he was moaning softly under him, kissing him back urgently.

Rollins brought his arms up so he could slide his hands into Jay's hair, his thumbs stroking his cheeks, his jaw. It seemed loud—their mouths moving against one another, their panting breaths.

Jay rolled his hips up and the long, thick line of his dick rubbed up against Rollins'.

"Yeah?" Jay broke away to ask.

Rollins kissed him fiercely, roughly; he didn't know where it was coming from, but he felt desperate. He wanted to say: *Please let me fuck you; I want to feel my cock inside you so bad it's driving me crazy.*

But Jay had made fun of his dirty talk before and that was an embarrassing thing to think, never mind say. So he tried to say all of that with his mouth, with his hips thrusting into Jay's groin.

Jay groaned underneath him, shuffled his hips until his dick was perfectly aligned with Rollins', so when they found a rhythm they were rubbing off in tandem, the feel of it so good even through the material.

Jay broke away again to gasp out, "Yeah? You wanna?"

Rollins sucked on the skin at Jay's throat. *I want to bury myself so deep inside you I don't know where I end and you begin.* He couldn't say it.

Jay slid his hands into Rollins' short hair, his hips frantic, his dick throbbing against Rollins'.

"Please," Jay said.

Rollins released the skin at his throat and took his mouth again, fumbling in his desperation. The bed creaked under their frantic movement, the sheets rustled, and Jay's breaths were loud each time he broke away to gasp for air before Rollins brought him back with rough hands.

"We should—

Rollins kissed him instead of replying—*I want to feel your skin against mine.*

"Fuck, dude, please—

Rollins took his mouth and shoved down hard—*I want to come inside you, I want to feel you dripping with it and then I want to do it again.*

"Pants off, please—

Rollins growled, bit Jay's lip, felt him gasp, push up and start to come—*Fuck yeah, baby, there you go, come for me.*

Rollins groaned into Jay's mouth and thrust against him until he was coming too, the feel of wetness seeping between them, the rush of it tingling through his groin, his throat, blooming warm in his abdomen.

"Shit, dude," Jay panted against his lips.

Rollins didn't say anything. He couldn't. He felt off kilter, unsure beneath the sated feeling. He rolled back to his side and dragged Jay with him.

"We should change," Jay said, his voice slurred.

Rollins breathed in deep, hugged Jay so tight against him he felt the breath rush out of Jay with a squeak.

Jay was asleep by the time Rollins answered. "In a minute. Just one more minute."

29

ROLLINS

Day 13... Somewhere in the middle of the Indian Ocean.

"**W**OW, DUDE, YOU WERE so into me," Jay's voice rasped against the skin at my throat.

It was cold, night falling around us, the constant lapping of the water against the dinghy sending me mad. Or maybe it was the memory of that night. Of how crazy I'd felt with wanting Jay.

"Shut up, I was just horny."

"*I want to bury myself so deep inside you, I don't know where I end—*

I used what energy I had to slap my hand over Jay's mouth.

"Shut. Up."

"I-think-it's-sweet-dude," Jay said, his voice vibrating against my palm.

I huffed a laugh down at him. What else could I do? It wasn't sweet, it was madness. I was slowly but surely going mad back then.

Jay brought his hand up and tugged gently at my wrist. I released him and slumped down. I was too tired to argue it.

"You know I love your dirty talk, right?" Jay asked.

I felt embarrassed. "No, you don't," I mumbled.

"I do, but. I shouldn't have said what I said and I wish..."

I could hear the sincerity in Jay's voice and I really needed to get over it, especially now. "You wish?"

"I wish you had said all that, 'cos then..." Jay's voice was a husk.

"'Cos then you wouldn't have fucked me over?"

Jay sighed. Neither of us had the energy to fight about it and I regretted bringing it up.

"Nah, dude, I still woulda done that, it wasn't personal."

I had the energy to clench my jaw though.

"Still wish you hadda said instead of, you know..."

"Yeah," I wished the morning after had gone better too.

But we were here now and that's all that mattered. Pity it wasn't going to be for much longer with the way things were looking—I was sure I wasn't imagining it was getting colder, the wind getting fiercer. We had the flares but not a goddamn soul to shoot them at.

"Keep going," Jay said softly into the darkness, the blue light of the moon catching his face so I could make out the little smile; it was a smile that said, sorry.

And I was sorry too. "I wish I could've been a better man, I wish—

"Nah, I like you like this. Tell it."

"Okay."

30

R OLLINS WOKE TO THE feel of soft sunlight on his face. It was early. He thought he'd wonder where he was, but he knew and the night before came back with immediate clarity and unsettling warmth.

Jay wasn't in bed, and Rollins knew the flat was empty. The unsettled feeling beat back the warmth.

He rolled to sit up, his pants pinching his skin painfully with the dry come. Nola looked up at him, tail wagging.

"Morning, Nols," he said roughly. He cleared his throat a few times and went to shower.

The bathroom was a discomfiting explosion of pink, female shit and hippy shit. There were plants fucking everywhere. Rollins closed his eyes and let the warm water soothe him.

It didn't work. He didn't know why, but the absence of Jay the morning after pissed him off. No, what had Jay said about anger? It was hurt. Yes, this fucking hurt.

And Rollins was god-fucking-damned if he was going to be hurt by a chubby shithead from Sydney. He turned the taps off viciously and dried himself with one of the hideous pink towels.

He stepped into the hallway just as Jay came in the front door.

"Woah," Jay said and looked Rollins' naked body up and down. "Warn a guy."

"Where the fuck have you been?" Rollins snapped.

Jay held up the polystyrene takeaway mugs. "Just getting coffee, dude. Keep your pants on. Or, well," he smirked, "not."

Rollins didn't drink coffee. And this is why he fucking hated Jay, he thought as he stormed into the bedroom and grabbed his pants off the floor. The boxers were a lost cause, so he'd be free balling it all the way back to Port Hedland, which was just fucking perfect.

"I got you a green tea," Jay said from behind him. He sounded unsure now.

Rollins felt a pang of hurt at making Jay sound like that. It made him angrier.

He buttoned up, grabbed his shirt and yanked it over his head.

"I'm out."

"Huh? Out where?" Jay asked.

Rollins sat and tugged on his socks, his boots. "Out of here, where else?"

"Oh," Jay said. And just fuck him for sounding all small and sad about it. "Okay."

Rollins didn't look at him as he reached for his phone, ripped it out of the charger in Jay's room—didn't have a charger did he?—and called a taxi.

He stood. Jay was still standing in the doorway, holding the cups.

"Dude, umm, did I..."

Rollins blew out a breath. He couldn't get the words out. And what words were there for this anyway? He couldn't come out and say: *You not being here when I woke up fucked with my head and now I'm furious and I don't know how to get it back under control.*

"You wanted to forget, right?" Rollins asked.

"Huh?"

"Last night, you said you wanted to forget. You wanted to fuck around with me to forget."

"Well, yeah, but—

"Job done then," Rollins said and turned to Nola. "C'mon, Nols."

He paused. Jay's mum was actually dying and, contrary to how bizarrely he was currently acting, he wasn't a complete fucking asshole.

"Do you need her to stay with you?"

Jay was shaking his head and looking at his sneakers. "Nah, she needs to stay with you."

Rollins clenched his jaw. He didn't know how to say how that made him feel, that Jay knew that, Jay fucking well cared about that. He grabbed her leash and her jacket from near the floor and went past Jay in the doorway.

"I'll see you when you get back," he said.

Jay didn't reply.

Rollins paused with his hand on the doorknob. He sucked in a breath. He thought he was going to cry and he didn't understand why. He hadn't cried since he went AWOL. Since he'd wandered out of Afghanistan into Pakistan, caught a train to India and sat on a beach and cried like a madman for months. When he got back they told him he'd been pronounced MIA, probably killed in action. When they asked where the fuck he'd been, he hadn't answered. So they chucked him in military prison before discharging him a year later with the dreaded tag: PTSD.

He hadn't cried since he wiped that last tear off his face on a beach in Goa.

So why was he about to start now?

"I'm sorry about your mum," he said, his voice cracking.

"Rollins," Jay started.

Rollins opened the door and slammed it behind him and Nola, slammed it on whatever the hell Jay was going to say next.

31

R OLLINS HAD CONSOLED HIMSELF the whole dreaded flight
back with the affirmation that Jay had been using him. It didn't
really work, the consoling part—he couldn't get the hurt sound in
Jay's voice out of his fucking head—but he did convince himself Jay
had been using him.

In fact, he thought as he boarded the flight to Port Hedland, Nola
trotting along beside him in her little jacket and keeping him calm, Jay
had always been using him. Jay had made his lack of interest in Rollins
clear on that front. Several times. Not wanting to fuck him. Saying
he wasn't boyfriend material. Mocking his dirty talk. Having a go at
his dick size. Calling paint drying on a wall more interesting than his
personality.

By the time he and Nola let themselves back into the house, Rollins
was at least convinced of that, even if he couldn't shake the guilt that
he'd lost his fucking mind at Jay when his bloody mum was dying.

The next morning, he still couldn't get past it.

He rolled over and sent a message before he could second guess himself.

I really am sorry about your mum.

He held the phone and waited for a reply.

Nothing.

And, well, fuck that.

He got up and took Nola for a run.

One line waited for him when he got back.

Thnx, dude.

Rollins panted and wiped the sweat off his face with his shirt. He typed.

Nola will be happy when you get back.

He wanted to ask when that would be but he couldn't.

He got a smiley face in return, a colon and bracket.

He wanted to say more, to keep talking, but the conversation was over.

He didn't want to acknowledge that he was actually scared Jay wouldn't come back at all. He threw himself into work, into working out, and every time his chest panged with the thought of Jay, he shoved it aside and worked harder. He looked at Jay's computer and reassured himself that he had to come back for that at least.

Rollins came in from a night shift a week later, let the door click shut behind him and felt someone else was in the house.

Jay stood from the couch when Rollins came in.

"Hey," Rollins breathed out.

"Hi."

"Your mum?"

"Dead."

Rollins nodded. Jay's face was blank, very carefully blank.

"You alright?" Rollins asked.

Jay shrugged. He sat back down. Nola was sitting on the couch with him and Jay sank his hand into her thick, black fur. She looked up at Rollins and beat her tail lazily in greeting.

"I'm sorry," Rollins said.

Jay didn't say anything, just watched his hand in Nola's coat.

"I can start back with you tonight if you want."

Rollins frowned. "You don't want some time off?"

"What for?" Jay looked at him then. His usually animated face was expressionless, his eyes dead. It hurt to look at him.

"Alright, well I could use you on it, so."

Jay snorted.

"What?"

"We both know you don't need to use me on anything, man. You're just tolerating my presence 'cos Horace said you had to."

"That's not true," Rollins replied but it sounded weak because that had been the truth. At the start. And now he didn't know what his relationship with Jay was, but it certainly wasn't tolerance. The relief he'd felt seeing Jay standing there when he came in? About as far from indifferent tolerance as a person could get.

"Whatever, dude. Let's just stay out of each other's way and get through this," he stood. He had his head down and he stumbled towards Rollins, heading for his room.

Rollins' hand shot out to stop him.

"What's the matter?" Rollins asked.

Jay tried to shrug him off, but it was half-assed. "Uh, my mum just died. Whaddya think is the matter?"

"And you're taking it out on me," Rollins nodded. That made sense. Sometimes he forgot how young Jay was.

Jay leapt away.

"Fuck you I'm not taking shit out on anyone. I'm not like you."

Rollins clenched his jaw. Jay was right of course, Rollins was self-aware enough to know that, but he didn't want Jay to be coming on out and saying it.

He crossed his arms over his chest and looked down at Jay in front of him—at least his eyes were alive again; he looked like a wild little animal, practically foaming at the mouth ready for a throwdown.

"Alright, you're just acting like we're acquaintances now because you believe that. Okay," Rollins said.

Jay growled at him. Actually growled. "Do you have like, the memory of a fish? Do you not recall storming out of my place like a fucking little bitch while my mum was fucking dying? I think treating you like an acquaintance after that is being polite!"

"You used me!" Rollins snapped. He dropped his arms and stepped forward so Jay was forced to back up against the wall.

"You've always used me!" Jay shouted.

"Hardly! Hardly at all and anyway, you're the one who wanted to stop and then you go and start up again and then fucking disappear like I'm some fucking slab of meat you can use when you feel like it!"

"You're fucking insane, you know that? I went to get coffee!"

"Well you could've left a note."

"Can you actually hear yourself right now? Can you hear the words coming out of your mouth?" Jay gave him a look like he was the stupidest person he'd ever met. "Dude, I'm not your fucking bitch."

"No shit, no fucking shit, I wouldn't want you to be."

"Oh, really? Then why are you so mad over *nothing*."

"Because," Rollins dropped his voice and stepped closer. Jay's eyes widened. Rollins liked that. Unfortunately, he didn't have anything further to say.

"Because?" Jay asked, only it was breathless.

Rollins kissed him. He expected Jay to push him off, punch him, he couldn't believe he was actually doing it, but once he was in it, he realised he'd been going mad wanting this again and now he had it, he wasn't going to stop.

Jay didn't push him off. No, Jay pushed into the kiss like a feral animal, his arms coming around Rollins' back and yanking him forward.

Rollins groaned into the kiss and shoved Jay into the wall. It was a messy kiss, vicious, too much tongue, too much teeth. Jay bit Rollins' bottom lip and Rollins growled and shoved him harder. Jay keened and tried to rub his dick on Rollins' thigh.

Rollins snaked his hand between them and undid his pants. He pulled back an inch and slipped his other hand onto Jay's shoulder to push him down.

"Suck me off," Rollins begged.

Jay brought up both palms and pushed against Rollins' chest. Rollins stumbled back.

"What?"

"I told you, I'm not doin' that unless you do it first."

"No, you said you'd do it if I did it too."

"Will you?"

Rollins couldn't hide his grimace.

"Exactly," Jay said and pushed off the wall. Rollins had heard this all before of course, but there was something quietly defeated about the way Jay was saying it now.

Rollins thought about that big dick in his mouth and had to hide his gag, his shudder. He couldn't do it. Jay wiped his mouth with the back of his hand. He didn't look at Rollins when he left the room.

32

"**W**HAT ARE YOU DOING?" Rollins asked, exasperated.

Jay was hauling the cable and knocking into the shit he'd left lying in the way.

"Sorry," Jay mumbled.

"Jesus," Rollins said under his breath. "You shouldn't be here."

"Alright, well, I'll just leave then!"

Rollins looked at him. He had red blotches on his face and his eyes were flashing with anger behind the glasses. He pushed them up his nose, his expression caught somewhere between anger and bursting into tears.

"Come on," Rollins said and dropped the cable, turned for the lift.

"Where are you going?"

"We're taking the night off."

"No we can't, we're already behind—

"You that keen to make a few million more for some wanker who ain't worked for shit since inheriting this pile of dirt?" Rollins stabbed the button.

Jay was beside him. Rollins glanced at him sideways. He could see Jay trying not to smile. Rollins felt so relieved, it took him by surprise.

"What about all our shit? We usually pack up."

"Yeah, well," Rollins stepped into the lift, "fuck it."

It'd been a week since Jay got back and they'd been snippy with each other or carefully avoiding each other. Rollins hated it. He hated it when Jay did this more—his usual confidence and ease replaced with this clumsy uncertainty. Jay might not want to hear it, but he needed to take a breather. Rollins might not know much, but he did know that when you lost someone, you needed to sit on a beach in Goa and cry about it until you didn't need to cry anymore. Even if it took months.

He headed for the jeep once they were back on the surface, Jay trudging along behind him.

"Let's go get Nols and go for a swim."

"It's night," Jay said as he pulled his seatbelt on. "Where we gonna go swimming?"

Rollins shrugged and started the car. "Reckon we should break into the pool."

Jay huffed a laugh like he thought Rollins was joking.

When they pulled up in the deserted carpark at the local pool, Jay said, "Dude," and laughed. Rollins smiled at him.

"Come on."

"How we gonna get in?" Jay asked.

"Bolt cutters," Rollins said and went to the back and got them out.

"You just carry around bolt cutters?"

"Course."

He didn't mention he carried a lot of other shit in his emergency post-apocalypse bag, of course he had bolt cutters. Jay shook his head around a smile and whistled for Nola to come on. She charged over to them from where she'd been sniffing around the palms.

The padlock fell away easily and they went in.

Rollins tugged his shirt off, shucked his pants until he was just in his boxers.

It was warm, humid, dark except for the soft blue of the streetlights beyond the fence.

"You comin'?" he asked as Jay stood there.

Nola jumped in with a splash and Jay laughed.

"She loves swimming," Rollins said and leapt off the edge, curling his body into a tight ball so he hit the water next to her with a huge splash.

As he broke the surface it was to Nola's happy dog face swimming towards him. He kept one eye on Jay while he swam at a leisurely pace to get Nola to follow him. He felt it when Jay jumped in, the water rippling over them.

They swam for a long time and didn't talk. It was nice. The moon was full above them next to a million stars, the distant clang of the never-ending work at the port, the pink-orange hue of the lights on the horizon against the black sky.

By the time Rollins dragged himself out and sat on the edge, legs dangling in the water, Jay was swimming over to him, his smile small but there. He came to rest on the edge next to Rollins' hip, head resting on his folded arms. Nola swam over and Rollins leaned down to heave her out so she could scamper onto the footpath.

"You're gonna have to grieve, you know," Rollins said after a while.

"Yeah, whaddya know about it," Jay replied without heat.

Rollins looked down at him. Jay was watching him back steadily.

"I lost my best friend, my partner. Got blown up by a landmine."

"Jesus," Jay breathed out.

"Yeah," Rollins said. He'd never said it out loud. He practically lived there, in that moment; whenever he had an episode, he was there. It was almost a second home, so real and alive in his head. Derek walking around looking for his arm. Bullets raining down on them from the mountain. The bullet going through Derek's torso from behind, the way he spun, the next hit in front, the next through his head. It happened quick but Rollins' memory always saw it in slow motion; Derek's body jerking forward, then back, then his head shot through before he fell.

He didn't remember running, but he must've. He didn't remember hitting the ground and crawling for miles in a filthy gutter, but he must've. He did remember the debilitating, gnawing guilt at leaving Derek there. He still remembered it. He'd choke on it if he didn't force himself to do something else.

"Anyway, I went and cried about it for a long time," Rollins said, his voice even, his eyes carefully forward. "Don't be telling anyone that."

Jay shook his head, his hair shaking droplets on Rollins' thighs. "Dude, I'd never, you know that."

Rollins nodded, met Jay's eyes. "I'm just telling you because you need to do that."

Jay sighed. "I can't. I got a tonne of shit to do, I can't... I can't let myself feel that."

"You ain't got shit to do more important than looking after yourself."

"But what I'm doing is looking after me... and her."

Rollins didn't know what to say to that. In his experience, the dead didn't really care what you did even if you tried to convince yourself it mattered to them somehow.

"Was he..." Jay started.

Rollins looked at him and raised both eyebrows.

"More than, you know," Jay said.

Rollins knew what he was asking. He thought about those years, holed up in abandoned buildings, the night freezing, his dick warm in Derek's mouth, the way he'd bite his fist to keep quiet as he panted. He thought about Derek telling him about all the fishing spots near his place in Katharine, about how he didn't understand his dad, about how he'd like to talk to him more when he got back.

"Yeah," Rollins finally said.

"I'm sorry, dude."

Rollins shrugged. "Yeah, me too, but it's not the point. You gotta deal with that shit."

"Yeah," Jay breathed out.

"C'mon," Rollins said and got up. "I'm hungry."

Jay laughed, he mumbled about how he'd always be hungry too if he ate like Rollins did, and went to pull himself out. Rollins leaned down and grabbed his hand. Jay took it and let himself be pulled out of the water, crashing into Rollins' chest, their wet skin slapping in the night. Rollins met Jay's eyes looking up at him. He wanted to kiss him so badly, but that never seemed to end well so he stepped back and let him go.

"C'mon," he said again and grabbed his clothes off the grass. "C'mon Nols."

"What're you gonna do about the padlock?"

"Nothin'," Rollins said and pulled his pants on, left his shirt off.

Jay grinned sideways at him, the cheesy one where his eyes got all squinty and his face transformed into a lazy look. Rollins loved that smile, had missed it.

He shook his head. "Get in the bloody car," he said around a smile.

"What, dude? I didn't say anything."

"Your face did."

"My face is an expressive masterpiece, true that, true that."

"Jesus," but Rollins reckoned his smile was so big he could proba-bly hurl a million insults at Jay and they'd sound like sonnets.

33

♥

J AY WAS GIGGLING.

"What?" I smiled down at him. My face was burnt from the sun and the wind, the salt, it felt like it would crack.

"Nothin', I was just thinking about your post-apocalypse bag."

I'd thought about that bag a lot since we'd been out here. I did not think of it with fond laughter—everything in that bag would be a godsend right now.

"And that's funny, why?"

"'Cos, like, didn't you ever think it was highly unlikely you'd be at your car when the apocalypse hit?"

"It's highly unlikely I wouldn't be."

"Nah, I mean, it'd be bedlam, right?"

"It could start slowly, be time to flee in your car, with the bag."

"What kinda apocalypse were you imagining? Locusts? Space invaders? A slow-moving storm?"

I clenched my jaw. I'd thought all of the above except the locusts.

"Locusts aren't apocalyptic."

Jay snickered. "You totally thought space invaders, didn't you?"

"It's more plausible than fleeing from locusts with a bunch of guns and power bars."

"Dude," Jay whined.

"What?"

"Don't talk about power bars."

"Sorry."

"It's alright... Tell the next bit, I like this part."

I smiled. I liked this part too.

34

THE HOUSE PHONE WAS ringing. It was the middle of the day, steaming hot, and Rollins had been drifting in that place somewhere between asleep and awake. He heard Jay's voice answering the phone. Only one person called the landline. He threw off the covers and went out.

Jay looked up and met his eyes and Rollins knew the answer without asking the question.

"Alright, thanks for letting us know, I'll tell him, yeah, he's right here. Thanks, yep, nice, alright, bye."

Jay hung up.

"Cancer," Rollins said.

"Yep, but benign, dude, so not so bad."

Rollins jerked his chin. "Whaddid she say."

"Suggested some chemo injections at the site, can do that with dogs, experiment like we can't on humans. Expensive, but," he finished and looked at Rollins like he knew Rollins was about to reply—

"I don't give a fuck how much it costs."

Jay smiled. "Yeah, I know, so does she. We can book her in, gotta do it in Perth, but."

"Alright, you got the number."

"She's sending it with a referral letter."

"Alright," Rollins nodded along, glanced out the window. "Alright."

"Yeah, dude, it's gonna be alright."

He bloody hoped so.

The only plus side Rollins could see to Nola's treatment was it got his missus off his back about all the wedding shit. The date was inching closer and every time he thought of it, he shoved it aside like he could ignore it and maybe if he did, the day would come, he'd get through it, be on the other side, and that would be that.

"Best thing is, you can fly down with her now," Jay said.

"Yeah," Rollins agreed but he was thinking about something else. "What're you gonna do? Come with?"

Jay looked surprised. "Wasn't planning on it. But—

"Fine, that's fine, you don't need to."

"I can if you want?" Jay asked gently.

It pissed Rollins off. Not Jay, not him asking, just the fact Rollins needed him to come.

"No, you got shit to do, we'll be alright," Rollins went back to his room before Jay could say anything else.

It was stupid to want Jay there and besides, he'd need Jay to cover a lot of work for him while he was away—banking the money, picking up and transferring the pseudo, hell, Jay was so good now, he could probably work the job running cable on his own. Rollins was surprised how much he'd come to depend on him.

As he lay back down, he realised it was the first time he'd depended on someone since Derek. More surprising? It didn't terrify him. It felt good. Calming.

When Rollins stepped out into the predawn to catch his flight with Nola, he expected to get in the taxi with no fanfare. Jay would be sleeping and he was happy for him to get a night off, to get a sleep in.

So when he saw Jay sitting on the top step of the porch, backpack beside him and cap pulled down over his face, he didn't know what to say.

"What," is what came out.

"Hey, dude," Jay yawned.

"What're you doing?"

Nola nudged Jay and he patted her.

"Gonna join you for the appointment—

"You can't, I already lined up the meet—

"Then fly back Sunday night."

"Oh."

Jay stood. Rollins hid his smile. That would work. His relief was palpable.

The taxi pulled into the driveway, the headlights washing over the three of them.

"C'mon, Nols," Jay said around another yawn. "Fuck, they better have some cokes in the vending machine."

"They serve them on the plane."

"Nah, dude, Pepsi."

"Same shit."

Jay sucked in a sharp breath. "Dude!"

Rollins laughed.

His relief was fucking palpable alright.

Nola limped out of the door into the reception area, the oncologist behind her. Rollins stood. Nola looked sad and sorry for herself, but she picked up the pace when she saw Rollins and Jay, the bandage on her side a large lump.

"All sorted," the oncologist smiled at Nola then at Jay and Rollins. He was a wiry guy, vibrating with energy. "We'll hit it again in three months, should take care of any possible further growth."

"Thank you," Rollins replied, his voice gruff.

Jay was leaning down and making a big fuss over Nola, but he straightened and ushered Rollins out the door like he did last time, telling him, "I'll take care of it."

Rollins still hadn't paid him back for the last time.

When Jay emerged and hopped in the passenger's seat of their rented car, Rollins said, "Give me the total. I'll get you some cash."

"Yeah, man, no rush," he leaned back to pat Nola. "She's got some pain meds. Wanna drive thru on the way back? I'm feelin' a veggie burger and we can get Nols some fries and a burger."

Rollins scrunched his face up, but for Jay and Nola, he'd drive thru.

Jay and Nola were looking thoroughly stuffed, sprawled out on the couch in Rollins' unit. Rollins shook his head at them.

"Scoot over," he said to Jay and was about to sit when there was a knock on the door.

Jay raised both eyebrows.

Rollins shrugged. He went to open the door.

"You said you'd call," Sarah said and started coming in.

Rollins stepped back. He'd messaged her he was coming down, then forgotten about it.

"Sorry, we just got back," he replied and shut the door after her, a jittery feeling in his limbs as he listened to her walk down the hall.

"Oh, hello?" she said to Jay.

"Yo," Jay said as Rollins came back in. He was smiling—the sleepy one—as he leaned up to take her hand. "Call me JC."

She shook it tentatively, barely concealing her distaste. "Thought it was Jayden?"

Jay shook his head. "Nah, JC mainly."

Rollins wondered why he introduced himself to him as Jay but otherwise went by JC. That woman at the hospital, Janet, his mum's friend, called him Jay as well.

"How is she?" Sarah nodded at Nola.

"Gonna be alright, eh," Jay patted her.

"Good," Sarah gave Nola a quick smile. "I thought we could go out?" she turned to Rollins.

"Can't leave Nola—

"She's good with me, dude," Jay cut him off.

"Or he could go out and we could stay here with her?" Sarah said quickly, turning slightly so she was giving Jay her back and talking about him like he wasn't even there.

It pissed Rollins off.

"He has a name."

"He is right here," Jay said and sat forward.

She glanced at him, gave him a tight smile. "Don't you have a girlfriend waiting for you somewhere?" she asked in a tone that said she thought someone like Jay would have a girlfriend when hell froze over.

Jay stood. "Nah, I'm gay, so no girls for me," he winked. "And single at the minute, but I got my crew."

"You don't have to go—

"You're gay?" Sarah asked, scandalised. "Does Horace know?"

Jay shrugged. "Dunno, probably not, ain't like we're braiding each other's hair."

He stepped around the coffee table and Sarah stepped back to give him an unnecessary amount of space as he went by.

"You don't have to go," Rollins said again.

"All good, dude," Jay said and brushed his arm as he went by, "gonna catch up with the crew."

"I'll drive you."

"Nah, I can bus it."

"Well," Rollins followed Jay as he went and grabbed his bag, "you'll come back later then. I gotta take you to the airport. It'd be better if you stayed here."

Jay shrugged his bag onto his shoulder. He smiled. "I'll text you later."

"Or you could just be back later."

Jay laughed. "Later, dude. Sarah," he said over Rollins' shoulder.

Rollins watched him shuffle down the hallway and disappear out the door.

He turned back to Sarah. "That was rude," he said to her. "You were rude to him."

"He's gay?" she asked again. "And he just goes around telling people?"

"Yeah, what of it? It's his business."

"Maybe he shouldn't be advertising it then. It's disgusting."

Rollins scowled at her. "How is it disgusting? So he likes guys, so what?"

"You don't think it's disgusting? Having a faggot in your house?"

"No," Rollins said slowly, "I knew a lot of 'faggots' in the army, top fucking blokes who'd die for you, way better people than those cunts at the clubhouse."

Sarah took a step back. And, yeah, that was seething. Rollins didn't know where it came from. It's not like he'd ever been on some pride crusade; he just didn't like the way she'd spoken to Jay.

She looked at him with disdain, but it was uncertain too. She was pretty, his missus, button nose and round eyes. She wore too much make-up and she wasn't a particularly nice person, as evidenced by this conversation. But she'd always been easy to be with—took control of shit Rollins didn't care about and never gave him too much grief over him being busy with his own shit.

But he looked at her now and for the first time, he didn't like her at all.

He really needed to break up with her.

She went over to the counter. "Want to order in?" she asked like nothing had happened.

He wiped his hand over his mouth. "Alright."

"I've got some invitation samples in the car, thought we could go over them..."

He stopped listening. He didn't like thinking about Jay catching all that public transport this late. He'd pick him up. He needed to figure out a way to break up with Sarah.

But as she settled in—pointedly taking the armchair and looking at Nola—while going over the invites, he thought about how he couldn't break it off, how this was what he was meant to be doing. What was he going to do? Break up with her and charge off into the sunset with Jay? He almost laughed out loud at the thought. Jay didn't even want him, and while he might not be a raging homophobic asshole, he wasn't going to date a guy. Jesus. How would that work? Dinner out and asking for a table for him and his boyfriend? He felt himself reddening at the thought.

No, he looked over at Sarah, her straight brown hair falling in her face as she pointed out the difference between this white and that white on the stationary—this was safe, this was what guys did.

35

J AY NEVER CAME BACK. Rollins texted him the following morning and then put his phone down, forced himself to pay attention to his missus as she told him about Tanya's latest indiscretion.

"I just can't believe she'd do that, you know? She knows as well as I bloody do that Cathy Kelly gets her hair dyed golden blonde every three months. Why would she go and use ash blonde?"

"I dunno," Rollins said and picked up his phone.

"She's trying me on, I'm sure of it," she crossed her legs, sipped her black coffee. "It's like she wants me to have to call her out and I can't think what I ever did…"

Rollins put his phone back down.

Squinted at Sarah and tried to pay attention.

It was noon when he finally got a reply.

Gaz givin me a lift dude. All good, c u soon.

Rollins gripped his phone tightly, then set it down. He was beginning to realise Jay—laid back, 'all good', I'm super chill Jay—wasn't all good when he said he was all good and instead of confrontation when he was hurting, he went away. He'd done this before. Quietly retreated. Rollins thought about him disappearing softly out the door last night.

"I'm just wondering if I should keep her in the wedding at all. She's supposed to be my maid of honour but if she keeps baiting me like this—

"I have to go," Rollins cut her off.

"Go where?" she looked up at him.

"Back to work."

"But I thought you were down for the week?"

He lifted his phone up. "Change of plans."

He went over to the couch. Nola looked up at him, tail wagging. It's not like she couldn't fly—she seemed fine—the vet had just said 'take it easy' for a week.

"Seriously?"

Rollins ignored that. Of course he was being serious, he wouldn't speak otherwise.

'Take it easy' Rollins had taken as: rest on the couch for a week, do not disturb, monitor 24/7. But she seemed fine. And it was Sunday night so they'd get a seat on the plane easily enough. Well, he was yet to see the flight full. He could head down now.

"I thought we could go down south, check out the venue..."

"I reckon you got it covered." He managed to stop himself before saying 'take Tanya'—that'd turn into a lecture on him not listening. He picked up his phone again. "If I don't get this sorted, Horace will be all over my ass and then there'll be no wedding."

She scoffed. "I'm going halves."

"I wasn't referring to the money."

She shook her head. "He wouldn't kill you over what? A few dollars."

"Yeah, he would," he leaned down and gave her a quick peck. "I better pack. I'll see you in a month."

And he jogged up the stairs before she could say anything else.

Jay was already in line waiting to board when Rollins arrived with his ticket in one hand, Nola padding along beside him in her little jacket, her lead in his other. Jay had his red hat tugged down over his face, his hand going up to tuck his hair behind his ear.

"Hope you don't mind sharing your leg room," Rollins said as he came up alongside him.

Jay startled, looked up, and the grin that broke out over his face was bright. "What're you doin' here?"

"Got shit to do, me and Nols."

"What shit?" he beamed up at him.

Rollins hoisted his duffel higher while Jay leaned down to pat Nola.

"You know, money laundering and drug running."

Jay barked a laugh and glanced around.

Rollins grinned at him. Yeah, nobody would take that seriously.

"Cool, cool, very busy and important," Jay smiled.

"Very."

Rollins bumped Jay's shoulder when the line started moving to board the plane. It was late afternoon as they crossed the tarmac—the sun sinking on the horizon and blaring one final golden blast over them—Nola charged ahead, her nails clicking on the asphalt as she made for the steps like she'd done it all her life.

"Oh, here," Rollins unzipped his duffel and got out the coke he'd bought at the vending machine near the ticket booth.

"Dude!"

"Yeah, well, just don't wanna hear you carryin' on about it."

"Nah," Jay held the can close and looked up at Rollins with a sleazy smile. "You love me."

"You wish."

"I reckon this is a sign of your undying affection—

"How're your geek mates?" Rollins cut him off as they went up the steps. "Finish writing your piece about Gaz doing fuck all?"

Jay cracked up and proceeded to tell him about how his story was already up and had a lot of interest from the US, thank you very much.

Rollins snorted and settled into his seat. He did up his seatbelt as Nola lay across his feet and settled in, Jay's bullshit story a comforting monologue as they taxied down the runway.

36

"DUDE, YOU AWAKE?"

"Yeah."

"What're you thinking about?"

I try to smother the groan, but Jay's gonna feel it with the way he's pressed up against my chest.

"Nola."

"Hmm," Jay's head rubbed back and forth against my sternum, the white in the blonde catching the first of the morning light behind us. At least it felt like we were drifting in the right direction now, the current pushing us west, the wind not as blisteringly cold.

"She'll be alright," Jay said eventually. "Gaz is good people."

I couldn't stop myself—I leaned down and pressed a rough kiss to the top of Jay's head.

"Stop talking," I said against his scalp. "You need rest."

And Jay always did know how to read a room—he did.

37

From the moment the humidity hit his face as he stepped off the plane, Rollins felt like he was home. It was stupid—this was so far from a nice place to be in, it made an uninhabitable planet look appealing—but as they stepped into the dank heat of the house, Nola charging around to check all was as she'd left it, Rollins felt it, the unmistakable feeling of letting his guard down. His shoulders eased and the familiar comfort had less to do with the actual place and more to do with what it'd come to mean from doing time in it. He'd felt this in the barracks on the edge of the desert; felt it on leave in Townsville with Derek; and now he felt it here with Jay.

"It's hot as fuckin' balls," Jay said and flopped down on the couch. He pulled his shirt up and wiped the sweat off his face, the soft creases in his abdomen glistening with sweat. It went beyond Rollins' understanding why seeing this turned him on. He went into the kitchen so he wouldn't have to look at it.

"Dude, get me a coke, please?"

"You can have water," Rollins replied and got them both a glass of water.

Jay took it, held the glass, his face scrunched up.

"I don't drink water."

"Who doesn't drink water? You have to drink water."

"Coke is made from water."

"Coke is sugar."

"Yeah, sugar made from water."

Jay held the glass and moved it this way and that, his eyes tracking the movement of the liquid before he looked back up at Rollins, eyes pleading behind the glasses.

"Fine, fuck, drink at least half of that and then I'll get you a coke."

"Thanks, dude."

Jay could just get up and grab it himself, but Rollins liked this, liked how Jay was sitting below him, gagging as he drank the water yet doing as he was told. Rollins smirked down at him.

"Ugh," Jay handed him the glass, spluttering. "That's half."

Rollins smiled, shook his head and went and got him a coke.

"Fuck, back to it tomorrow," Jay said after they'd been sitting in companionable silence for a while, the house settling around them, the night loud with insects and the animated feel hot nights seemed to have.

"Yeah," Rollins slumped further into the couch, his bicep resting against Jay's. He glanced down at Jay's crotch, the bagginess of his jeans.

"You wantin' somethin', dude?" Jay asked.

Rollins could hear him smiling. He thought he was being discreet.

"Yeah, yeah," Rollins felt his face reddening at getting caught. "You ain't gonna do anything with me unless I admit to all my faults and worship at the altar of your dick. I got it."

Jay giggled and pressed himself further into Rollins' side. "That's not what I said at all, man. And besides, I think you got most of it. I said—

"Fine," Rollins took a deep breath, his eyes on Jay's bulge where his dick was clearly hardening from all the attention. "I'll suck you off if you suck me off first."

Jay nudged him. Rollins met his eyes, serious behind the glasses.

"You're gonna have to suck it first," Jay said.

Rollins shook his head. "You don't trust me to keep my word?"

Jay twisted his lips. "I dunno, I reckon you'll intend to, but it might get too much and then I'll be left with a hard cock and a mouth full of come won't I?"

"Jesus," Rollins said and adjusted himself.

He was nervous. He felt a skittishness racing up and down his limbs as he shuffled forward and went to his knees on the carpet, pushed himself between Jay's spread thighs.

"Fuck, really?" Jay panted above him.

"Yes, really," Rollins snapped. "You better hit me back."

"Fuck, I'm gonna, man, I'm gonna."

Jay unfastened his pants quickly, shoved his jeans and boxers down so he could get his half hard dick out.

Fuck, it was huge. Thick, decent length, really white with delicate blue veins. Uncut but the head was already peeking out as it got harder in front of Rollins' eyes.

Rollins brought both hands up and gripped Jay's hipbones, shoved him hard into the couch.

"I'm gonna hold you there," Rollins flicked his eyes up to meet Jay's. "Don't fucking move."

"I won't, dude. Promise, I won't," Jay gasped.

Rollins would've laughed, but he was too nervous. He leaned forward, his mouth hovering over Jay's dick. Jay was holding the base, holding it towards Rollins' lips but not moving otherwise. Rollins exhaled, wet his lips, shoved his nerves and his disgust aside and licked the tip.

Jay groaned, his body wriggling but staying within the confines Rollins had set for him. Rollins liked that, liked how much harder Jay's dick was getting from one swipe.

He did it again, a gentle lick around the crown, then pressed his tongue into the slit.

"Fuck, dude, fuck, please, more."

Rollins smirked around his dick. He liked that too.

He wrapped his lips tentatively around the head, gave a little suck.

"Ah, fuck."

Rollins sucked a little harder, let his mouth get wetter and went a tiny bit lower.

"Oh, shit, man, you're fucking killing me."

Rollins huffed a laugh.

"Haven't even done anything yet," he said against Jay's skin.

He sucked the head into his mouth again—braced for the gagging—then pushed down.

Jay groaned loudly above him.

Rollins pulled back, then did it again, really slowly. He was only going halfway down, his fingers digging into Jay's hipbones in a death grip, but Jay was panting and whining like Rollins was going to town on him.

He went down a bit further, still waiting for the moment he'd have to abandon it, only Jay moaned, cried out, "Fuck, feels so good, so good," and Rollins could almost feel how good it was feeling for him.

He increased his suction and went as far as he could—not quite to the base, but right down the shaft—laved the length with his tongue while he was down there, pulled back again. He was awkward, he knew it, but he was getting so turned on as he listened to Jay losing his mind above him, staying so still, letting Rollins take his time and, to his horror, enjoy himself.

He pulled off.

"Good?"

"Fuck! Don't fucking stop!"

Jay was a red, sweaty, panting mess.

Rollins smirked.

"Fuck you, fuck—

Rollins sucked him right down. And there was the gag reflex, but Jay was crying out and Rollins relished in it. He stayed as low as he could manage and bobbed his head in small increments, dug his fingers into those hipbones and heard his own moaning answer Jay's.

He liked making Jay feel good. He sped up. He wanted Jay to come. He wanted to do that to him.

"Fuck, I'm gonna, pull off now, if you don't want—

Rollins sped up.

Jay groaned and Rollins felt the first pulse of come hit the back of his throat. His instinct was to retreat, but he fought against it, pushed on by how much Jay was losing it. He sucked harder, swallowed around him, felt the tip of Jay's dick move against the muscle at the back of his throat. He smiled to himself when it made Jay make this embarrassing high-pitched squeal.

Jay slumped back. Rollins gave him another tight suck just to feel Jay whine out "Too much, too much."

He pulled back and looked up. Jay was blissed out above him, his lips parted as he caught his breath.

Rollins stood and unfastened his pants. His dick was rock hard. He got it in hand, stroked and leaned forward.

Jay didn't miss a beat—he sat forward and took Rollins into his mouth, down to the hilt and sucked him off with expert suction and speed.

"Jesus," Rollins panted as he rocked his hips into Jay's mouth.

He was so keyed up, there was no way he was going to last. A part of him realised just how shit he was at this when he felt just how fucking good Jay was. He was just taking it as Rollins fucked his mouth, laving the length of his dick with regular swipes of his tongue as he sucked him down.

"Jesus," Rollins said again and started to come.

Jay moaned around him and the sound and the vibration sent him over the edge with an even deeper thrust into Jay's mouth.

Rollins rocked his hips forward as he finished and Jay took it, licking around him. He pulled out and Jay slumped back.

"Fucking nice, dude," Jay said.

"Yeah," Rollins replied, breathless. Nice was one word for it. Earth shattering was another—he could still taste Jay's come in his mouth and he... liked it.

"See how much better it is when you hit your partner back?" Jay asked as Rollins flopped back on the couch next to him.

Rollins groaned. "Shut up."

"It's good to talk after sex, cement the bond."

"Jesus," Rollins huffed.

"Now we can do it again."

Rollins groaned, mainly so he wouldn't say: *when?* His dick was already interested in 'again'.

38

AGAIN TURNED OUT TO be when they woke up after accidentally napping on the couch. Rollins woke to the feel of Jay's head resting on his chest, his breath soft through the material of his shirt, warming his skin beneath. Rollins was hard, his pants still unbuttoned. He was groggy, but as he blinked away the sleep he saw Jay's bulge pressing against the material of his jeans. He slipped his hand down and rubbed him without thinking about it.

Jay groaned softly against his chest, rocked into his hand, still asleep.

Rollins felt around Jay's cock, the weight of it, the length; he gripped him, released him, then snaked his hand inside his pants until he was touching skin.

Jay rocked into it, waking up slowly.

Rollins shuffled down, carefully dislodging Jay from his chest and stretching him out on the couch beside him. He pulled Jay's dick out and got his mouth on him.

Jay groaned.

Rollins held his hip steady and sucked him slowly, got him all wet, got used to the feel of that cock hardening in his mouth, throbbing, felt out the way he liked the feel of it, liked the sounds Jay made as he woke up to the feel of himself in Rollins' mouth.

Jay's hand went into the short strands of his hair, caressing him as he moaned and rolled his hips up. Rollins pushed down to meet him, his tongue caressing the tip before he sank all the way down.

"Rollins?" Jay's voice was sleepy.

"Hmmm," Rollins replied around his dick.

Jay groaned and pushed his dick forward with a slow, gentle grind.

Rollins reached up and brushed his fingers over Jay's belly.

Jay sucked in a breath.

Rollins lay his palm flat and ran it back and forth, his mouth moving slowly up and down Jay's length, suction tight.

Jay made little sounds in reply, moved his body in response to what Rollins was doing to him.

Rollins liked it, with each sweep of his hand and brush of his tongue he felt how good Jay was feeling and that made him feel good—it made him harder, it made him warm in his chest.

"I'm—

Rollins groaned and swallowed around him.

When Jay shuffled down to reciprocate, Rollins stopped him with a hand on his hip, met Jay's sleepy eyes and then kissed him. Jay kissed him back with a sleepy moan. Rollins rolled Jay under him, rutted into him on the couch, kissed him in time with his groin rubbing up against the smooth, soft surface of Jay's skin.

Jay broke away, kept his lips close.

"Yeah, dude, c'mon," he said.

Rollins made an embarrassing little gasp and came all over Jay's belly.

He slumped down and the last thing he remembered was the gentle, reassuring feel of Jay's hand sweeping up and down the planes of his back, the soft sound of Jay's breath fanning his throat.

39

"**I** GOT THE STRANGEST message from Horace," Rollins said when Jay walked into the kitchen in his bare feet, his baggy jeans too long and covering all but his toes, his blonde hair sticking up everywhere as he rubbed his eyes, replaced his glasses, looked over at Rollins sitting at the kitchen table.

"Huh?"

"Look at this," Rollins held his phone out.

Jay glanced at it, raised an eyebrow. "Short how much?"

"Doesn't say, but I reckon the fuckstick can't count. I ain't short. I cleaned forty-three last month, forty-three exactly. That's thirteen more than I was doin' in Perth."

Jay shrugged and put the kettle on. "I reckon he might be losing his mind a bit. He's been drinkin' for a long time, probably getting dementia, the booze hound version."

"Yeah, maybe," Rollins looked at the message again.

You're fucking short.

But Horace was shrewd and even if he had dementia—whatever the fuck the booze hound version of that was—he wasn't the kind to miss a single dollar.

The sound of the gas clicker made Rollins look up. Jay was at the stove, yawning, scratching his calf over his jeans with one toe, the stuff for Rollins' breakfast at his elbow, his own shit next to it.

Rollins tossed his phone on the table and stood. He came up behind Jay and slipped his hands around his waist, kissed his nape.

"Oh, hello," Jay said.

"Hmmm," Rollins kissed around his neck, up to his ear, nibbled on the lobe, slipped his hand to Jay's front, ghosted his fingers over his dick.

Jay giggled, leaned back against Rollins' chest; he craned his head back so when he spoke, the words whistled over Rollins cheek. "You wanna go again already?"

Rollins kissed him, slid his tongue into Jay's mouth and gripped his dick more firmly. Jay responded with his tongue sliding over Rollins'.

Rollins broke away. "What already? It's been days." He brought his hand to Jay's ass and massaged him over his jeans. He got impatient and brought both hands to the front and undid Jay's pants, shoved them down.

"Jesus, dude," Jay clicked the stove off.

Rollins brought his hand up and slipped two fingers into Jay's mouth.

Jay got the message and sucked them, got them all wet, moaned as Rollins slipped them in and out.

Rollins groaned and rubbed his hard-on against Jay's ass, kissed his cheek, pulled back to watch Jay sucking on his fingers. He pulled them out and slipped them down between Jay's crack, found his hole and slid in with one. Jay gasped.

"You wanna move, oh—

Rollins snickered and shoved in again. Jay rolled his hips into Rollins' hand and made breathy little moans.

"Enjoying yourself?" Rollins said against his ear.

Jay huffed. "Fuck off, dude, like you wouldn't—

He cut off when Rollins pushed in with the second finger.

He brought his other hand up and slipped it under Jay's chin, tilted his head back so he could kiss him, fuck his mouth with his tongue like his fingers were doing to his ass. Jay spread his legs wider, rolled his hips in time with the thrusts, and kissed him back.

He pulled his fingers out, got his dick out and nudged up against Jay's hole.

"Yeah?" he asked.

Jay rolled back so the tip popped inside.

Rollins groaned and slid both arms around his waist, hugged him back against his chest and thrust up into him.

It was a dirty grind—something obscene about it there in the early evening light of the kitchen, the sound of his dick sliding in and out of Jay's hole, the slap of his hips against Jay's ass, the groans he couldn't stop and the punched-out breaths Jay made as he met Rollins' dick, fucked back against him like he was as desperate for it as Rollins was.

Rollins bit his throat, sucked his skin, kissed his way back to Jay's mouth until Jay met him again. He was going to come, but he wanted to get Jay there first. He reached around and wrapped Jay's big dick in his dry palm, squeezed him, jerked him off roughly. Jay tried to break the kiss to pant, to cry out, but Rollins forced him back, tongue fucked his mouth as he pounded his ass until Jay was moaning into the kiss, coming, saying something unintelligible into Rollins' lips.

Rollins broke away and yanked Jay against him; he rested his forehead on his nape as he started to come, tried to bury his dick as deep as he could get it.

"Geez, dude, wake up horny?"

Rollins huffed a laugh, his dick still twitching in Jay's ass.

"You love it."

"I ain't objecting, no."

Rollins pulled out slowly. He gave Jay's ass a friendly slap then a squeeze before he bent and tugged his pants back up, refastened them with gentle sweeps of his fingers over Jay's belly.

"Reckon I'm gonna need a shower," Jay said.

"Or you could stay like that?"

Rollins stepped back, did up his pants. Jay looked at him over his shoulder, eyes squinting, mouth quirked in a smile.

"Ass full of come all night?"

Rollins felt the weirdest butterflies at that. "Yeah."

Jay laughed, shook his head, but he turned the stove back on and didn't shower before they left for the night and Rollins liked that, he liked that a lot.

A NOTHER MESSAGE WAS WAITING for Rollins when he met with the truckie that weekend. Contrary to Horace's orders, he never brought Jay with him. He liked to think it was because Jay would be a liability—looking like he did and so bloody young—but in his heart he knew it was because he didn't really want to drag Jay into this shit.

"The boss says you gotta make up the short fall," the driver said.

"What?" Rollins looked at the guy in front of him in his stubby shorts, rolling his cigarette. The flies buzzing around their heads were more invested in the conversation than this guy.

"Shortfall," he said as he licked the edges of the paper, put the tip in his mouth and lit it. "That's all I got told," he blew out the smoke and hoisted himself back into the cabin.

Rollins was left standing in the puffs of red dirt, incredulous. There was no fucking shortfall. Horace was insane.

When he walked back into the house, he meant to talk to Jay about it, but Jay looked up, pushed those stupid glasses up his nose, smiled small and welcoming, and Rollins needed to blow him more.

After, lying on Jay's futon, he finally brought it up. "Got another message from Horace. Short."

"Serious?" Jay panted and rolled his head to the side to look at him.

Rollins mirrored the pose, leaned over and kissed him.

"Yeah," he said when he pulled away. "I got the weirdest feeling he's trying to play me."

"How d'ya mean?" Jay rolled onto his side, rested his head in his palm.

"Like, fuck with my head by saying this so I'll end up paying more out of my own pocket."

"He'd do that?"

"Course."

"Well, you can't fucking pay him with your own money, fuck that," Jay said and sat up.

"Where're you going?" Rollins asked as he reached up and ran his hand up and down Jay's back.

"I was working," Jay smirked at him over his shoulder.

"Oh, my apologies, Stephen King, busy writing about your friend's latest shit?"

Jay laughed, bounced himself down the mattress, stood and buttoned up his pants.

"No, that's a bit weird, even for us."

"Hmm," Rollins watched Jay slide back into his chair, put his glasses back on and squint at the screen.

He'd miss this, he realised with a pang. Once this job was done and he and Jay went their separate ways, he'd miss him.

"You going back to Sydney after this?" he asked.

"Huh?" Jay looked at him. "Oh, yeah, probably."

"You should think about staying," Rollins sat up and got busy refastening his pants.

"Where? In Port Hedland?"

"No," Rollins rolled to his feet and stood. "In Perth."

"God, why?" Jay asked.

Rollins met his eyes and shrugged, headed for the kitchen. "Why not? You got mates here."

"I can talk to them from Sydney," Jay called after him.

But you can't talk to me, Rollins thought but of course didn't say. It was a stupid thing to think, never mind say. Plus, he was getting married for fuck's sake—at which point, no more dick for him.

It was better that Jay was going. Even if the realisation made him feel like shit.

IT WAS STILL EARLY the next morning when Rollins got Jay under him in his bed, his dick like steel as he pushed inside. Jay's soft thighs wrapped around his hips as Rollins kissed him in time with his thrusts. Rollins could feel how good of a fuck it was going to be—slow, deep; tongues meeting and tangling; the pleasure building between them as Rollins ground in and Jay rocked up to meet him—when there was a pounding on the front door.

"The fuck?" Rollins jerked back.

"Who—

A key turning in the door told them exactly who.

Rollins slid out and was off the bed, reaching for his pants and yanking them on faster than he ever had in his life, Jay not far behind him.

By the time he skittered into the living room, he could see Horace's back in the kitchen.

"Horace?" he called.

Horace turned. "Were you fuckin' sleepin'?"

"I'm on nights," Rollins replied and walked into the kitchen, forcing Horace to track him with his eyes as he powered past him for the fridge. "Want a beer?"

"It's not even ten," Horace said. "Where's that shit kicker son of mine?"

"Here," Jay said from the door in the kitchen. "Horace."

"Jayden," Horace sneered at him. "See workin' it up here has done nothin' for ya, ya all red and sweaty, what've you been doin? Jerkin' it?" Horace laughed.

Jay smiled, easy-going, and Rollins saw it for the mask it was.

"Yeah, you know, gotta come to get any sleep after a night shift," Jay replied.

"Jesus, ain't no one wanna hear that shit."

Jay shrugged, looked at Rollins. "I'll have a beer."

"Really?"

"Yes, Dad," Jay mocked.

Horace laughed. "Get me one too. I'm gonna need it to sort your pansy ass out," he turned to Rollins.

Rollins was grinding his jaw, but he got three beers and followed Horace outside, felt Jay behind him a moment later. Nola was there, sprawled under the sprinkler, which would explain why she didn't bark at the door. She thumped her tail when they came out, but otherwise didn't move.

"You're short," Horace said.

"I'm fucking not," Rollins snapped.

Horace took a swig of his beer, wiped his mouth with the back of his hand. "Ya know, I mightn't have finished school, but I sure as fuck know how to count and you're short. Thirteen grand. Now," he leaned forward, adjusted his bulk in the chair, then sat back, "I gotta ask, you tryin' to fleece me or you honestly can't fucking count?"

Rollins shook his head, worked his jaw. "I ain't sure what you're fucking smoking," he stood, "but I sure as fuck ain't short. I cleaned forty-three, deposited forty-fucking-three."

"Thirty," Horace said and looked up at him. The position didn't appear to intimidate him at all. He swigged his beer, his eyes never leaving Rollins. "Get me another one and bring me your fucking books while you're at it."

"His books are tight," Jay said from Horace's other side.

Horace turned a really mean smile on him. "And I ain't takin' the word of a son of a whore on that one."

Rollins would've wanted to clock him for that, he reckoned most guys would, but Jay just smiled—genuine and bright like he hadn't since Horace walked in. "And I reckon all the good DNA flowing through my veins comes from that whore."

"Yeah, well," Horace sat forward and adjusted himself again. Jesus, Rollins had a moment to wonder if he had a bladder infection. "You would, pansying it up in that brothel your whole life." He looked up at Rollins. "Get the books."

"No," Jay said before Rollins could move.

Horace turned back to him. "You wanna go, sonny?"

"Nah," and now Jay's smile was downright mean. "That wouldn't be a fair fight, would it?"

"Damn straight, smartest thing ya ever—

"'Cos I'd slit your fucking throat with the kitchen knife I brought out here with me before you could even move from your chair."

Rollins' eyebrows flew up and he scanned the ground for a knife. Surely Jay was kidding, but he had a hoodie on the ground next to him. He didn't usually have that hoodie out; it was way too hot.

But Horace just laughed. "Seems like ya got a bit of the good bits too then, eh?"

Jay grinned. "Yeah, I ain't afraid of killing if someone insults my mother."

Horace snorted. "Every man with a dick has insulted that slut. Or, well, used to," he slid a sly grin over to Jay.

Rollins watched Jay's smile grow, which was pretty weird—Horace would've known she had just died, he clearly didn't think Jay was going to put his money where his mouth was. And for the first time ever, Rollins had no idea what Jay was going to do, he really didn't.

"We're not short," Jay said now.

"Oh, it's we now, is it?" He glanced at Rollins. "How's that beer comin'?"

"I reckon you've had enough," Jay said.

"And I reckon it's high time you shut your fuckin' mouth."

"Alright," Rollins interjected. "You, out," he said to Horace, "I'll check the accounts again."

Horace looked up at him, and Rollins reckoned he was doing a good job of throwing off the 'remember I can kill a man with my bare hands and if you insult my Jay any further, I might just get over my fucking PTSD and follow through for once' vibe.

Horace stood, putting himself right in Rollins' space.

Rollins didn't move.

"You do that," he said. "I'm gonna head on down to the pub if you pussies feel like seeing the show later."

And then he sauntered back inside, the sound of his boots heavy on the carpet, then the linoleum in the kitchen before the front door slammed.

"Do you really have a fucking kitchen knife under there?" Rollins asked as Jay said, "He's got fucking bipolar, I swear to God, did you see—

Jay cut off and glanced at his hoodie. He shrugged. "Maybe."

"Do you even know how to use it?"

"Think it's pretty intuitive, you know, stab-stab-stab," he replied and made a stabbing motion with his hand.

"And then what?"

"And then what, what?"

"What're you gonna do with the big, fat-ass dead body in your yard?"

Jay shrugged. "I dunno, feed it to the crocs."

"So, your master plan here was to stab him and then drive ten plus hours with the body in the boot and feed it to some crocodiles?"

"I hadn't thought that far ahead, but yeah, something like that."

"Jesus, and he ain't got bipolar, he just doesn't give a fuck."

"I know," Jay said, quite seriously.

"You can't let him get to you."

"It's not me I'm worried about."

Rollins sighed. "I know him talking all that shit about your mum isn't right, okay, but you can't just go around stabbing people."

"I ain't worried about what he says about her, she already told me when I was little—every time your daddy says something about me, you'll be hearing how much I love you, okay?" he mimicked a woman's voice as he said it and it was meant to be funny, but his voice cracked.

Rollins gusted out a frustrated breath.

"Well, alright, don't do it for your sake then—

"He's not gonna threaten you while I'm around," Jay said.

Rollins would've laughed. A few months ago, he definitely would've laughed. But Jay wasn't joking and Rollins had to wonder for a second if he really would go on a stabbing rampage for Rollins' honour.

"I can handle myself, c'mon, you know that."

Jay shrugged and looked at his hands.

"Do you reckon he'll come back?" he asked.

"I dunno, maybe."

Jay nodded, his eyes still on his hands. "Guess we can't finish then."

Rollins smiled down at him. "Guess not, unless..."

"Unless?" Jay looked up, his eyes bright.

"Unless we do it in the living room, facing the window."

"Fuck yeah, doggy style," Jay got up.

"Please don't call it that," Rollins said and followed him.

"What? You're the porn connoisseur, that's what it's called. You don't like it?"

Rollins liked it just fine, liked it with Jay even more.

"I like it," he gritted out as he watched Jay—his baggy jeans and awkward gait as he jogged inside—and wondered at how much he liked it. "I just hate that term."

"Well, alright," Jay said and locked the front door before undoing his pants, pushing them off and getting onto the couch on his knees, his bare ass covered by his singlet. "Lovingly boning from the rear."

"Oh my God, shut up," Rollins said and kneeled behind him, his thighs widening so Jay was cradled between them.

"Getting dicked down from behind."

Rollins got his dick out, nudged up against Jay's hole and brought his hand up to cover his mouth.

"How about," he said as he pushed in, "taking it like a man."

"I like that," Jay murmured against his palm, tickling his skin.

Rollins started to fuck him and let his hand fall away. When Jay craned his head back for a kiss, Rollins met him.

42

Horace didn't come back. Rollins wasn't surprised—Horace might be a demented, unscrupulous piece of shit, but like Jay, he could read a room. And when the room was blaring—fuck off my mum just died—you read it right and stayed away.

But Rollins had an uneasy feeling around Jay after that. Not like he was scared of him or something crazy, more like, he reckoned there was a bit more going on beneath the surface with his grief and it could make him do something crazy if he wasn't careful.

On the plus side, he wanted to fuck. All the time. Rollins wanted to fuck all the time too. Win-win.

"Hey, you wanna?" Jay was saying to him now while Rollins cleaned and sorted all the gear from his post-apocalypse bag.

Rollins put down the torch, turned, hoisted Jay up with two big palms under his thighs.

Jay chuckled in his ear. "Fuck, you're strong, I'm like super heavy, dude," Jay said and kissed Rollins' throat.

"Nah," Rollins replied and carried him inside to the futon, kneeled down and pressed Jay into the mattress as he kissed him.

He loved kissing Jay. He could do it for hours—bury his dick in him, cradle his head with his palms, and just kiss him. He reckoned it was the stress—he knew the money was fine, Jay knew it was fine, but Horace's certainty was unsettling.

Rollins took Jay's mouth now, enjoyed the feel of Jay's hands brushing his abs as he got his pants undone, and deduced that losing himself in Jay's body constantly was a coping mechanism. Maybe for both of them.

"Hey," Jay said pulling back.

"Yeah," Rollins kissed his clavicle, his shoulder.

"Can I fuck you?"

Rollins jerked back. "I don't do that."

"Yeah, but you don't suck dick either and I lost count."

Rollins frowned. Jay was right, he'd had Jay's dick in his mouth so much he'd lost count as well. He fucking loved it.

"This is different."

"How?"

Rollins rolled to the side, tucked Jay in next to him and ran his hand up under his singlet, back down over his bare hip and thigh.

"It's just so fucking gay," Rollins said.

Jay squinted up at him. Rollins prepared for an argument.

"Is it so gay or are you just scared?"

"Scared of what?"

"Scared it's gonna hurt. 'Cos dude, it will at first but then it like, feels real good."

Rollins glanced away. His hand rubbed and squeezed up and down Jay's side, and he pushed his dick against Jay's hip like he couldn't help himself.

"I like to fuck," he eventually said. "Not get fucked."

Jay rolled his eyes. "You're missing out."

"Have you even done it that way?"

"Yeah, course."

"With who?" Rollins paused his caress and gripped Jay's hip.

"Both my boyfriends, some random dudes, I like it both ways."

"Jesus, you're like twenty, how have you fucked around this much?"

Jay laughed. Rollins didn't think it was funny, he didn't like it at all.

"Dunno, guess I'm just irresistible."

Rollins rolled his eyes but he wasn't feeling it; he had an uneasy feeling about all these guys and whether or not he measured up. Worse, he hated the thought of them touching Jay, kissing him.

"Do you kiss all these blokes?" he asked and instantly regretted it.

Jay stopped laughing and tilted his head like he was thinking about it. "Yeah, most of them I guess, be a bit weird to fuck and not kiss."

Rollins didn't mention that Jay was the only dude he'd ever kissed, but maybe it was different if you were actually gay.

He let Jay go and rolled onto his back.

"You don't wanna anymore?" Jay asked, leaning over to peer down at him. "You can fuck me, I'm just saying, think about it 'cos I'd like to fuck you."

Rollins groaned and his dick twitched.

"Yeah, I reckon your body likes it."

"Shut up," he said and slipped his hand behind Jay's head to drag him down for a kiss.

Jay straddled his waist without breaking the kiss, started up a nice grind between their dicks.

"I'm gonna ride you," Jay said against his lips.

Rollins groaned again and kissed him.

Jay laughed against his lips. "You gotta let me go so I can get our pants off."

"Okay," Rollins said and kissed him again, tugged him into his chest so they were pressed together. Jay was still laughing into the kiss, but he shut up when Rollins deepened it.

Rollins broke away this time. "Did they kiss you like that?" he asked.

Jay made a tiny space between them, searched Rollins' eyes. Rollins watched him back, steady.

"Nobody kisses me like that," Jay replied, his gaze level.

"Good," Rollins said gruffly and kissed him hard.

Jay managed to wriggle his pants off and get Rollins' cock out, with no help from Rollins. But Rollins was all for making Jay fuck his fingers for a while, watching him roll his hips back, rub his dick along Rollins' abs in the same movement. The whole thing felt so tight—like they both didn't want to move too far away from the other. Rollins removed his fingers and slid in with his dick in a single movement, bringing his hands to rest on Jay's hips so he could control how far off his cock Jay could go.

"Feel good?" he asked.

"Yeah, dude. Yeah," Jay whispered. "Feels real good."

It was quiet in the house, hot and sweaty between them, their own little cocoon on the futon in the middle of the day.

Rollins lifted Jay up until he was half out, then dragged him back down. His fingers dug into his hips, thumbs pressing indents into the soft flesh of his ass. He loved Jay's skin, loved how soft he was, how he was so white he went red really easily, how he hid nothing when they fucked. It was nothing like other guys Rollins had fucked—Jay was all there with him, showing him every gasp, every moan, biting his lip and throwing his head back.

"Let me," Jay said and pushed his hips back.

Rollins loosened his grip and groaned when Jay started to ride him, dragging Rollins' cock in and out of himself slowly, his hair falling on Rollins' chest and dancing lightly over his nipples.

Rollins slipped a hand between them and wrapped it around Jay's cock. It was so thick, so long, and it felt so good in his palm—veiny, heavy, impressive. He thought about it in his mouth and had to kiss Jay while he dragged his hand up and down his shaft, just the way he liked it—tight but not too tight, teasing, then firm, stroking him like he could and would pull the orgasm right out of him.

"Oh," Jay said, his eyes widening like it was a surprise.

"Yeah, baby, there you go."

"Oh," Jay said again and squeezed his eyes shut as he started to come.

Rollins bucked his hips up, getting himself there just as Jay finished.

He groaned into Jay's shoulder and neck.

"Mm," Jay's voice whistled across his collar bone where he had his head resting on Rollins' chest. "Wanna get take-away?"

"Uh, no."

"Fish and chips? I can get a cornjack."

"No."

"They'll grill the fish for you."

"Ugh, fine."

Jay laughed. Rollins tightened his arms around his waist, his dick still buried inside him as he went soft.

"Nap first."

"Slacker," Jay murmured but didn't move.

"I T'D BE GOOD IF it could've ended there," Jay murmured.

He looked better. He'd made disgusted sounds when I first started catching the fish, but he'd begrudgingly eaten the flesh. And, yeah, I had to agree—it was far from sushi out here when you picked it off the bones with your fingernails. But it was food and it'd buy us some time. Because no, Jay, you can't shoot the cans open with the flares.

"I dunno, I reckon I could've done without a lot of what came next, especially when you were getting hurt, but you know..."

Jay lifted his head to look up at me, eyebrow raised. "You know?"

"I don't reckon I'd, you know, give up the last part."

Jay smiled, his head nodding, eyes bright. "Sap."

"Ah, shut it."

Jay's smile dropped and his eyes dimmed.

"What is it?" I asked, shaking him gently.

"Nothin', just, I never said thanks for, you know, bailing me out. Both times."

I squeezed him close. "Ain't no need for the thanks."

"Yeah?" Jay craned his head back again, expression hopeful.

"Course," I said, my voice rough.

Jay smiled and leaned up. I met him. "Thanks," he said against my lips.

The water lapped the sides of the dinghy and I hugged Jay between the cradle of my thighs, wrapped my arms around his waist. It was getting cold again, which made me worry we were drifting too far south.

"I can feel it, dude," Jay murmured.

"Feel what?"

"Land."

"Hmm," I looked around, nothing but ocean. Not a bird in sight. "Alright."

T HEY WERE FINISHING UP on the level where Rollins had started, the contract to do the one below secured the day before, and Rollins was right up in his head. He had been all week. This thing with Jay was eating at him.

Sarah had called and asked what time his flight would be in. He'd told her he wasn't coming down, needed to get the job done. She'd lost it, and he'd hung up. He realised then he had cold feet. Which meant this thing with Jay? Cold fucking feet.

Then why was the thought of Jay saying all on the level—*Nobody kisses me like that*—eating away at him so much?

Then there was Horace. More money disappearing.

Rollins threw the last of the copper into the trolley with so much force the whole thing crashed over.

"Geez, dude, save it for the gym."

"You fucking save it."

"What's with you?" Jay wandered into his line of sight.

"Fuck, nothing, alright. Fuck all. Just get your ass over there and finish this so we can go home," he looked away from Jay's face, the streak of grease on his cheek.

"Alright, alright," Jay said, palms raised, but did as he was told.

"Seriously, man, what's up?" Jay asked when they pulled up at home. "You're like, worse than usual."

"What worse than usual? I'm nice as fuck."

Jay scoffed. "Who told you that?"

Rollins glared at him. "I'm plenty nice to you."

"Eh, you've warmed up. But for real. What's doin'?"

Rollins shook his head, opened his door, stretched his leg out but made no move to get out. He wasn't going to talk about his impending nuptials with the side of impending doom, but he could talk about the money.

"Just fucking Horace, reckons I'm still shorting him."

"Fuck's sake," Jay said. "Why don't you like, just say someone else is doing it."

Rollins looked at him. "The fuck? And put someone else in this position?"

"Better than you being in it. What about Chad?"

"Chad?" Rollins scoffed. "Regular old brain's trust right there, siphoning off almost a hundred thousand now, yeah, might as well just say you're doing it."

Jay huffed. "He could draw the heat."

"Draw the heat? Where did you hear that?"

Jay opened his mouth.

"Don't answer that. No, I ain't doing that to anyone, least of all Chad, fuck's sake."

"Why not?"

"It's completely unbelievable for one thing and it's a fucked up thing to do to someone for another. You'd do that to someone?"

"To get him off your ass? Yeah."

Rollins shook his head. "Not cool," he said and got out.

"Also," Jay said as he followed him, the car door slamming. "I'm way smarter than Chad."

"I never said you weren't."

"You just implied it like five seconds ago."

"It's not smarts that are needed to steal that much cash, it's balls," Rollins stepped back and let Jay go into the house before him.

"So now you're saying I haven't got the balls."

"Have you?" Rollins slammed the door and greeted Nola.

"Course."

"Well then are you?"

"Dude!" Jay spun to look at him.

Rollins shrugged. "I'm kidding. Anyway, no, I'm not getting someone else beaten to death over it."

Jay rolled his eyes. "That isn't gonna happen."

"It really is."

"Are you stealing it?"

Rollins scoffed.

"Exactly," Jay said and went back to getting himself a coke. "Don't go around accusing man, not cool. Not cool."

"You just did," Rollins said and grabbed the coke out of his hand.

"What the fuck."

"Water first and you were just about to accuse Chad."

"It was just an idea."

Jay went and got himself a glass of water and drank it like it was poison. Rollins tried and failed to suppress his smile.

"It's a stupid fucking idea," he replied as Jay handed him the empty glass. Rollins gave him his coke.

"I'm checking in with the dudes," Jay said and wandered into the back room.

Rollins had been planning to tell him—right then and there—that they couldn't fuck anymore, really put his foot down. But turns out Jay wasn't in the mood to fuck anyway. And that pissed Rollins off more.

He kicked his boots off and decided to take a shower, maybe he'd jerk off to take the edge off wanting to do it with Jay so bad. It was embarrassing because clearly, he thought as he listened to sound of the keyboard clicking, Jay wasn't having the same problem.

He got out of the shower and yanked his towel off the hanger so hard the bracket ripped out of the wall. This fucking dump. He dried himself off and went and put shorts on. When he went into the back room, Jay glanced up at him and whistled.

"Didn't realise I got an invite to the show," he said and went back to typing something.

"What?"

Jay waved his hand but didn't look again. "Half naked and glistening with water."

"Glistening?"

"Yeah, you know, your skin is glistening with droplets and sweat."

Rollins shook his head and came up behind Jay. He looked at the screen—a series of black boxes and some kind of code he couldn't understand.

"I can't sleep yet," he said.

"Yeah, dude, we usually eat and fuck."

Rollins worked his jaw, he wanted to say a lot of things to that. *Not anymore* came to mind but he couldn't get the words out. *Well, what're you waiting for?* came a close second.

"My ass is sore," Jay said as he continued to type gibberish.

"I could blow you," Rollins said and slipped his hand around Jay's nape, ran his fingers along the skin.

Jay leaned into the touch. "I really wanna fuck you, dude."

Rollins squeezed and his dick twitched.

"I'm not doing that."

Jay shrugged. "Okay."

Rollins loosened his grip and resumed the caress. Jay kept on typing, yawned, pushed his glasses up.

"You're not gonna argue?"

"Nah, that's not cool, gotta respect your partner's boundaries."

Rollins shook his head and let him go.

"We ain't partners," he said as he headed for the kitchen. "I'm cooking and you'll eat it."

"Not fucking spinach, dude! I can't do it, I just can't," Jay called.

Rollins scoffed. "You'll eat it if I fucking salt it and fry it."

There was a long silence.

"Alright!" Jay yelled.

"This guy," Rollins said to Nola at his feet. Her tail thumped on the linoleum.

They were laying on the futon later, Rollins sweeping his hand up and down Jay's inner thigh while Jay read some manual, Rollins' sleepy eyes on the horizon beyond the door. He'd been sleeping out here more days than not and he was surprised he could—Jay hadn't bothered with blacking out the room and yet Rollins slept like the dead, cuddled up to Jay every day, his chest expanding and relaxing against Jay's back.

"You still want me to blow you?" he asked.

"Yeah, in a minute," Jay said and turned the page.

Rollins huffed and then he couldn't help it, he laughed.

"What?" Jay smiled over at him.

"Nothin', just, with that level of enthusiasm I'm not sure I can be assed."

"Liar, you love having my dick in your mouth."

Rollins clenched his jaw. He did. He didn't need it fucking pointed out.

Jay went back to reading.

Rollins didn't like not having his full attention.

"Or," he said, nervous, "you could fuck me."

Jay whipped his head back. "Yeah?"

"But if I say stop, you stop."

Jay tossed the manual aside and crawled up Rollins' body. Rollins lay back with the motion and slid his hands up Jay's side under his singlet.

"Course, dude, course. Gotta respect my partner's wishes."

"We ain't—

But Jay cut him off with a fierce kiss.

Rollins kissed him back, his hands sliding into his hair to control his head. He was already hard and he could feel Jay's big dick getting there against his own.

Jay broke away.

"How do you want it? Best to take it like a man your first time," Jay gave him a cheeky grin.

Rollins ignored that and traced Jay's bottom lip with his forefinger, slipped it into his mouth. Jay licked around the digit.

"No, like this," he said and pulled his finger out, kissed him again.

He felt Jay's hand scrambling around the side of the mattress. Rollins broke the kiss.

"If you're reaching for your fucking book again—

Jay cracked up and rested his head on Rollins' chest.

"Lube, dude."

"Ah," Rollins sat up and held Jay against him with his other hand as he reached behind the pillow. "Here."

"What's it doing under there?"

"Didn't want to just leave it lying around."

"Why?" Jay asked as he slid down Rollins' body and tugged his shorts down as he went.

"In case someone comes round and sees it?"

"Whose gonna come round?" he yanked his shirt off, got his pants off and slid between Rollins' thighs.

"Horace?"

"Could just be for jerking it."

"Still," Rollins said and moved his legs apart easily enough, but he was nervous, really fucking nervous.

Jay pressed a gentle kiss to his inner thigh. "Relax, I'll stop as soon as you say the word."

"Okay," Rollins said on a breath. He knew Jay would. He was scared he wouldn't be able to make him if it came to it.

Jay kissed up his inner thigh until he was kissing along the skin of his ass, and then he kept going until he was kissing Rollins' asshole.

"What?" Rollins jerked.

"Shh," Jay said against his skin and kissed him there again. He stuck his tongue out and licked; soft swipes of his tongue that zinged up Rollins' spine, made him shiver.

"Are you tonguing my asshole?"

"Not yet," Jay said against his rim and then pushed in with his tongue.

"Oh, fuck," Rollins said and brought his hand down on instinct and gripped the back of Jay's head. He didn't know if he wanted to push him away or drag him closer.

Jay pressed in and then Rollins could feel it—a tongue in his ass, penetrating him, thrusting in and out gently. It felt strange. It felt strangely fucking good. He panted, found his hips rocking into the touch to get more. Jay responded by pushing in deeper, really fucking him with his tongue.

"Oh," Rollins groaned out, his hand wrapping Jay's hair to make a loose fist, to tug him deeper.

Jay got the message and fucked him more insistently, his little moans vibrating against Rollins' rim. He pressed his tongue right in and then pushed in so his lips were against Rollins' hole, his tongue moving inside.

"Oh, God," Rollins bucked down.

Jay pulled out and huffed a laugh against him.

Rollins would tell him to shut up but he was scared if he spoke what would come out was—*don't fucking stop!*

Jay cracked open the lube and squirted some on his fingers, pushed one inside.

"Oh, shit," Rollins said. It felt weird, but good weird.

"Yeah, feels good doesn't it?"

Rollins closed his eyes and pushed into the touch. Jay added another, then another quickly.

"Jesus, don't put your hand up there," Rollins bit out.

Jay snickered. "Don't reckon we're at fisting yet, buddy."

"Fisting?" Oh, he got it then. "*Fisting?*"

Jay was laughing as he pulled his fingers out, went up onto his knees.

"Who you been fisting?" Rollins asked as he looked up at Jay above him. He lost the train of thought at the sight of Jay rubbing lube up and down his big cock. There was no way that thing going up there was going to feel good. He wanted to ask Jay to go back to the tongue. The fingers. That felt good. But he didn't want to seem chicken shit.

"Never tried it," Jay said as he planted one hand next to Rollins' head, the other one wrapped around his dick as he guided it to Rollins' entrance. "Deep breath," he said and smiled.

"Shut up—

Jay pushed forward and the tip popped inside.

"Oh, fuck," Rollins squeezed his eyes shut.

Jay brought his other hand next to Rollins' head, leaned down and ghosted his lips over Rollins'.

"Fuck, feels so tight, I'm gonna nut right now," he hissed.

"No, you're fucking not," Rollins said and brought his thighs up and tugged him in.

Jay crashed into his chest and pushed all the way in.

"Oh, Jesus," Rollins gasped as he felt that thing wedge right up inside him. But fucked if he was backing out now.

Jay groaned.

Rollins slipped his hand into his hair and lifted his head.

Jay's dazed eyes met him.

"Fuck. Me."

Jay nodded and got to it, pulling his hips back and then pushing back in. He was being gentle, careful. Rollins appreciated it—it didn't feel good or bad yet, just strange, like he had a foreign object lodged inside him.

Jay pulled out again, pushed in, his breaths coming short; he got a measured pace going and Rollins felt it then, a tingling, a pleasurable sensation around that big dick. He moaned and brought his hands down to plant them on Jay's ass and started forcing him inside himself harder, faster.

"Oh, fuck, there you go," Jay said and let Rollins set the pace, use that big dick.

"Jesus," Rollins rolled his ass down to meet that dick fucking into him.

"You need a—

Rollins arched, cried out and started to come.

"Holy shit, holy shit, untouched," Jay fucked him through it.

Rollins felt him starting to come, felt it warm and wet inside. Fuck, he liked that too.

"Jesus, dude, you're a porn star," Jay said breathlessly. He propped himself onto his elbows, his hips still rocking into Rollins' groin as he finished.

Rollins laughed, spent.

"Seriously, you're hot and you're an ass man. Could be in porn."

"Shut up," Rollins said.

"Shit, we gotta do that again."

Rollins groaned. It was better than saying: *fuck, yeah*.

R OLLINS WAS GETTING FUEL the next evening, the eve of a
night off, and he needed to go to the shop and fulfil the list
Jay had given him, when a burly guy stepped into his line of sight. He
wasn't alone.

Rollins knew what this was. He put the nozzle back, walked inside,
paid, strolled out again. Five of them. He had weapons in the back of
his car. He knew they probably knew that. He could probably take
them, but the burly guy lifted his shirt an inch, the butt of his gun
resting against his fat gut. And all Rollins could think was he didn't
want them taking this to the house.

He headed for the side of the building, behind the toilets.

And then he took the beating.

"Where have you ... What the fuck!" Jay said when Rollins staggered
in.

"Horace," Rollins collapsed onto the couch.

"I'm gonna fucking kill him," Jay went to march outside.

Rollins lurched forward and grabbed his wrist. "No."

"Let me go, dude. He's not pulling this shit any fucking more."

"I need you," Rollins bit out.

Jay spun back and pressed into his space. "Are you alright?"

Rollins got the hem of his shirt in his hand and tried to tug it off. He groaned. Jay got the message. He lifted it, gently, and sucked in a sharp breath.

"Hospital."

Rollins shook his head. "Back of my car, the black duffel, get it."

Jay looked at him, searched his eyes. "Okay," he said and raced out.

Rollins closed his eyes and Nola came and sat beside him.

"You shoulda had her with you," Jay said as he came back in with the bag.

"Boil some water, get the kit out, can you sew?"

"No," Jay said.

Rollins jerked his chin. "Get everything ready, I'll do it."

"You're gonna stitch yourself up?"

"Not the first time," he said and cracked his eyes open.

Jay shook his head at him. "Dude, you're like fucking MacGyver."

Rollins laughed, but it hurt so he told Jay, "Shut up and get the fucking water."

"Yes, boss," Jay hustled into the kitchen.

He leaned back, rolled up his shirt and surveyed the wound. Knife. He'd reckoned they wouldn't kill him and he'd been right. It was a warning. But they'd wanted to make the warning clear—return the money quietly now or you're a dead man—and a few jabs with a knife in his abdomen to finish the night completed that message.

The cuts were clean, not too deep and not puncturing anything vital. He'd be fine.

Jay came in with a steaming bowl of water. Rollins walked him through sterilising his needle while he cleaned the wounds.

Then he splashed iodine everywhere and sewed them up.

By the time he finished, he was sweating, shaking.

"Now—

But Jay was already leaning forward with a wound dressing, pressing one firmly over each patch of stitches until the adhesive stuck.

"Thanks," Rollins breathed out and slumped back.

"What're you thanking me for? I didn't do anything."

Rollins frowned at him. He wasn't meeting Rollins' eyes.

"This isn't your fault," he said because it absolutely wasn't. "Horace is just a one-track-mind fuckwit."

Jay shook his head. "Still, I shoulda been there."

"I'm fucking glad you weren't."

"I coulda helped."

"You really couldn't. Listen," Rollins knocked his knee into Jay's where Jay was sitting in front of him on the coffee table. He waited for Jay to look up. When he did, Rollins went on. "When five guys are sent to take care of you like that, you just get through it, you hear me? You don't fight back."

Jay frowned. "Why?"

"All they been sent to do is give you a warning, but they might accidentally kill you if you go and antagonise them. Take the beating, then regroup."

Jay didn't say anything.

Rollins was beat. Well, he was literally beaten, but he was really feeling it now. He let his eyes slip closed.

"Always?" Jay asked.

"Always what," Rollins murmured.

"Always take the beating?"

Rollins let out a long breath. "No, sometimes you should kill 'em all."

"When?"

"You'll know."

Jay was nodding his head. Rollins didn't have to see him, he could feel it in the way the air shifted, knew it in the way he knew Jay.

"I'm gonna get you something to drink, make you some soup."

"I'm fine," Rollins murmured.

"Soup," Jay said firmly and squeezed his thigh.

Rollins placed his hand over Jay's before he could pull away. He gripped him and Jay slid their fingers together.

"You need to eat something," Jay said softly.

He squeezed Jay's hand.

Jay turned their palms over so his was on top and slid his fingers tightly into Rollins' grip before he slipped his hand away, placed Rollins' hand back on his thigh with a gentle squeeze.

Rollins listened to him moving around in the kitchen, let it ground him back in their house, in the here, now.

ROLLINS HAD TWO CLEAR problems after that night. The first
was Horace's demented obsession with this missing money. If
the beating hadn't been clear enough, the text waiting for him the next
morning was: *last warning*. The second was his insatiable need to fuck
and the wounds that made it impossible. He'd liked to have said the
first was the most pressing. It wasn't.

He was lying on Jay's futon, thinking about fucking him, when the
man himself walked in.

Jay took one look at Rollins' hard dick pressing against his pants
and snorted.

"Shut up," Rollins said.

"I didn't say anything, but you need to settle down, man. You need
to heal."

"Jesus, shut up."

Jay laughed and sat down at his computer.

Rollins watched him and palmed his dick idly as he did so.

"Stop it, geez," Jay snickered over at him.

"'M not doing anything," Rollins cracked a smile.

"I need to concentrate."

"Writing more about Gaz doing fuck all?"

Jay gave him a mocking smile, but then went back to typing.

Rollins looked him up and down, assessing. He could get Jay to blow him, even though Jay had shot that down on account of Rollins "shifting his torso too much."

He scanned down to his ass in the chair. Maybe he could finger him? He liked doing that.

"Dude," Jay whined over at him.

"What?" Rollins squeezed his dick.

"I can feel your eyes on me. It's tough for me too."

"Is it?" Rollins asked and rubbed himself with a firmer grip. "Tell me about it."

Jay laughed, shook his head. "We can't."

"What about if I just like, played with your ass."

Jay spun in his chair to face him, spread his legs. "You mean like, rimming?"

Rollins scrunched his face up.

Jay laughed again. "Not into licking ass?"

Rollins huffed, but his dick twitched. "You like that?"

"Love it," Jay quipped. "Getting my partner all wet and ready for my dick, my partner getting me ready." He was palming himself now too.

"Shit..."

"But we can't," he said and stopped.

"Why?" Rollins couldn't believe how whiny he sounded.

"Because, your stitches—

"What if I laid on my stomach. They'd be protected."

"You want me to rim you again?"

Rollins scrunched his face up again, but it was half-assed. He did. He really did.

"I can if you want, but..."

"But?"

"But you don't gotta do it back this time."

"Fuck that," Rollins said. "You said we have to hit each other back."

"Yeah, but you're like, incapacitated."

"I'm fine. You could... sit-on-my-face," he rushed out.

Jay's mouth dropped open. "Yeah?"

"Yeah," he breathed out.

Jay was up and undoing his pants. "You sure?"

"Yeah, c'mere," Rollins said and reached out.

"Okay, but if those stitches even so much as stretch, we're stopping."

"Yes, Mum," Rollins said, eyes fixed on Jay's half-hard dick coming towards him.

"Eww," Jay said but straddled Rollins' face.

It was a lot, but Rollins liked it. He liked how much smaller than him Jay was. Jay was a tubby little thing, but he was small—soft and easily man-handled. Rollins ran his hands up Jay's thighs and gripped him by the hips, then slid his hands down to bring his ass over his face, using his thumbs to open him up.

He told himself—*Thank Christ Jay just got out of the shower.* And—*This is disgusting, I can't believe I'm doing this.* But he was so full of shit—Jay could've been a sweaty mess after a shift and Rollins still would've been salivating for it like he was now.

He stretched his tongue out and licked over Jay's hole. Jay jolted like he'd been electrocuted. Rollins tightened his fingers on his hips, pressed his thumbs in harder.

"Thought you'd done this before?" he asked against Jay's skin.

"I have," Jay already sounded breathless. "Just, not a lot."

"Why?" Rollins asked and licked again, getting him nice and wet.

"It's a, oh shit," he gasped; Rollins could feel his thighs trembling at the side of his face.

"It's a?" Rollins prodded his hole with his tongue. His voice was muffled but he liked that too; he felt surrounded by Jay.

"Ah, shit, it's a boyfriend thing."

Rollins pushed in, pulled out. "You've had boyfriends." He laved Jay's hole with his tongue, softening him up.

"They weren't," Jay tried to rock down, realised he couldn't and panted. "That into it."

"Hmm," Rollins penetrated him again, fucked in and out with his tongue. Jay gasped and moaned above him. He pulled back. "But you are."

"Yeah, fuck, please don't stop."

"Actual manners," Rollins smirked between his ass cheeks, pressed so all his fingers were digging into his skin.

"Fuck, please," Jay said again, not a trace of humour in his voice.

"I got you," Rollins replied and started to fuck in and out with his tongue with real purpose, like it was his dick. His dick, which was hard and rolling into the air against nothing.

But Jay was pushing down, really losing it above him and Rollins found himself enjoying that more. There's no way it would be enough to get him anywhere—it was a tease more than anything—but Rollins liked that too, liked that he could keep Jay on edge like this for hours if the little shit had the stamina.

"God, that feels so good, so good," Jay said above him.

"Hmm," Rollins said into his skin, tongue buried deep as he wriggled it around.

"Maybe I could just, ah, fuck," Jay panted, "sit on your dick, if you don't move..."

Rollins groaned against him.

"You wanna use me?" he asked as he pulled out.

"If you stay still..."

"You wanna use my dick?" God, why did that turn him on so much?

"I'll be careful."

Rollins lifted him up and brought him down.

Jay huffed a laugh. "Fuck, I always forget how strong you are."

Rollins looked at his red face, his smile, his stupid glasses he hadn't taken off, not to mention the cap.

He reached up with his hand as he lowered him with the other, prepared to remove the glasses and the hat and kiss him, when Jay stopped him.

"You don't want to kiss?" Rollins asked, a little disappointed, but that was fair—his tongue had just been in Jay's ass.

Jay snorted. "No, I don't want you to move. I always want to kiss."

"I'm barely moving," Rollins said and pushed his hips up so his clothed dick rubbed over Jay's ass.

"Stop it," Jay said and braced himself over Rollins' hips. He got his fingers in Rollins' waistband and freed his dick. "You're just gonna have to lay there and take it," he stroked Rollins' cock a few times, "and I'll kiss you if you're good."

Rollins laughed. Jay paused and stared at him.

"What?" Rollins asked, smiling.

"Nothing, dude," Jay shook his head.

It was clearly something, but Rollins didn't a get chance to press it because Jay was sinking down on his dick.

"Don't move," he said as he impaled himself.

Rollins groaned. He wanted to buck up so badly, but he knew Jay was right so he stayed completely still and let Jay sink all the way down, then rise up slowly, build a measured, torturous pace with his hips.

"Oh, fuck yeah," Jay said as he used Rollins' dick, his thighs straddled around his waist, his soft belly and chest undulating where he sat upwards and brought himself up and down. "Feels so fucking good," he looked at Rollins, "does it feel good?"

"Yeah," Rollins breathed out, his voice embarrassingly awed.

Jay smiled down at him, groaned, and took his time.

It was slow, intimate with the way they were watching each other, Jay moving up and down carefully, agonisingly drawing the pleasure out. His big dick was hard, stretching up and hitting his stomach with each roll of his hips, but he didn't move a hand to touch himself, and Rollins found his own hands running up and down Jay's thighs, reluctant to touch him as well, to finish this.

Rollins didn't think either of them could get there at this pace, so he was surprised when he felt it building inside him; he wanted to push up, to get himself there, but as it intensified, he wanted to let Jay drag it out of him like this.

When he did, Rollins was still watching him and Jay was watching him back. The orgasm rippled up his spine and as he started to come Jay's eyes widened, then he smiled, "Fuck, I can feel it," he said and Rollins groaned.

Jay stopped moving, sat with Rollins' dick coming inside him as he jerked off in carefully tight movements. Rollins gripped his hips and watched him arch and come. He looked so good like that—his white skin blotchy red, his eyes closed behind his glasses, his sweat tacky above his lip; objectively, it wasn't hot, but as Rollins watched him coming into his fist, watched him suck in air, listened to his voice catch, he couldn't think of anything turning him on more. It was the abandonment Jay brought to it, the honesty. It was Jay.

Rollins ran his hands up and down his thighs in a settling caress.

Jay's eyes flicked open. "Your stitches."

"Fine," Rollins replied, hands still moving. "You owe me a kiss."

Jay gave him a small smile. "That I do, dude. That I do," he leaned down and kissed him softly, and Rollins let himself be kissed.

47

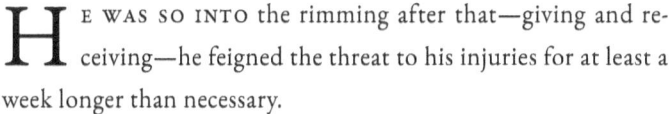

H E WAS SO INTO the rimming after that—giving and re-
ceiving—he feigned the threat to his injuries for at least a
week longer than necessary.

But Jay was no fool; he gave Rollins a knowing smile when
Rollins rolled onto his stomach so Jay could hit him back.

He was less into the message he received from Horace after the
latest cleaning and the news more money was missing.

"He's fucking deranged!" Rollins threw his phone onto the
futon and headed for the yard.

Nola and Jay both startled and looked over at him from where
they were sitting just outside the door.

"Who?"

"Who else?" Rollins blew out a breath.

"More money?" Jay asked.

"Apparently."

"Fucking seriously?"

"No, I'm lying."

"No, but, have you got the message."

"Yeah," Rollins looked at him sprawled in the lawn chair, his coke beside him, a pair of garish sunglasses he'd actually ordered on prescription hiding his eyes.

"Can I see it?"

Rollins frowned. "It just says twenty-three k."

"Twenty-three…" Jay said around a breath.

"More bullshit," Rollins crouched down for Nola's ball and tossed it. "Maybe he has got dementia, but I reckon it's a mind-fuck…" he trailed off. Jay was so still beside him, it was sparking Rollins' senses. "What?"

"This doesn't make any sense."

"No shit."

"No, but…" Jay didn't finish. He got up and went inside.

Rollins craned his head back and watched him booting up his computer. Nola brought the ball back. Rollins patted her, picked it up, threw it and watched her bound after it. He turned back to look at Jay. His leg was bouncing. Nola came back with the ball. Rollins picked it up. Jay started typing something. Rollins stood with the ball in his hand. Jay bit his bottom lip and squinted at the screen. Rollins stepped inside. Jay looked over at him and his face said what Rollins thought in the exact same moment.

"You…" he trailed off.

"I can explain," Jay said.

So many feelings hit Rollins in that moment, but the one that won out was not betrayal or shock, it was terror.

"He's going to fucking kill you."

Jay scoffed. "No, he's not."

"He is, he fucking is. Jesus fucking… how?"

Jay bit his lip and glanced at his computer.

Rollins looked at the screen like it could answer him.

"We hacked him," Jay shrugged.

"We…" Rollins breathed out slowly, who was we? More importantly: "I don't know what that means, but you need to put it back," Rollins was frozen. The ball still in his hand. "He might still kill you, but it's a fucking start."

Jay looked up at him. He looked guilty, yes, but defiant too.

"You used me," Rollins said, the words just popping out like he had Tourette's.

Jay shook his head, but he dropped his gaze.

"Put it back."

"No," Jay said, his voice small but firm.

"Jay, this isn't fucking around, this is fucking serious—

"I can't."

"Whaddyamean you can't?"

"I don't have it."

"Who the fuck does?"

Jay looked up at him; he looked so guilty.

"Who the fuck has the money, Jay?"

Jay sucked in a breath. "My mum."

"But she's dead…"

Jay was shaking his head.

Then Rollins remembered the woman outside the hospital.

"Her best friend died," Jay glanced up. "She was more than that, but… Mum's fine."

Rollins didn't know how to process any of this. Jay and his mother were stealing all the money. Jay had used Rollins to work the accounts. Jay's mother wasn't fucking dead. But one thing was paramount.

"He's going to kill you if you don't fix this. Tell her that," he snapped but Jay was shaking his head.

"Jesus Christ," Rollins said and went for his keys and phone.

"Where are you going?" Jay called after him.

Rollins didn't answer him. He was going to fucking fix this before Horace killed both of them.

Between the money he had set aside for the wedding, his savings to start the build on Sarah's dream house and buy his boat, he had enough. He went to the bank and made the transfer. He went to drive home and found himself accelerating out of town. He drove for a long time. His mind worked over the same ground and didn't come up with a different answer. He searched for a way to put this together in a different arrangement with a different outcome and he couldn't find one. He slowed, made a U-turn, and drove back.

Jay stood from the couch when Rollins walked in.

"I can explain—

"You have to leave."

Jay's lips parted. "You want me to go?"

Rollins' jaw clenched. It wasn't a matter of what he fucking well wanted. "Sydney. Horace doesn't know where you live in Sydney, right?"

Jay nodded his head. "Yeah, but—

"You need to go and never come back."

"But what about you?"

"I'll be fine."

Well, his plan to get enough to build the house and then quit was now thoroughly fucked, and he was probably going to have to work even more to get enough to cover his end of the wedding, but he doubted Horace would kill him outright over this if he kept a low profile.

"Please let me explain," Jay shoved his hands in his pockets, shrunk in on himself.

"I think I get the picture," Rollins said. "And now you need to go."

Jay was shaking his head.

"You don't though, I never meant to get you hurt and I felt so bad. I'll fix it somehow, I'll talk to Mum and we'll get the money—

"The money's sorted."

Rollins left him in the living room and went to get his things. He needed Jay gone now or he was going to do something stupid like try and figure out a way to make it so he could stay. He was hurting over Jay using him, but he got it; sometimes things start out one way and end up another.

"Whaddyamean the money's sorted?" Jay came up behind him. "And what are you doing?"

"Packing," Rollins said and shoved all Jay's shit into his backpack. "You need the computer, you'll have to wait until I can get it sent."

"Would you just stop. Dude. Rollins."

Jay hardly ever said his name. Rollins liked the sound of it. He shook himself. There was no time for sentimentality now.

"C'mon," he zipped the bag up roughly, eyes on the zipper. "You can make the last flight."

Jay's hand covered his suddenly. "Don't make me go."

Rollins breathed out roughly. He wanted to shove Jay away. He wanted to shake him. He wanted him to not have done this. But the only way to keep him safe now was to make him leave.

"Get the next flight to Sydney. If you think Horace won't think you got a hand in this after that time he visited..." he trailed off. "Fuck, I'm stupid," he said to himself.

"You're not, dude. I'm... fuck..."

Rollins stood, stepped back. He averted his eyes and got his keys.

"Say bye to Nols, I'll meet you in the car."

And he went out and told himself to get his shit together.

Rollins was almost about to get back out of the car, go back inside and drag Jay into the car when he trudged out.

He opened the door. "Can we at least wait until—

"No." Rollins turned the key.

Jay got in and Rollins ignored him wiping his eyes under his glasses with his sleeve.

He was prepared to mount all the counter arguments if Jay said a word. Jay didn't. He sniffed a few times, but kept his eyes outside his own window. When they pulled up at the airport Rollins had to bite his tongue on saying too many stupid things—*Let's sleep on it* or *Why didn't you tell me?* or, worst of all, *Fuck this, let's just disappear to New Orleans together*.

"You better hurry," he finally managed.

He could see Jay's head nodding in his periphery, listened as the car door opened. Jay didn't get out.

Rollins kept his eyes forward and focused on breathing.

"I'm really—

"It's fine."

Jay got out, dragged his bag onto his shoulder but didn't shut the door.

"I..." Jay trailed off.

Rollins waited, but Jay slammed the door and Rollins watched him and tried not to watch him as he crossed the front of the bonnet, head down.

He exhaled roughly and drove back onto the road. He pulled onto the shoulder, cut the engine. He watched the runway, the stretch of red dirt, the little triangular parachute lifting limply in the breeze.

He stayed there until the plane pulled out, trudged down the dirt and made a large turn before revving at the top. He watched as it accelerated, gained speed, barrelled down that stretch of dirt before the tyres left the ground and the nose pointed up. He watched it take flight and climb into the sky.

He watched it until it was nothing more than a speck on the horizon.

And then he watched as it became nothing against the twilight blue of an empty sky.

48

"I DIDN'T KNOW YOU did that," Jay murmured.

He was lying flat on the bottom of the dinghy, eyes squinting up at the sky through the hole.

I shrugged. It was embarrassing—pining after a plane—but the memory still made me ache. The terror of what came next was worse.

"I never told you why I did it," Jay said.

I nudged his side with my foot, in time with the rocking of the water—we'd been undulating like this for so long, I didn't reckon I'd ever know what it felt like to be still again.

"I figured it was revenge," I replied, dug my toes into Jay's side.

He gripped my foot and exhaled.

"Yeah, but, it wasn't Mum. It was me."

"He beat you too?" I felt a surge of anger and wanted to live just so I could kill him again.

"Yeah, course, sometimes, but not like he beat Mum. But that's not why," Jay said. His voice was slow. Everything felt slow, sleepy, like a dream. "Mum let it go. She said, 'we got another life here, why dwell on it?' But I was like, I can't, you know? I'd think of him, of that house, of how terrified we always were and I'd imagine bumping into him in like, a bar, and he'd say, 'Oh, hi, Jayden,'" Jay mimicked a lady's voice and I snickered. Jay shot me a smile. "Anyway, I pictured, you know, smashing the beer bottle in my hand and glassing him."

"Jesus, you never even order beer."

Jay giggled. "You know what I mean, dude, it was a fantasy. Anyway, so Mum said, you either gotta let it go or you gotta do something, can't go on living your life carrying all that around inside you."

Jay clasped his hands over his stomach and exhaled. "So, I was like, I can't let it go. And she said, alright, well you ain't gonna go round glassing people, so here's what you do," Jay looked up. "'Cos those guys? Mum said, 'we saw them, but they never really saw us.' She meant—

"I know what she meant," I grabbed Jay's foot and squeezed.

"Yeah, so, she saw everything, she knew where the bodies were buried."

"And I was an easy mark."

Jay frowned. "At first, maybe? Mum said get to the courier, she knew Horace woulda got them on cleaning 'cos that's what he used to do, but when I got Horace to put me with you, put the idea in his head, I never wanted, even then, I never wanted to get you hurt."

I snorted. "You had no love lost for me, don't lie."

"Nah, dude, it's true I thought you were expendable, but I always kinda liked you."

"Hmm," the boat rocked and I slipped my eyes closed. I didn't believe that and I didn't like how hearing it made me ache, made me wish everything could've been different. Then maybe we wouldn't be here facing certain death. But then that was bullshit; I'd been a pussy about my feelings for Jay until the very end. And now it really was almost the end.

"Why do you think I introduced myself as Jay?"

"'Cos you're deranged."

Jay giggled. "Nah, I reckon my subconscious knew, you know? It just popped out. Only my people call me Jay. And like, I said 'Jay.' To you."

"Hmm," I tickled his foot.

Jay smiled, tired but fond. "I guess I kinda liked you from the start too."

I laughed and dropped my head.

"That laugh, man," Jay huffed.

"What?"

"Kills me. Every time."

"Ah, shut it," I said, smiling.

49

T HE HOUSE WAS EMPTY after that. Literally and in the clichéd sense—Jay's presence had been everything. Rollins decided not to take the second contract on the mine. After he turned it down, he looked at Nola and said, "I just can't."

She looked up at him, eyes understanding, but berating him too, for sending Jay away.

"Get it together. Jesus," Rollins muttered. "She's a dog, she's not saying that with her eyes, for fuck's sake."

He packed up and drove out of Port Hedland with Nola on the front seat not two hours later. He'd figure it out back in Perth. Get a big job—they were looking for subbies on the new stadium, something like that and he could remake the money lost and get Horace off his ass.

He'd been back a week when he got the call. Horace was the same fat asshole he'd always been, sitting behind his desk and wearing a mean smirk.

"I should kill ya for that," he said when Rollins walked in.

Rollins snorted. "You'd never get your hands that dirty."

"Watch it," Horace's expression shifted to just mean. "I've decided to be the bigger man about it, even let Jayden off the hook, but if you wanna antagonise me, I can change my mind."

Rollins froze at the sound of Jay's name. "Whaddyamean, Jayden?"

"Christ, how hard did those guys hit your head?"

"Jayden?"

"What about him," Horace leaned back, clasped his hands over his gut. "Got him back on cutting. Oh, don't worry, I had him smacked around a bit for helping you cause all that trouble, but I let him keep working, no point wasting a decent set of hands."

"He's here?" Rollins was going to kill him.

"Where else would he be?"

Rollins walked out.

"Hey, where the fuck are you going, we ain't finished yet—

But Rollins was out the door. He was going round to Jay's place and he was going to strangle him.

Gaz opened the door. "Yo."

"Where the fuck is Jay?" Rollins asked.

"Woah, dude, I ain't letting you in with that attitude," Gaz replied, both hands up.

And he was right, Rollins needed to settle down.

"I need to speak to him, that's all," Rollins toned it down.

Gaz shook his head. "JC said you're alright, but he's not here."

"Where is he."

Rollins knew he wasn't at the clubhouse, the place was empty save for Horace.

"He went to the food court, got a friend over from Sydney, so maybe—

"Thanks," Rollins snapped and turned back for his car.

The food court at the shopping centre near Jay's house was a bustling hive of noise and awful neon lights—the cavernous ceiling made everything worse, echoing with the sounds of too many voices, cutlery hitting plates, and kids screaming. It ricocheted through Rollins' brain painfully. Every table was full. He scanned the room, looking for Jay and that woman from the hospital who was clearly his mother.

When he spotted his red cap he saw it wasn't a woman with him, but a guy—mid-twenties, slight, slimy-looking and smiling at Jay with real interest.

What. The. Fuck.

Rollins really was going to kill him.

He marched over. Stopped beside Jay and glared at the guy.

"Umm, hi?" the guy said as he looked up. He had an accent.

"Rollins?" Jay asked.

"Who are you?" Rollins asked the guy.

"Dude," Jay said. Rollins could hear he was surprised, nervous even, but Mr Dickfuck having lunch with him needed to answer the fucking question.

"Umm, Jayden, who is this?" the guy flicked his eyes to Jay. The question was laced with disgust. And the accent was South African.

"I asked you a question," Rollins said.

"This is Simon," Jay said.

"And how the fuck do you know Jay, Simon?"

This Simon rolled his eyes. Oh, I don't fucking think so, Rollins thought and stepped closer. Simon's face flashed with real fear.

"Okay," Jay jumped up, stepped in front of Rollins. "Simon was my boyfriend back in Sydney. He's in Perth for work."

"Thought your boyfriend was called Aiden."

"That tosser," Simon scoffed as Jay asked, "You remembered that?"

"And I thought this fuckwit didn't have a name."

Rollins finally looked down at Jay. He had a black eye. Rollins sucked in a breath and grabbed him by the biceps.

"Are you okay?"

Jay's mouth dropped open—probably because Rollins was acting like a lunatic—but he replied, "Yeah, dude, I'm fine."

"Jayden, who is this guy?" Simon asked.

Rollins didn't drop his hands but shifted his gaze to Simon. "I'm the guy who wants to know what the fuck you did."

"Rollins," Jay squeaked. "It's cool, dude, it's in the past."

"So is this a fucking date?" Rollins asked.

"No—

"So what if it is?" Simon piped up.

Rollins tightened his grip on Jay and ignored the wanker. "You didn't even want to speak his name."

Jay winced. Simon scoffed.

"It was nothing, I got hurt and you know," Jay dropped his gaze, "but it's all good now, dude. So, do you need something?"

"You wouldn't speak my name because of that?" Simon asked, laughing.

Jay shrugged and Rollins let him go, but stayed in his space.

"'Cos of what?" Rollins asked, eyes on Jay.

"I asked him not to come to my family shit," Simon stated.

"Why?" Rollins asked.

"Because I didn't want to introduce him as my boyfriend."

Rollins shifted his head to look down on him. "Why?"

"Because," Simon waved his hand at Jay and sat back.

Rollins clenched his jaw. "Why are you having lunch with this fuckstick, Jay?"

"Dude, it's fine, really."

"It ain't."

"What're you, his bodyguard?" Simon asked.

Rollins had to hand it to the slick fucker—he was half Rollins' size, and Rollins could snap him in half if he wanted to—but this guy was cool, like the slime just rolled off him.

Still, Rollins only had one answer to that question. "I'm his partner and we got business to discuss, so if you could fuck off."

"I'll wait," Simon smiled, sleazy. And oh, Rollins got it then, this jackass thought he was about to get laid.

Over Rollins' dead fucking body.

"No, you ain't got the balls to stand beside Jay? You got nothing left to say to him. Go on, get," Rollins said.

"Oh, come on, Jayden gets it, we had an understanding."

"Jay," Rollins looked at him. He'd been suspiciously quiet.

"Yeah?"

"Ask fucktard here to leave now or I'm gonna take him outside and take care of him."

Simon scoffed again.

Jay searched Rollins' eyes. He didn't look away when he said, "Better go, man, he's not kidding."

"I'm not getting run out by a white trash thug and his wannabe gangster boyfriend—

Rollins stepped forward. Simon almost fell out of the chair.

"Alright, alright," he got up and started to walk away backwards. "And fuck you too, Jayden, you'd think the son of a whore could fuck better!"

Rollins lunged, but Jay put his body in front of him so Rollins was forced to grab him or they'd both topple to the floor.

"You dated that cunt?" Rollins spat.

Jay struggled in his hold. Rollins tugged him in and hugged him. Then he shoved him away.

"What the fuck are you doing here?"

"In the food court?"

"No," Rollins said. "In Perth."

Rollins noticed the people at the nearby tables looking at them, people in the lines to eat the sludge steaming under the buffet lights as well. He didn't give a shit.

"Working?" Jay asked.

"I told you to leave."

"I know, dude, I get it. But I went to Horace and when he asked, I just said it was me and he got me beat up and that was the end of it," he shrugged.

"That's not the fucking end of it," Rollins grabbed him by the bicep and marched him out of there.

A few people watched, but no one intervened.

Rollins let him go once they were in the carpark.

Jay stumbled forward and then turned to squint up at him against the sunshine.

"I told you to leave because it ain't safe for you here now."

"And it's safe for you?"

"I can handle myself."

"And I can't?" Jay stepped forward, pushing his glasses up his nose as he came closer. He was tiny, out of shape—certainly no fighter—but he wasn't fucking stupid, as Rollins' drained bank accounts could attest.

"I reckon you underestimate what you're up against."

Jay shook his head at him. "I reckon I know it better than you do."

Rollins folded his arms over his chest and took Jay's measure. Jay watched him back. What he really wanted to do was hug him again. He didn't think he'd ever see him again, and he was surprised by how good it felt to be seeing him live and in colour in his psychedelic hoodie and baggy jeans, his scuffed sneakers.

"But you don't need to stay. You did what you came to do—

"And then you went and fucked it all!" Jay yelled.

Rollins recoiled. "I saved your fucking life."

"No, now I gotta go and pay you back, I gotta stay and work it off."

"No, you don't," Rollins replied, both eyebrows raised. He never even thought of that. "You really don't."

"And also," Jay ignored him, "I gotta do it all again."

"Jesus," Rollins shook his head at him. He looked over the rows of the cars, the steady hum of traffic beyond it, the concrete rows of shops on the opposite side of the road. "Do you want to die, is that it?"

"Course not, but I gotta finish this."

"It's gonna finish you."

Jay shrugged. "Have a little faith in me, dude, come on."

"I got more faith in you than that cunt you were just having lunch with. Maybe you need to have a little more faith in yourself and go and get yourself a life while you still can."

"In Sydney," Jay said like the place was a tombstone.

"Anywhere but here."

"Why, 'cos you're here?"

"It ain't got nothing to do with me."

"I reckon it's got everything to do with you," Jay said like a dare.

And, well, in a way, it was the crux of it. Sure, it was highly likely Horace would now use Jay as a punching bag and mentally torture him, but Jay was right—he could handle that. And while Rollins was certain Horace was not just going to let this go—he was playing them while he waited to execute his next move—they'd certainly bought some time to make a counter move if that's what Jay really wanted to do.

But. Rollins was getting married soon. Rollins hated having Jay here and that event at the same time. And he really couldn't think about that.

So, he said, "If you're staying, you're on your own."

Jay gave a sharp jerk of his head. "I know."

"Jesus Christ," Rollins breathed out.

"Bye," Jay said and started walking towards his place.

"Don't go and hook up with that fuckwit!" Rollins yelled after him.

Jay held up his hand in a wave but kept walking.

Rollins jogged to his car, got in, sped out of his spot and drove alongside Jay before he made it to the road.

"Get in."

"Dude," Jay huffed at him. "I can walk."

"And I can give you a lift."

"Not very on my own if you're giving me a lift, is it?" he asked but got in. "I'm not going to hook up with him," he continued as he put his seatbelt on.

"You better fucking not. Can't believe you even had lunch with him," Rollins said and headed out of the carpark. "Why did you have lunch with him? He wanted to fuck you."

"Nah, I reckon he just wanted to catch up."

Rollins shot him an incredulous look. "You're not that dumb."

"Why do you even care?"

"Why do I care that you're out carousing with a guy you can't even speak the name of?"

"Carousing? Who says that."

"I do."

Jay chuckled. "Nah, it was like, closure. When he called, I thought, let's close this. Don't wanna go through my whole life collecting up these grudges."

"One's enough for the time being, is it?"

Jay smiled over at him and Rollins couldn't stop the smile he shot him.

"You really are gonna be on your own if you pursue this, I'm not kidding," he said as he turned onto Jay's street.

"Yeah, I get it. It's not your fight."

Rollins pulled into his driveway. "That's not why—

"And I fucked you over."

"Also not why—

"And you're getting married."

Rollins zipped his mouth shut. So, Jay was a more perceptive little fucker than Rollins gave him credit for. They sat in silence and it felt unbearably loaded. Jay broke it with a loud exhale and opened his door.

"Later, Rollins," he said and shut the door quietly behind him, something final in it.

Rollins let out a deep breath, tapped his fingers on the steering wheel. He watched Jay unlock the screen door, then the front door. He wanted to go after him. To fuck him again. To hold him. To kiss him.

He put it in reverse and sped out of there.

50

H E DIDN'T WIN ONE of the jobs on the stadium, but he did secure the entire shopping complex in Rockingham south of Perth. It was enough to get him a loan with the bank and not have to tell Sarah about losing all that money, enough to cover his end of the wedding. Fucked if he knew what he was going to say when she asked about building the house.

But he had bigger concerns. True to his word, he'd left Jay to it. They crossed paths at the clubhouse. The first time they crossed paths, Jay wouldn't meet his eyes. It was so surprising, Rollins turned and followed him out into the street.

"Jay," he said to his back.

"Hey, dude, I'm out, gotta get some sleep," he said and quickened his pace.

Rollins jogged up to him, past him and in front of him. The streetlight illuminated his face and Rollins saw the busted lip. It was fresh.

"Jesus fucking Christ," Rollins planted himself in front of him.

"It's fine," Jay said and licked his tooth. It was bloody.

"It's not fine, nothing about this is fine," Rollins said.

"I know what I'm doing," Jay replied and grinned up at him; the blood between his white teeth should've been disgusting, but it was oddly charming, hysterically funny.

Rollins tried to suppress his smile.

"I saw that," Jay said, smile widening; but then he seemed to clamp down—his hands going into his pockets as he stepped around Rollins and kept walking.

"I'll drive you," Rollins called after him.

"Nah, dude. Gaz," he waved his hand at the beat-up Corolla idling in the street.

Rollins watched him get in and leave.

The next time he saw him, nothing was visible, but he was hobbling. He shot Rollins a grin, winked. Rollins shook his head. He wanted to kill Horace. But this was Jay's fight and he had to leave him to it.

He worked out. He ran with Nola. He worked the job. He agreed to all the wedding plans. When he heard that all the security at the clubhouse was no longer working, he knew it was Jay and he kept his mouth shut. When Horace went apoplectic with rage because all of his cheques had bounced and then corrected twenty-four hours later, he knew it was Jay and wondered how close to the sun the kid was planning to fly.

But when he walked in and found Jay taking a beating from three guys twice his size, he got between them, picked Jay up and walked out.

"Dude, put me down."

"No," Rollins said.

Jay squirmed in the hold Rollins had on him over his shoulder.

"You're really fucking pushing it, you know that?" he opened his passenger door and dumped Jay in the seat, slammed the door.

He got in; he half expected Jay to jump out, but he was examining his bruised face in the mirror.

"You're still pretty, don't worry," Rollins said with a smirk.

Jay laughed and put the sun visor back up. "Thank you, sir, where to?"

Rollins shook his head and started the car. "I'm taking you home, we gotta talk."

"We really don't."

Rollins ignored him and drove to his place. He followed Jay up the steps and stood close behind him as he unlocked the door. He could hear voices farther inside the house as he went in and pulled the door closed behind him. Jay still hadn't said anything and as Rollins followed him down the hallway, he reached out and stopped him with his hands on his waist. Jay stilled. Rollins nudged the strands of hair away from Jay's neck with his nose and kissed his nape. There was a laugh from the backroom, a murmured voice. Rollins kissed his way up to Jay's ear, kissed his jaw, slid his hands around him and pulled him back against his chest.

"Ah, fuck it," Jay said and reached back to kiss him properly.

Rollins met him. He pushed his tongue into Jay's mouth, felt Jay's sliding alongside his own and groaned into the kiss. He spun Jay with a hand on his waist and backed him into the wall, using the leverage

from his height and build to overpower him—kiss him harder, run
his hands under his shirt, touch his soft skin—not that he needed
to; Jay was meeting him like he wanted to crawl inside Rollins, his
own groans desperate, needy.

Jay pulled back suddenly and hissed.

"What is it?" Rollins asked hushed between them.

"Lip," Jay tongued his lip. "It's healed but still got a sore spot."

Rollins traced his bottom lip with his thumb. Jay sucked it into
his mouth.

"I can be gentle," Rollins said.

Jay let go of his thumb. "I don't want you to be."

"Hmm," Rollins brought both his arms up and bracketed them
over Jay, crowding him into the wall. "You don't, do you? Don't
want anyone to go easy on you."

"No," Jay breathed out.

Rollins brought his head down and ran his nose up the side of
Jay's neck, fanned his breath over the skin, inhaled the smell of him.

"Maybe I want to," he said and kissed his throat softly. "Maybe,"
he pressed his lips behind his ear, "I want to fuck you," he kissed
his cheek, "real slow."

Jay was panting, shaking under the gentle touch. "Dude,
c'mon."

"I'm gonna take my time," Rollins whispered against his ear,
then took his hand and tugged him into his bedroom, kicked the
door shut with his boot behind them.

He got Jay under him, felt his whole body trembling as he un-
dressed him, kissing each bit of skin as he got to it. Jay let him—his
hands running over Rollins scalp, tracing the shell of his ear when
Rollins looked up and met his eyes as he kissed over his stomach,
laved his nipples with his tongue, felt Jay panting under him.

Once Jay was naked, he slid back down between his thighs and pushed him open, tongued his hole until Jay was begging for it.

By the time he slid inside, Jay was arching and coming, his eyes squeezed closed and his moan a long, drawn-out whine. Rollins kissed his neck, pressed a kiss to his shoulder, rocked his hips forward agonisingly slowly, pulled back just as slow.

"You can go faster," Jay panted out.

"Don't want to," Rollins said into his neck and took his time.

Jay sighed and wrapped his legs around him, ran his hands up and down Rollins' back.

His orgasm rolled up and over him and he came with his lips pressed to Jay's, their puffs of air mingling together.

"Shit," he said as he came back to earth slowly, "I needed that."

Jay pressed a hard kiss to the side of his head. "And now you need to go."

"Huh?" Rollins lifted his head up. He hadn't even gone soft yet. "We need to talk."

Jay closed his eyes. "I reckon we have."

Rollins pulled out and flopped onto his back with a groan.

"You really want me to go?"

Jay pulled the doona over himself. "It's not a matter of want. C'mon, Rollins, you know that."

Rollins shut his eyes, caught his breath. He did know that.

"Okay," he said and got up.

He pulled on his boxers, pants, looked for his shirt. "Just, can you stop taking it so far? Or even think about what I said, about going home."

"Can't, dude, you know that."

"Fuck's sake," Rollins said as he yanked on his shirt. "You deserve better than an early grave, you get that, right?"

"I'm not planning on getting dead."

Rollins shook his head and sat on the edge of the bed as he put his boots on. His breathing was rough and he realised he was furious.

No, he was scared. He was scared of coming in one day and hearing Jay was dead.

He finished lacing up and then sat forward and held his head in his hands.

"It's gonna be alright, I know what I'm doing," Jay said and nudged him with his foot.

Rollins turned to him. Jay was sitting up, his thighs propped up under the doona, his hands dangling over each knee. He was serious—those green eyes sharp and certain.

Rollins pressed forward and gave him a bruising kiss.

"You better," he said against his lips and stood.

Rollins grabbed his keys, patted his pockets for his phone and wallet and went for the door.

"Wedding's soon," Jay said.

Rollins tensed. "Yeah."

"Don't forget my invite," Jay said, a forced lightness to his tone.

Rollins felt a bolt of anxiety at the thought of Jay there.

But Jay was his friend. More than—since Derek, Jay was probably his only friend.

Of course he would invite him.

"Yeah," he replied and left.

51

R OLLINS LOOKED FOR JAY every time he went to the clubhouse in the month leading up to the wedding but never
saw him. He reckoned Jay was avoiding him. He idled on Jay's
street with the invitation on the passenger's seat for a good while.

Then he told himself to stop being fucking stupid, parked, got
out and jogged up the steps.

Bloody Gaz again.

"He's not here, eh," he said, really dragging that 'eh' out.

"Do you know when he'll be back?" Rollins asked, tapping the
heavy envelope against his thigh.

"Dunno, probably not for a while."

"Where is he?"

"Dunno. You coulda just left that in the letterbox," Gaz jerked
his chin at the envelope. "Unless it's cash? Yeah, nah, don't wanna
be leaving cash outside around here."

Gaz was unlocking the flyscreen and Rollins was handing the
invite over.

"Later," Gaz said and shut the door.

Rollins was left dazed and disappointed. Delivering that had been the only real excuse he had to come round. He realised he'd done it just to see Jay.

He turned around and walked back to his car. The sun was too hot on his face.

He guessed he'd see him at the wedding.

52

THE SHIRT FELT CONSTRICTING.

"It's perfectly fitted," Tom said like Rollins was dense. Rollins was used to the tone; Tom had been talking to him like he was stupid since they were kids, but it was always fond too. "You want a beer?"

"No, I don't want a fucking beer; Jesus, it's ten in the morning," Rollins yanked one sleeve down, then the other.

"Yeah, but I think you can make an exception for your wedding day," Tom said and wandered into the kitchen. Rollins could hear the fridge opening, the can cracking open. So, he'd be shitfaced by noon. How wonderful.

"Don't you look nice?" his mum said as she came in through the sliding door at the back of the cabin he'd rented. Tonight, they'd all leave and he'd come back here with Sarah. Married. The thought of it was something he couldn't think about. For some reason, he suddenly thought of Nola. But Sarah had put her foot down on Rollins bringing her, said she might get out of control. Rollins was beginning to wonder if Sarah had even met Nola. He'd had to leave her with Gaz—well, he could've used his regular dog sitting service, but part of him was hoping to run into Jay and he knew Jay trusted Gaz, so, win-win. Or lose-win since Jay wasn't there when he dropped her off.

"I look like I always do," he said to his mum.

"None of that," she smiled at him as she came behind him and started to fix the collar. "Your dad and I are so proud of you," she said as she patted his shoulders. "Tom, really?" she went on as she moved away.

Rollins wondered what Jay would say about his mum being proud of him for getting married—it was hardly a fucking achievement; it was an expense, a big fucking expense. But he wasn't thinking about Jay, who'd failed to RSVP, who'd all but disappeared from his life over the last month save for the odd update when Rollins broke and asked Chad how he was doing.

"He's real good, eh? Kickin' it, ya know?" Chad had said.

Rollins had no idea what that meant but it was the best he could get. Jay being alive was currently a real win in his book.

"Can we get going already? It's too hot in here," Rollins said and yanked his suit jacket on.

"We've got time," his dad said from the little kitchen. Rollins didn't even hear him come in—he was standing in the kitchen with Tom, sipping some sort of drink.

Rollins looked at his family, dressed in their Sunday best, his mum's acquiescent yet fixed smile, his dad red-faced from years of steady drinking, and Tom, a younger version of his dad, and he wondered who these people were, wondered why they were here with him getting ready as if any of them really cared about each other beyond the socially dictated necessity of acting like they cared about what happened to the other.

"I'll be outside," he said and got out of there.

By the time he got some time to himself, he was sweating for real. He told Tom, "Give me a minute," and ducked into an empty room at the back of the church.

The door creaked open behind him.

"I said give me a minute, for fuck's sake," he lifted his head.

Jay was standing there in his suit, hands stuffed in his pockets, smile easy but timid. He was wearing his sneakers. Jesus, Rollins thought, goes all the way with the suit but then doesn't change the fucking shoes. But he was so full of shit—he thought that in lieu of dealing with how seeing Jay made his heart pound, his palms tingle, how it brought profound relief and overwhelming affection over him all at once.

"You never RSVPed."

Jay shrugged, tilted his head to the side. "You look nice."

"Nice?"

Jay's smile widened, but there was something guarded in it. "You know what I mean, dude."

Rollins shrugged. "Any monkey can put on a suit. Have you seen the gang out there? All wearing suits, still fucking clowns."

Jay snorted a laugh. "Yeah."

There was a beam of sunlight cutting across the floor from the high window beside them, cutting a line between them. The echo of voices outside were muted yet loud against the thick stone walls.

"Yo, you ready—

Tom cut off as he pushed in the door.

"Give me a minute," Rollins shoved him out and shut the door, his eyes shooting back to Jay.

Jay took a deep breath. "Don't do it, man."

"Do what?"

"Marry her."

Rollins raised both eyebrows. "You reckon I should call it off. Now?" he was incredulous; imagine Sarah's face?

"I do, yeah," Jay said. "You don't even love her," he finished, eyes dropping down to his sneakers.

Rollins snorted. Jay wasn't wrong, but it's not like he could back out now.

"What am I gonna do, Jay? Marry you instead?"

Jay looked up. He pushed his glasses up his nose, straightened. "Yeah."

Rollins was sure he must've been joking. "I was kidding."

"Why? We love each other, why shouldn't it be me?"

"This ain't no gay romance, this is real life—dudes don't just marry fucking dudes."

"They could if they had the balls to fucking do it."

Rollins shook his head, scoffed. "I'm marrying a woman, a fucking woman."

"Oh, so you're marrying her and not me 'cos she's got a pussy and I don't? Yeah, that makes sense."

"We can't get fucking married. Jesus Christ, what's with you?"

Jay looked away, eyes on the wall, he was nodding his head to that invisible beat again, but there was something small about him now. Jay *was* small, but he'd never looked it. Not like this.

Rollins realised it'd taken every bit of courage Jay had to come in here and say this, and his heart clenched in his chest at the thought of it.

"Look, I'll see you after, okay? We'll just get through this then talk later."

Jay looked back at him, his smile sad. "Nah, reckon this was it, eh?"

He shrugged to himself and went for the door. "Bye, Rollins."

Rollins stepped in front of him.

"Later," he said and gripped Jay by the shoulders.

Jay didn't look up. "Nah, I reckon this is goodbye," he shook his head, "I can't watch you with someone else."

Rollins sucked in a breath. He wanted to berate Jay for talking like this, for coming in here, saying all of these stupid feelings. He gripped him instead.

Tom barrelled back in. "We really gotta..."

Rollins let Jay go and stepped aside. He listened to Jay take a deep breath, heard the soft tread of his sneakers as he left.

"Yeah, I'm comin'," Rollins said, his eyes on the shard of sunlight.

"I do," Rollins said.

Sarah tittered, and the priest chuckled as if Rollins was an adorably nervous moron.

"Not yet, eh," Tom nudged him, his voice condescending but embarrassed.

"No, I mean, I do."

"You do, what?" Sarah asked, her perfectly made-up face was bewildered yet telling Rollins he was one wrong word away from her absolutely losing her shit.

"I do have a problem with it. I can't," he looked away from her to the priest, whose face was shifting from a man addressing a nervous groom to slowly realising there was a real problem, "keep my peace," he finished.

"You have a problem with this union?" the priest asked.

"Don't fucking do this to me," Sarah hissed.

Rollins looked back at her—carefully styled hair, sleeveless gown with the boning pushing her breasts up enticingly, perfect face—and he felt nothing for her beyond the guilt of one human to another when you were about to royally fuck them over. He felt like he was having an out of body experience; the hushed twittering of the crowd felt periphery to his awareness. But he felt sure too.

"I do," he said again, eyes on Sarah. "I'm sorry, I love someone else."

"Is it that fucking skank Tanya!" Sarah screamed and before Rollins could reply, Sarah was wheeling on Tanya and lunging.

"Jesus Christ," Tom said.

But Rollins wasn't paying attention, he was sidestepping them and marching out of the church.

"That was quick," Horace's voice came from behind him as he made his way up the path to the cabins where most of the guys were staying.

He turned. Horace was leaning against the trunk of one of the massive trees, smoking a cigarette, his fat gut hanging over his belt, bursting the white buttons of his shirt.

"Where's Jay?" Rollins asked, a feeling of dread seeping in.

"Never mind about that little faggot," Horace said and dropped the cigarette, crushed it under his boot. "Was gonna do this after, but since I got you alone now—

"What the fuck have you done to Jay?"

He never heard the answer. Someone clocked him over the head from behind and the world went black.

53

HE CAME TO SLOWLY, but he'd been in this situation before and as consciousness dawned, he knew to keep it to
himself. He kept his eyes closed and assessed the situation. He was
in a lawn chair, arms bound but not his legs—first mistake. His
head was pounding from the hit, but nothing else had been done
to him—second mistake. And there were two other people in here
with him—third mistake.

He lifted his head, opened his eyes.

"He lives," Horace smiled. He was standing with Slater—big,
but not a trained fighter. Rollins saw two Glock 9mm on the
table—cop guns, which meant they were stolen, which meant
Horace was doing worse shit than he thought. They were next to
a little screen; a box like what was used for surveillance footage.

"Where's Jay?" he asked, voice raspy.

"Jesus, you're like a broken fucking record," Horace said and
dragged a chair to sit in front of him. "Wouldn't worry about that
little faggot anymore, he's about to take a swim with the fishes."

Rollins felt like his heart stopped.

Horace laughed.

"Ya know, when I realised it was that little piece of shit behind the money, I was like, alright, Horace, bit of respect, eh? Kid's not as much of a pussy as I thought the old whore had made him."

"You can't just kill him," Rollins tried. "He's got people in Sydney—

"A dead whore and her whore mates?" Horace laughed. "Anyway, I wasn't plannin' on it, just punishing him a bit, ya know how it is with kids these days."

Rollins thought about the myriad injuries Jay had been carrying since they got back from Port Hedland and very much did not know. He wanted to kill Horace back then; he really wanted to fucking kill him now.

"But then I saw this," he waved his hand at the box. "Ya know I got surveillance put in up there?"

Rollins felt all the life drain right out of him.

"Yeah," Horace gave him a disgusted look. "Have you seen my missus, Rollins? Hottest piece of ass in Perth and even I don't fuck her as much as you two disgusting faggots."

He turned and flicked the screen on.

It was black and white, small, but Rollins knew what it was. He remembered that day. He'd just eaten Jay out for what felt like hours, fucked him frantically on the futon. When Jay had come into the kitchen in nothing but his baggy jeans afterwards, Rollins had followed, naked, and slipped his hands around Jay's waist where he stood at the stove, heating up the pan.

"I'm not hungry," he'd murmured into Jay's hair as he kissed his nape, ran his hands over his bare stomach.

"Dude," Jay had laughed, "we gotta eat."

"Nah," Rollins kissed his neck, spun him, kissed his mouth.

They'd fucked again—Jay bent over the kitchen table, Rollins hugging him tight and close against his chest—and as Rollins watched it now, all he could think was how fucking stupid he was. He loved Jay. He'd been in love with him for a long time. Jay was right—they were in love.

Which meant Jay had just told him he loved him back.

Christ, but he was stupid.

"Earth to fucking Rollins," Horace was saying.

"Where's Jay now?" he asked.

"Jesus fucking Christ, you'll be happy to know you'll be seein' him right soon if you believe in that shit," Horace turned to Slater.

Rollins kicked out with his leg and knocked the chair out from under Horace. As Horace hit the ground with an "Oof," Rollins charged Slater—he knocked him hard with a hip and shoulder, then brought the chair tied to his back up to the table and smashed the screen off so it hit Horace in the face, skittered the guns across the room. He watched both men scrambling to get up and worked on wriggling his hands free.

Slater recovered first.

"You're a fucking dead cunt—

Rollins kicked him with a clean blow right to the stomach. His hands were burning on the rope and as he slid one free, he felt all the skin tear off with it. He shook his hand out and grabbed for the gun.

Horace was sitting up; he saw the gun and raised both palms.

Slater stood. Rollins faced him and shot twice, both knee caps clean, and he hit the ground with a scream.

Rollins shook his other hand free, tossed the chair and picked up the other gun, tucked it into his waistband.

"Where is he," he said and trained the gun on Horace's face.

"Dead."

"Where."

"Boat."

"I don't believe you'd let them kill him yet, you'd wanna see that."

Horace shrugged, but his face was indulgent.

"If he's really dead, you're fucking dead. Tell me where he is," he said and stepped closer.

"Even if I tell ya, don't mean I'm not gonna be back for more."

And Rollins always did know, deep down, Horace was fucking stupid. Or maybe he knew he was already dead.

"Tell me."

"Busso, they're waiting on me," Horace smiled.

Rollins moved the gun down and shot him in the groin. Injury like that and he'd bleed out and be dead soon enough. He tucked the gun in the back of his pants and jogged out to the sound of both men screaming behind him.

As he tore down Caves Road in Horace's car—the high beams illuminating the old growth forest on the edge of the empty, pitch-black road, the two guns on the passenger's seat—all Rollins could hope for was that he'd guessed right and Horace hadn't lied. They'd wait. They'd have to wait.

He gunned it to the marina and slowed as he approached. One boat lit up at the end of a jetty. A lot of noise. It's like these clowns had never heard of the word discreet, had so much arrogance they never thought that hanging a neon sign above their activities might, as Jay put it, draw the heat. Rollins shook his head and parked a good distance away. He grabbed both guns, got out, shut the door softly and let his eyes adjust to the jetty, the edge of the boat. No one outside. Morons.

He jogged down the side of the jetty just in case, kicked off his shoes and socks once he hit sand. Tucking both guns in his waistband at his back, he lifted himself up and lay flat on the jetty and listened. Voices. Laughter. A smacking sound. He couldn't hear Jay, but he knew what that was—they were beating him. He clenched his jaw, crouched and thanked a God he didn't believe in that meant Jay was probably still alive.

There was a crackling in the distance. He looked up. Fireworks.

His heart started thumping harder in his chest. He squeezed his eyes closed against the memories. Not now, not fucking now. The water lapped against the jetty, the voices laughed, jeered, and he couldn't feel this now; it was tugging at him, trying to drag him back and spit him out from a jetty in the night into the desert in the day with gunfire raining down on him.

A rope hitting the deck made him blink it all back and he saw one of them tossing the ropes off the boat at the same time as the engine started. So, they'd decided not to wait, or maybe Horace had managed, even with his balls bleeding out, to make the call.

Rollins sucked in a deep breath.

That's your Jay in there, he said to himself, *get your fucking shit together.*

He got up, stayed low, jogged alongside the boat and jumped onto the deck.

His heart was in his throat at the same time as the guy on the deck met his eyes. Rollins swallowed, lifted the gun and started shooting.

"Y OU ALMOST HAD AN episode?" Jay reached up and stroked his fingers along my jaw.

"Yeah," it was still weird to talk about them so openly. Even here and now, facing certain death, I'd almost prefer death than acknowledge this weakness.

But this was Jay. And if I could be honest with anyone, it was Jay.

"Is that why you blew up the boat?"

I had the energy to scoff, loudly. "For the last time, it wasn't meant to totally blow up, that part was an accident."

"You accidentally shot the fuel tank twenty times?"

"Okay, first of all, there weren't twenty rounds left in those guns, and it's not like I made a mag change on either of 'em..."

Jay chuckled, pressed his head back against my chest. I wrapped my legs around him and went on. "And that guy had you in a headlock, he was going to shoot you, chuck you overboard, I panicked..."

55

ROLLINS BURST INTO THE cabin and clocked five guys, Jay a huddled mess at the rear of the small space. Rollins shot the first two—right then left, kill shots, straight through the heart—then skidded under the table as the third guy shot.

As expected, he was a terrible shot and the bullet zinged wide and shattered the window.

Rollins only had eyes for Jay. The guy next to him was dragging him out the front door to the front of the boat. He could feel the boat moving out at a quick clip and he knew if that guy threw Jay off, he'd have a hell of a time finding him in the dark.

He rolled onto his stomach and fired two quick shots—a kneecap, a thigh—and the two remaining guys collapsed. Rollins saw the horrified face of the first one and recognised him vaguely; he shot him between the eyes. He saw the second one rolling around, holding his thigh, wailing. Rollins dragged himself up enough to take the shot—the guy rolled and Rollins hit his stomach. He'd bleed out.

He shuffled forward to the edge of the door. The wood splintered near his head. His heart gave a panicked thump and he told himself to shut the fuck up and find the shot. He looked up and caught the reflection in the window of the guy holding Jay in a headlock, a gun in his hand. He recognised him. Terry? Terrance? Some fucking name that started with a T. Didn't matter. What did matter was that Rollins had a vague recollection of the guy being ex-army. So, he could probably shoot.

"Drop it, Rollins," T-banger yelled, "or I'll kill him."

Rollins looked up at the reflection.

He had the gun against Jay's head.

Then Rollins noticed the forty-gallon drum of fuel.

"Kill him and I'll kill you," Rollins replied as he shuffled out of the cabin, onto the starboard deck. The lifeboat was in one of the white pods—he lifted it, cut the painter line, tossed it over the edge and pulled the end of the painter hard until he saw it inflating. He dropped the line and crawled back inside. He had two rounds left in the Glock in his hand; he pulled the second one out from the back of his waistband. Fourteen rounds with a gun in both hands.

"I mean it, Rollins, give me the gun—

"Jay?" he called out.

"He ain't got nothin' to say unless—

"Yeah?"

"Jump," Rollins said. He watched Jay's reflection, saw the slight widening of his eyes. He took a deep breath, turned and started firing low.

T-fuck shoved Jay away at the same time as the fuel ignited.

Rollins raced back through the cabin and launched himself off the stern as the thing exploded.

He hit the water and his heart was in his throat but all he could think was—did he fucking jump?

He breached the surface, gasping, the boat still zipping along in front of him, flames spitting up from the front of it. Rollins thrashed around looking for Jay.

Oh, fuck, oh no.

"Dude!"

He heard splashing and swam for it.

"Jay!"

"Fuck, dude!"

Rollins swam in the dark to the voice.

Jay was there, treading water, a stupid grin on his face.

"You're fucking MacGyver!"

Rollins grabbed him and held on.

"You alright?"

"Yeah," Jay said as they trod water. "Now what?"

Rollins let him go and looked around. The white pod was bobbing not a few metres away, the life raft floating beside it.

"Now we get on that thing and wait until we wash back up on shore."

"Fucking MacGyver," Jay said again.

Rollins huffed a laugh. He didn't let Jay go as they swam for the lifeboat.

"It wasn't a perfect plan, yes, Jay," Rollins thought or said, he wasn't sure anymore, but he could fucking admit that now.

"Nah, dude, this is alright, eh. At least we're together and you didn't get married. I couldn't have beared it."

"Hmm," Rollins kissed the top of Jay's head. "Me neither."

56

Day 31. Present moment... off the coast of Africa.

"**D**UDE," JAY RASPED.

"Huh?"

"Land."

Rollins craned his head up. White gulls flying high, diving down, water breaking foam against rocks, and right there, land, fucking land.

57

A WOMAN IN CAMO fatigues appeared above them on the beach.

"What do we have here?" she asked, her white teeth blinding against her black skin. She nudged Jay with the butt of her rifle.

That got Rollins moving. He sat up, put his body in front of Jay's.

"We just need some water," he rasped. "And maybe something to eat."

"Hmm, Australian?"

"Yeah?" Jay said from behind him, poking his head around Rollins' body. "Just popping in, you know."

She cracked a smile.

"Hmm, I can help you, but then I'll take you to the commander."

"Uh—

"Okay," Rollins said and reached back and grabbed Jay's wrist; he hoped it effectively communicated—just go with it, then I'll get us out of it.

They were eating soup after drinking a litre of water when a white guy in camo fatigues walked in.

"Rollins?" he asked with surprise.

Rollins looked up at the guy in the doorway flanked in bright sunshine against the dimness off the space.

His eyes adjusted and then he recognised him. He couldn't believe it.

"Shit, Damon, what're you doing here?"

"Killing poachers, what're you doing here?"

Rollins laughed, he shot a smile at Jay. "Had some trouble back home."

"Kiara says she found you on the beach? Did you come by fucking boat?"

"Kind of," Rollins scratched his head; he couldn't stop smiling. He knew Damon from the SAS.

"Do you need to get back?" Damon asked as he came further inside the hut.

Rollins read the play and stood to accept the hug.

"Umm," he stepped back and looked down at Jay.

Jay shrugged. "Probably not a good idea since you just murdered like, seven people."

"Jesus," Rollins said. "You don't just go and say that."

"Who's this?" Damon jerked his chin at Jay.

"I'm Jay," Jay stood and extended his hand. "Rollins'—

"Boyfriend," Rollins cut him off, voice gruff. "Soon to be husband if the offer still stands." He glanced at Jay.

Jay's mouth was hanging open. "Fuck yeah, dude," he breathed out. "Yeah."

"Cool," Rollins said and looked back to Damon.

Damon raised an eyebrow, but took it in stride. "Cool, well, you can stay if you want, could use you if you can't go home?"

Rollins looked to Jay. Jay was beaming at him.

"Well, what'd you reckon, Jay? Wanna shoot some poachers?"

"Fuck, yeah!"

Rollins frowned. "Or maybe you could just write about it, I dunno about you and a gun."

"Dude," Jay wrapped his arms around Rollins' waist. "Yes, to all of the above, and c'mon, let me shoot, I'll be good at it, I promise."

Rollins wrapped his arms around him, kissed him before turning back to Damon.

"That would be a yes," he said and held Jay tight.

Epilogue

Zimbabwe ... One year later...

R OLLINS EMERGED OUT OF the brush and Jay jumped him.

"Oof," Rollins laughed, his big arms coming up to wrap under Jay's thighs and hoist him up.

"Where have you been?" Jay asked.

Rollins kissed him. "Had some shit to do in town."

"What shit?" Jay asked as Rollins carried him to their hut.

"Never you mind shit," Rollins replied as he deposited Jay on the bed and slipped his backpack off, placed his gun beside it before blanketing Jay's body and kissing him for real.

He'd have thought after a year of living together in their little hut he'd get tired of fucking Jay, that his obsession would wane. It had not, as evidenced by the desperate way his hands were rucking Jay's shirt up and encouraging him to get the damn thing off.

"Why aren't you naked already?"

Jay scoffed and ripped his shirt off. He pulled off the Clark Kent glasses he'd picked out after they got settled, then pushed up and resumed the kiss. "Can't just lay around naked waiting for you to get back when you take your damn time doing God knows what," Jay said against his lips.

Rollins ran his hands over Jay's belly, squeezed the flesh; he'd lost a bit in the year since they arrived after Rollins had lectured him incessantly on the dangers of drinking so much coke. Jay ignored that, but when Rollins begged him to do it for his health, told him quietly that he couldn't bear to lose him, Jay rolled his eyes and told Rollins he was the old man here and he'd probably be dead before Jay succumbed to his sugar addiction, but, "Fine, fine, I'll cut back." Rollins kissed him. Rollins always kissed him.

But Jay would always be soft, plump, and Rollins would never get tired of digging his fingers into him, then caressing his soft skin in the places he'd just squeezed. He kissed his belly button, kissed his way up to his pink nipples, sucked on one while teasing the other one with a slow circle of his finger.

Jay ran his hands over Rollins' head, down his neck.

"C'mon, Rollins, you been gone for days," Jay whined and rolled his hips up.

"Hmm," he switched to the other nipple, slid his hand down and rubbed Jay's dick. "I know. So, I need to take my time, make sure all is as I left it."

Jay laughed, his hands sliding further down to pull Rollins' shirt up. Rollins got the hint and moved away an inch so Jay could drag it off.

"You're so difficult," Jay huffed.

Rollins met his eyes; Jay's eyes were soft on him, his smile easy and indulgent. Rollins smiled back and kissed his sternum, squeezed his hips.

"I'm gonna eat you out for hours."

"No, dude, c'mon, fuck me first, then you can."

"Needy," Rollins said and bracketed himself over him, their clothed dicks rubbing off against each other. "Maybe I want you to fuck me?"

Jay gripped Rollins' ass. "Yeah? Wanna get my dick in you?"

Rollins groaned and dropped his head between Jay's neck and shoulder. "Your dirty talk is awful."

"Is it?" Jay brought his hands to the front of Rollins' pants, got them undone and then slipped his fingers down the back of his waist band, ran his fingers over the bare skin. "You're not an ass man begging for my come?"

Rollins groaned and rolled his hips against Jay's.

"I think you've misunderstood what ass man means."

"It means you love getting fucked up the ass."

Rollins laughed and turned his head. Jay tilted his head to the side so their eyes met. They were so close—Jay was smiling and Rollins knew he was smiling stupidly back.

"I know you know that's not what it means," Rollins said as Jay continued to play with his ass and Rollins continued to push into it and rub off against him.

"I'm taking it back," Jay said.

"It never got taken."

"It did. It used to mean dudes into getting fucked up the ass."

"It never meant that."

"It probably did."

"Probably is not actually."

Jay slipped a finger down and teased Rollins' entrance. Rollins buried his face in Jay's shoulder to hide his groan.

"Total ass man," Jay said. Rollins laughed into his shoulder.

"Pants off," Rollins said as he rocked down onto Jay's cock and Jay fingered him dry.

"You gotta move if we're gonna get to it."

"Don't wanna move."

Jay laughed, fucked him with that finger before pushing him off.

Rollins made it very difficult for Jay to get his pants off and his own with how he wouldn't let him go. But Jay huffed, laughed, managed to get himself naked and Rollins' ass free with his pants bunched around his thighs so he didn't have to deal with getting his boots off.

Jay rolled him to his stomach and pushed inside with his tongue, no messing around. Rollins groaned, brought his hand back and pushed Jay's face into himself, trying to get more inside him. But Jay wasn't lying about being keyed up—he tongued him, fingered him, lubed up his big dick and pushed in, his body blanketing Rollins, fucking him deep and fast.

"Don't come," he said against Rollins' ear.

Rollins groaned. "I'm gonna."

"No, wanna get fucked after."

Rollins shuddered. He wasn't going to hold out, there was no way—Jay was nailing him right where he lived and his dick was rubbing up against the mattress—but then Jay was pulling out, right in time, and Rollins was flipping over and grabbing him.

"You little shit," he said as he shoved Jay under him, hoisted his thigh up.

"C'mon, dude, fuck me already, fuck me," Jay yanked him in with hands on his ass.

Rollins grappled around for the lube, poured it on Jay's hole and then pushed in.

"Ah, fuck, yeah, there," Jay said as he arched.

Rollins fucked in deep, brought his hands up so he could slide his fingers under Jay's skull and hold him steady while he kissed him roughly. Having his pants around his thighs restricted his movements, made everything tight and close. Jay urged him on with his hands on his ass, kissed him back fiercely.

When Jay slid one hand down and shoved a finger inside him, Rollins was coming with a gasp, shoving into Jay hard and fast, fucking back onto the finger, fucking into the warm heat.

He felt like he came for a long time and when he was finished, he felt Jay hard between them, rocking his dick up against Rollins' abs.

Rollins slipped his hand between them and jerked him off roughly, his kisses lazy against Jay's desperate ones.

"You gonna come?" he asked against Jay's lips.

Jay keened and pushed into his touch.

"Yeah, you're gonna come, total slut for my dick aren't you, baby?"

Jay moaned, giggled. Rollins tightened his grip, smiled against Jay's lips.

"My little slut, gonna come with my dick still inside you, need it don't you?"

Jay was caught between rutting into his hand and laughing. "Dude, stop, more, please, ah—

"What've I said about calling me dude while we fuck," Rollins loosened his grip.

"Rollins, Rollins, please, babe, please."

Rollins kissed him, then jerked him just the way he knew would get Jay there in one, two, three more strokes and he was arching and coming, his breaths mingling with Rollins' own.

Rollins kissed him through it, made a small space between them so he could run his hand up and down Jay's body from hip to nipple.

"Good?" Rollins broke away to ask.

Jay huffed, smiled. "Always."

Rollins kissed him again.

"But," Jay leaned back, "seriously, dude, where you been?"

"Hmm," Rollins gave him one last bruising kiss before pulling away. He sat up and got his boots off, used his shirt to wipe himself down before standing and bringing his pants up over his ass, leaving them undone.

He crouched over his backpack and heard Jay sitting up behind him.

"Went to get you a present," he said and rummaged around for the coke.

"Dude!" Jay cheered when he handed it to him. "I love you!"

Rollins laughed and slid back beside him on the bed.

"You might wanna put it in the cooler—

But Jay was cracking the can open and drinking.

Rollins laughed and tucked his body alongside Jay sitting up on the bed, rested his head on his chest. Jay drank his coke, made pornographic noises over it, and ran his other hand over Rollins' shaved head, traced the shell of his ear, stroked his neck.

It felt nice.

"I love you too," Rollins said after a while.

Jay snorted. "Bit of a delayed reaction, but yeah, I got that already."

"Still gonna marry you when we can."

"Yeah? I'm gonna marry the shit out of you back."

Rollins huffed a laugh into his skin, dragged himself closer. "That doesn't make sense."

"It does, but, because when we get up there, I'm gonna be all like: I fucking do, seriously, are you guys looking at my dude, here? Hot as fuck, fucks like a porn star—total ass man—and he's the kindest son of a bitch in the world."

"You are not saying any of that. And if you say ass man, everyone's gonna think I'm totally into your ass."

"You are, but you know what I mean; you love getting fucked up the ass and licked out and just ass play in general."

Rollins groaned. "Please stop talking. On the day all you have to say is, I do."

"Nah, man, can embellish, write my own vows. I've been writing 'em already, getting Gaz's input."

Rollins huffed but settled in and listened to Jay giving him updates on his mum's new place with a huge backyard and a garden, on how Nola was doing living with Jay's crew in Perth. Jay had been into town to use the internet café while Rollins was out on a mission to deal with elephant poachers—he'd managed to scare them off without having to kill them, but he'd needed to stay and keep an eye on the elephants for a few days, before making his way to town to get Jay's coke.

"The whole crew is spoiling her, dude, it's all good."

Rollins squeezed him close. He knew that. He sent money for her. He knew she was well and very well taken care of. But.

"I know it's not the same," Jay said and crushed his can, pitched it into the bin, hitting his target before bringing that hand down to stroke Rollins' back. "But at least you don't gotta worry on it, she's all good."

"Unlike with you," Rollins grumbled.

"Don't start," Jay squeezed his neck.

They'd had variations of this argument since Jay stopped working with Rollins and partnered up with Kiara. He'd been on a mission to protect a pride of lions while Rollins was dealing with the elephants. They couldn't keep working together on account of being actual partners. Damon had been the one to stop it, but Rollins knew it anyway—just like husband-and-wife teams couldn't snipe together, neither could future husband and husband teams. Too distracting, too much worry.

Rollins had hoped Jay would want to quit. Of course Jay didn't. Rollins also knew he was being irrational and selfish. He knew all this and still he worried.

"You're not gonna lose me, man, I can shoot real well now."

Rollins squeezed him closer.

"I know."

Jay shook the back of his neck until Rollins looked up.

"I ain't ever gonna leave you; you get that, right?"

"Maybe it won't be your choice."

Jay smiled at him, easy and fond. "Nah, see, I know something you don't."

"What's that?" Rollins couldn't help his answering smile.

"This is a bloody gay romance—

Rollins scoffed.

"Which means," Jay barrelled on, "we're getting married, adopting some hyenas and riding off into the sunset."

Rollins rolled his eyes. "You can't adopt hyenas."

"You can, I heard about this guy who's feeding 'em…"

And Rollins rested his head against Jay's chest, felt the vibrations as he talked. He leaned into Jay's hand stroking his head, and he reckoned Jay was probably right—this all felt pretty fucking gay. And pretty fucking romantic.

It was totally a gay romance.

Acknowledgments

Huge thank you to my three betas—Ana, DF, and KP. They've taken a decent book and made it so much better. I cannot thank them enough: they see things I don't, offer insightful suggestions, and make the process so much fun—it was such a pleasure to work with them on this book. Special shout out to Kath, for another marvellous edit, and to Cate Ashwood designs for the magnificent cover. Thanks as well to my mailing list for keeping me accountable and sending me encouragement—these emails give me life, they truly do. Finally, to my beloved galah, Mippy the Misogynist: currently dying of cancer, she should've been dead months ago; but, in keeping on brand, she's refusing to meet that deadline. This one's for you, Mippy—you keep doing you.

About Author

Sasha Avice is the author of nine novels (and counting!) and one PhD (which is enough). She lives with a changing cast of birds and a dog. When she's not writing or teaching, she's fostering birds. She loves hearing from readers! Email direct at sasha@sashaavice.com or join her mailing list at sashaavice.com for regular updates.

Also By

Perimeter
Series

"Out there on the perimeter, he ain't interested in love... but goddamn if it don't keep on finding him."

Set in Western Australia at the turn of the millennium, each book is a standalone featuring guys who don't want love, don't seek it.

They drift, they work... and then some guy turns up and the dull isolation goes bright, blinds them like a splinter of sun caught in the eye.

Fox

A Perimeter Novel

Sometimes it takes falling in love to realise who you are...

Working as a dish pig and selling drugs on the side, Fox is just trying to survive the tension at home while not looking too closely at himself and his lack of ambition.

Then he meets Taylor. Cool, hot, and did he mention, the cousin of the head of a bikie gang? Paired together to do drug runs, Fox intends to keep his guard up. But Taylor talks to him and listens to him. Taylor sees him, and Fox finds himself looking back with a lot more interest than a straight boy should have.

But Taylor is an enigma with a complicated debt, and Fox has family drama that drags him back in. Together, they must weigh the desire to escape against the price of being free.

You Were My Ride Or Die

A Perimeter Novella

"You were my ride or die...
And you just left!"

When Bain catches the head of a rival bikie gang—who also happens
to be his ex-best friend—in a compromising position with another
man, he knows he just scored a blank cheque for blackmail...

When Ash is caught, he knows he'll do anything to stop this getting
out.

But when Bain cashes that cheque with an outrageous request for a
straight man, the stakes just got raised much higher than Ash getting
outed. Ash knows he has everything to lose and nothing to gain if Bain
discovers the real reason behind their decade long feud.

But how far will Ash go to avoid the question he knows Bain wants to
ask: why did you leave me?

The Cook

A Perimeter Novel

"Guys touch in threeways, you know."
"Do they? Like that?"

When Tim drops out of university in the early 2000s to cook meth for the bikies, he doesn't expect to drag his best friend, Jake, into this mess with him.

But Jake is the mechanic who works on their bikes. Jake is a useful target to get Tim to do what they want.

Another thing about Jake? Tim's been in love with him since high school, but Jake doesn't even know Tim's gay. And Jake's so straight he sleeps with different women several times a week, often where Tim can hear.

So when one of Jake's girls invites Tim to join them, Tim sees the perfect opportunity to scare Jake off, to keep him safe for good.

But if Jake is repulsed, he's got an odd way of showing it... Should Tim try again?

After the Show

A Perimeter Novel

Some guy is making moves on the man he loves but won't have?
Over his dead body...

Working the club scene in the 1990s, Cisco is a queen-glam-rocker
with anger management issues. Swimming in booze and sex to forget
the dream job he lost—principal with The Australian Ballet—Cisco
has zero interest in relationships.

Franco, the hot new bouncer with a heart of gold and an
un-swiped V-card, is completely smitten. Shy, illiterate, and working
poor—there's no way Cisco will go for him.

But Cisco gives him a shot. And Franco blows it. Literally.

When Cisco agrees to train him to be better in bed, he doesn't expect
these sessions to turn into real conversation and—to his horror—actual feelings. For Franco, these nights confirm he was right to wait for
The One.

But if Cisco's toxic aversion to relationships succeeds, Franco will be
forced to let him go...

And since the hot new glassy just asked him out... will Franco finally
move on?

Contested Possession
Series

"... possession is achieved as a result of winning a contest." *Australian rules football*.

Each book features a football player whose possession of the guy he wants is... contested.

Shop now at Amazon.com for current books and future releases in this series.